12

GOBLIN SLAYER

©Noboru Kannatuki

©Noboru Kannatuki

"*Yeah, this is how an adventure should be!*"

Contents

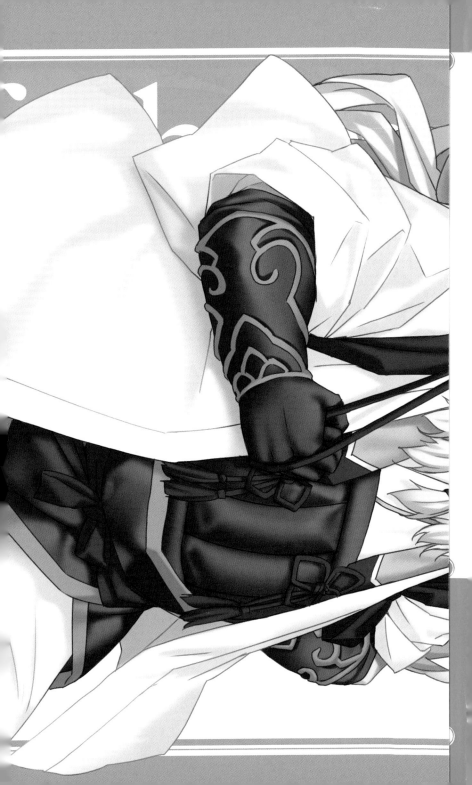

GOBLIN SLAYER

VOLUME 12

KUMO KAGYU

Illustration by
NOBORU KANNATUKI

YEN
ON

NEW YORK

GOBLIN SLAYER

KUMO KAGYU

Translation by Kevin Steinbach ✛ Cover art by Noboru Kannatuki

GOBLIN SLAYER vol. 12
Copyright © 2020 Kumo Kagyu
Illustrations copyright © 2020 Noboru Kannatuki
All rights reserved.
Original Japanese edition published in 2020 by SB Creative Corp.
This English edition is published by arrangement with SB Creative Corp., Tokyo, in care of Tuttle-Mori Agency, Inc., Tokyo.

English translation © 2021 by Yen Press, LLC

Yen On
150 West 30th Street, 19th Floor
New York, NY 10001

Visit us at yenpress.com ✛ facebook.com/yenpress ✛ twitter.com/yenpress
        yenpress.tumblr.com ✛ instagram.com/yenpress

First Yen On Edition: July 2021

Yen On is an imprint of Yen Press, LLC.
The Yen On name and logo are trademarks of Yen Press, LLC.

The publisher is not responsible for websites (or their content) that are not owned by the publisher.

Library of Congress Cataloging-in-Publication Data
Names: Kagyū, Kumo, author. | Kannatuki, Noboru, illustrator.
Title: Goblin slayer / Kumo Kagyu ; illustration by Noboru Kannatuki.
Other titles: Goburin sureiyā. English
Description: New York, NY : Yen On, 2016–
Identifiers: LCCN 2016033529 | ISBN 9780316501590 (v. 1 : pbk.) | ISBN 9780316553223 (v. 2 : pbk.) |
    ISBN 9780316553230 (v. 3 : pbk.) | ISBN 9780316411882 (v. 4 : pbk.) | ISBN 9781975326487 (v. 5 : pbk.) |
    ISBN 9781975327842 (v. 6 : pbk.) | ISBN 9781975330781 (v. 7 : pbk.) | ISBN 9781975331788 (v. 8 : pbk.) |
    ISBN 9781975331801 (v. 9 : pbk.) | ISBN 9781975314033 (v. 10 : pbk.) | ISBN 9781975322526 (v. 11 : pbk.) |
    ISBN 9781975325022 (v. 12 : pbk.)
Subjects: LCSH: Goblins—Fiction. | GSAFD: Fantasy fiction.
Classification: LCC PL872.5.A367 G6313 2016 | DDC 895.63/6—dc23
LC record available at https://lccn.loc.gov/2016033529

ISBNs: 978-1-9753-2502-2 (paperback)
        978-1-9753-2503-9 (ebook)

10 9 8 7 6 5 4 3 2 1

LSC-C

Printed in the United States of America

GOBLIN SLAYER

VOLUME 12

GOBLIN SLAYER

✝

CHARACTER PROFILES

"I am to goblins what goblins are to us."

GOBLIN SLAYER

A strange adventurer active on the frontier. He is famous for reaching Silver (3rd) rank hunting only goblins.

"Protect, heal, save."
—The Three Holy Tenets of the Earth Mother

PRIESTESS

Works with Goblin Slayer. A sweet young woman who must put up with her partner's antics.

"Ignorance is bliss, for learning is the highest joy." —Elven proverb

HIGH ELF ARCHER

An elf girl who adventures with Goblin Slayer. A ranger and a skilled archer.

The only things that matter to her are the weather, the animals, the crops...and him.

COW GIRL

A girl who works on the farm where Goblin Slayer lives. The two are old friends.

"How can you go adventuring without pen and paper?"

GUILD GIRL

A girl who works at the Adventurers Guild. Goblin Slayer's preference for goblin slaying always helps her out.

"Before they're polished, jewels and precious metals all look like rocks. No dwarf would judge a thing by its appearance alone."

DWARF SHAMAN

A dwarf spell caster who adventures with Goblin Slayer.

"A naga does not run."

LIZARD PRIEST

A lizardman priest who adventures with Goblin Slayer.

"Train yourself: Kill with the blade. If blood flows, let it be the enemy's."—First of the "Secrets of Steel."

HEAVY WARRIOR

A Silver-ranked adventurer associated with the Guild in the frontier town. Along with Female Knight and his other companions, his party is one of the best on the frontier.

"Only a tangled skein awaits those who carelessly spin tales about love or the universe's mysteries...not to mention a woman's beauty."

WITCH

A Silver-ranked adventurer at the frontier town's Adventurers Guild.

"I won't make friends tomorrow with an enemy I respect. I'll do it today."

SPEARMAN

A Silver-ranked adventurer at the frontier town's Adventurers Guild.

"Love does not consist in gazing at each other, but in looking outward in the same direction." —A poet

SWORD MAIDEN

Archbishop of the Supreme God in the water town. Also a Gold-ranked adventurer who once fought with the Demon Lord.

©Noboru Kannatuki

OF STARTING A CAMPAIGN

We did it! Illusion, Life, and Death cried, throwing their hands in the air.

Upon the table of the stars of the Four-Cornered World, a vast diagram lay unfurled.

The three great deities smiled to see it, nodding at one another in satisfaction.

Illusion, of course, but also Life and Death, were generous and merciful gods—they gave all things in this world as gifts, and finally, welcomed them all back again.

When these three grew excited, how could the other gods not take an interest?

Truth and Abundance were quick to appear, eager to know what was going on.

But a flustered Illusion promptly exclaimed, *Don't look!* reaching to cover the diagram as Life and Death stood between it and the newcomers.

What's this? A new adventure scenario?

No, it's a campaign.

A campaign! That word got the gods talking.

A campaign! A tale of heroism! A story of battle!

Even a single adventure was such fun, a series of them connected to one another would clearly be even more so.

That was why the gods loved campaigns.

They would start with one or two, but some gods kept adding and adding, until they had seven or eight campaigns running at once.

And yet, even so, they couldn't sit idly by at the proposal of a new saga.

They forgot whatever they had been about to do, raising their hands and saying they wanted to be a part of it.

Life and Death watched all this with a mixture of pleasure and concern.

It would, of course, be lonely if no one wanted to be part of your session.

The excited gods were enough to convince them that it had been worth it to ask Illusion for her help designing the scenario.

Illusion shouted angrily, bringing some order to the scene, then she picked the gods who had the most time in their schedules at the moment.

Life and Death chuckled happily to themselves as they watched this unfold.

They were, after all, both very busy gods, and had few opportunities to play like this.

But of course, gods alone did not an adventure make.

Now they needed adventurers to decide to take on the adventure of their own free will.

They had an idea—what a fine thing, ideas!—of which adventurers would suit which monsters.

They would start with the invitations—giving "handouts," revelations, here and there that would intimate the destiny of adventure to each person.

Whether that person reached forward or drew back was up to them. An adventure had no meaning if the adventurer was dragged into it.

But the gods had faith that these people, being adventurers, would take on the adventures.

And the gods had faith that the monsters, being monsters, would stand in their way.

Nobody involved would offer silly excuses or find a pretext to run away.

All that remained, then, was to say a prayer and roll the dice.

Even the gods didn't know how this adventure would turn out.

Everything would be determined by each adventurer's karma—and the dice of Fate and Chance.

CHAPTER 1

Of When You're Right in the Middle of an Adventure and a Wyvern Shows Up

Just then—well, you saw the chapter title.

"Yeeeeeek!"

"Run, run, run-run-run!! It's gonna eat us!"

"Gosh, we are truly done for now, I daresay…!"

At the screech from behind them, the warrior with the club and sword gave a scream and began beating a desperate retreat out of the forest. The cleric, tears welling in her eyes, ran alongside him as they followed the white-furred hunter bouncing ahead.

How did this happen…*?!*

Frustration filled his mind, along with a profound commitment to keep his eyes forward. *Don't look back.*

From above came what seemed to him the shadow of death. That wasn't the wind howling; it was a cry of murderous intent.

Why did the air seem so hot and thick? It wasn't because he was sweating.

"GYAAAAAAAAAAAOSSSSSSS!!!!"

It was because a massive, airborne predator was swooping at them from behind!

Which idiot was it who said that wyverns are just failed dragons?!

Then again, the statement wasn't exactly wrong. They weren't quite as strong as dragons, but dragons were so strong to begin with that it hardly made a difference. Especially when the wyvern's prey was a trio of adventurers who barely had any proverbial hair on their chests!

He hadn't wanted to use the ploy he'd picked up recently quite like this, but...

"T-tell me what we're supposed to do now!" his old friend, almost out of breath, shouted at him.

The shadow overhead half-flapped and half-coasted along, vastly quicker than they were down on the ground. The trees gave them some small measure of cover, but the end would come soon.

"What do we do...?!"

There was only one thing *to* do: Run. They weren't going to fight that thing and win. But where to run to?

The young man, Club Fighter, thought as fast as he could, but he knew perfectly well that he wasn't likely to come up with any bright ideas for turning the situation around. He had never really been the thinking type.

Harefolk Hunter looked back at him and frowned. Padfoots were quick and nimble, but they lacked endurance. Harefolk, in particular, could be quite acrobatic so long as they had something to eat, but they weren't made to run very long without stopping for a snack or a tipple.

"I—I don't think...I can last...much longer..." Harefolk Hunter said.

"Aw, *gygax!*"

"Hey, no sweari— Agh!" No sooner had the boy seen her white paws slipping than he grabbed Harefolk Hunter by the belt, hefting her up and seating her astride his shoulders. Despite her girlish shouting, she was both softer and heavier than she appeared, but the warrior hardly noticed.

This farmer's third son is stronger than you think!

It was only after he let out a breath that he noticed something that made his eyes widen in realization. The first thing he saw was the girl's ears, bobbing above him from where he had placed her on his shoulders, a position she apparently objected to.

He seemed to recall this happening once before. Only that time, his cleric friend had been huffing and puffing alongside him, and they had been in the sewers. That adventure had been quite an ordeal, in part because it had been only the two of them then. It was still an ordeal now. Even though they were a trio.

A trio?

"Oh…" That was when he was gripped with a flash of insight. "That's it—*ears!*"

"Huh?!"

"You remember—on our way here—the river! The sound of water! Can't you hear it?! Which way? Can you tell?!" He knew he wasn't being entirely coherent, but Harefolk Hunter got the gist of what he was thinking. She collected herself, then *hmm*ed thoughtfully, listening, and finally pointed to the right. "Think it's prob'ly that way, but…"

"Okay…!" That settled it, then. With his free hand he grabbed that of the cleric of the Supreme God and ran like his life depended on it. His childhood friend's hand was smaller than he remembered, and it was trembling—but he couldn't think about that now.

"The river— Wh-what are you going to do at the river?!" she yelped, her face pale—both things he might have teased her about under other circumstances, but now…

"I don't— I don't know, but…something…!" A strained smile crossed his face as he realized his pallor at the moment was probably no better than hers.

Shortly thereafter, his field of vision expanded; they must have left the forest. A river spread out before them—well, not exactly *before* them; it was at the bottom of a narrow ravine—a thin line snaking its way between sheer cliffsides. Normally, he might have come screeching to a halt from sheer terror. He would never have picked this for his staging ground. Certainly not in the middle of an adventure.

"GYAAAAAAAAAAAOSSSSSSS!!!!"

But they had nowhere to turn and not a single second to spare. Now that they were beyond the shelter of the trees, the wyvern made a beeline for them.

"It's coming— You know it's coming, right?!" Harefolk Hunter shouted. From her perch on Club Fighter's back, she could well see it overhead.

"Don't blame me if we all die, okay?!"

"Of *course* I'm going to blame you!" Cleric shouted. "I'll give you a piece of my mind right there in front of the Supreme God!"

At least she was going to follow him. Such, in any case, was how Club Fighter chose to interpret the little squeeze she gave his hand.

And then he jumped.

One great leap, with an old friend beside him and a new one on his shoulders, right off the cliff.

He had no sense of floating; it was more like the ground was sucking him toward itself. The wind whipped in his ears. The girls— and the warrior himself—screamed at the top of their lungs. It was chaos. The young warrior pulled the girls close, hoping to save them from being bashed against the cliffsides if nothing else, then wrapped his arms over his own head. The fast-approaching surface of the water was still terrifying. He closed his eyes for an instant, then opened them and tried to look anywhere else but down.

He twisted his neck around; it took all his strength to look up, but he was just in time to see the wyvern gnashing its beak where it had plowed into and was stuck between the cliff walls.

Too big to fit? Even a roach could get in here, sucker!

If the wyvern could have read his mind at that moment, it would certainly have been incensed by its findings. Instead, it had to settle for an enraged howl at the escape of its prey, the ear-piercing noise reverberating through the ravine.

The next thing he heard was the rush of water…

Then there was pain and cold, as if he had been struck with a ball of ice, and the warrior fainted.

§

"I guess this is, what, the third time we've done this? Goblins really are small fry…"

"GBBOR?!"

He caught the goblin's dagger on the blade of the sword he called Chestburster II, then crushed its skull with a flourish of his club, Roach Slayer II. He never got used to the wet, gooey feeling of the brain giving way; it was always unpleasant. It wasn't like killing bugs.

The cave floor was damp, but there was none of the slime that was perpetually present in the sewers. Plenty of traction. Club Fighter kicked off the ground, firmly planting his feet ensconced in his tall boots, and pulling his weapons in close. Fighting in the club-and-sword-both-at-once style—"dual wielding," maybe—had felt profoundly strange at first, but he was getting used to it.

How many more?

"Probably five or six left, I think! Stay sharp…!" called a sprightly voice to his side. It was Supreme God's Cleric, her back against the rock wall. She held the sword and scales in one hand and a lantern in the other, and was watching the battle closely. Until recently, it had always been just the two of them, so she was always on her guard, taking nothing for granted. After all, their only ranged attack was a single miracle she had been granted by the Supreme God.

It was also their only ace. A precious resource not to be spent lightly.

Yeah, gotta use it carefully, Club Fighter thought.

"Meh, think we can handle this much," Harefolk Hunter said, sounding utterly unconcerned, despite the fact that they were in a cave hunting goblins. Even as her hands worked her bow *rat-a-tat-tat*, the string snapping sharply again and again.

Harefolk Hunter—she was what made this so different from the days when they had been hunting roaches in the sewers. She seemed to be able to keep track of everything that was happening at once; she could stand on the front line—and look at her shoot! She could jump back, bring her bow to bear, and nock in an arrow all in a single turn. And as long as she had a turn to take, she could keep shooting—unlike with magic! (Even though she had once chuckled, her ears bobbing shyly, and admitted, "Well, t'ain't like arrows come free, y'know. Take too many shots and I might not be able t'make my next meal!")

"Taaaake that!" An especially heavy arrow went flying with a sound like chopping wood, landing a bull's-eye on a goblin far in the back of the battle line. The creature looked amazed at the bolt suddenly sprouting from his neck and tumbled backward, rolling over once before coming to a stop and not moving again.

"GGOROGB!!"

"GROB! GOOROGB!!"

The goblins made a terrible racket at that, but they must have believed they could still win, because their morale remained high. Or maybe they had simply realized that the adventurers had nowhere to go but through them.

It was easy to get distracted by the opponents right up at the front, but luckily Cleric was there to warn them. "There's more coming from deeper in…!"

"Aw, that's just what we need! My bowstring's startin' to feel awfully heavy!" Nonetheless, Harefolk Hunter gave a great pull on the bow, which seemed far too large for such a small creature. She had to brace herself and tilt it to one side; it took a certain amount of time.

And it's my job to buy her that time…!

"I'm on it!" Club Fighter shouted and rushed in. His hands were slippery with sweat, and the protective metal plate strapped to his forehead felt heavy, almost making it hard to see. But he had the tethers of his club and sword wrapped around his wrists. And his friends were watching out for him. So he stayed faithful to his role, lashing out with the club in his left hand as he drove forward.

"GOOBGG?!"

"Rrrahh!!"

The goblin in front of him gave an incoherent screech, his throat crushed, and Club Fighter finished him off with a stroke of the sword in his right hand. He tilted his head down so that the splatter of blood wouldn't get in his eyes, catching it instead on his forehead guard. He remembered how he always used to flinch backward at the various fluids that squeezed out of the rats and roaches on his earlier hunts.

Is this what you call "experience" at work?

"GORB! GOBBGB!!"

"Hrngh…?!"

No time to be thinking about that. Better be thinking about the dagger of the goblin who'd just made a leap for him, totally unperturbed by the death of his comrade.

Club Fighter was too late to catch the dagger with his weapon; the blade pierced the simple leather glove covering his left arm.

"Eeyow, that hurts!" he cried, more from surprise than pain. He inadvertently let go of his club, but the thong securing it to his wrist caught it for him.

"GORRGBB!!"

Even that didn't matter—this goblin did. Club Fighter pulled his arm back forcefully, away from the mocking, triumphant creature.

"You stinking son of a—"

"Here I go!!"

"GOBGB?!"

There was a great *ker-ack* and one of Harefolk Hunter's thick arrows came flying. It pierced the goblin through the eyeball, stabbing him in the brain and taking his life as if it were the simplest thing in the world.

Club Fighter kicked the corpse out of his way, knocking it back into the encroaching goblins, then stepped back, panting. "Sorry—hold the line for a moment…!"

"Y'all can leave it to me!" Harefolk Hunter said with a flick of her ears, stowing the bow across her back and producing a large hunting knife as she advanced on the goblins.

He and Cleric could never have this when it was just the two of them. The boy pulled the dagger out of his arm and threw it away.

"Hey, are you okay?!" His partner's face as she hustled over to him was tight with worry. He shook his head. "I dunno…! I'm too scared to look…!"

"I don't think you have a choice!" She put the lantern on the ground and pulled off his gauntlet, inspecting the wound. Thankfully, the leather had taken the brunt of the attack, the tip of the blade just grazing his forearm. There was only a small trickle of blood. "Okay, I… Let's see… I need to put antiseptic on it, then bandage it… Press it down tight to stop the bleeding!"

"Y-yeah, got it…!"

A good, firm press would stop minor wounds from bleeding. A blessing from the gods, perhaps.

He had only learned about this since he had started adventuring, and he followed his old friend's instructions to the letter. The squeezing honestly seemed more painful than the stab wound, but Cleric wasn't going to take it easy on him.

"Was it poisoned?!"

"Dunno…!" He frowned when he realized it might have been. "No choice, I guess— Gotta drink one of these…"

They both hated to see expenses mount, but if he ended up paralyzed here and now, costs would be the least of their worries. He glanced toward the front line, where Harefolk Hunter was shouting and brandishing her dagger at a group of goblins.

How many did we kill? How many are left…?!

He wasn't sure anymore. Slightly panicked, the boy took out an antidote bottle and drank it in a single gulp. "Damn, that's bitter! Okay, I'm going in again!"

"I'll watch your back—you just take care of those goblins!" Supreme God's Cleric gave him a slap on the back, and Club Fighter, holding his weapons in his hands again, ran through the cave.

"Sorry to keep you waiting!" he called to Harefolk Hunter, who shouted back, "You oughtta be! Argh!" A goblin with a gaping slash in his chest was lying at her feet, but Harefolk Hunter herself was covered in small scratches. Specks of blood were visible in her white fur, and her breath was ragged. She was obviously nearing exhaustion.

"GOROGBB!"

"GBBGB! GORGBB!!"

Two goblins remained, which meant she had been fighting three on one. The goblins' eyes glinted with lust; they made no effort to hide their hideous appetites. Their awful little brains must have been imagining all the fun they would have with the rabbit girl, all the many ways they would trample on her dignity. No doubt they were having similar imaginings about Supreme God's Cleric in the back row. But Harefolk Hunter was between her and them.

It must have been terrifying for her to have all the force of this lust turned upon her. The young man frowned with this understanding. *I have to get a better grasp of the situation—give better directions…!*

If Harefolk Hunter had made any kind of slipup, the goblins would have been upon her now, might already have had her on the ground. "I'll take your place!" he thundered, sorry he had forced her to hold the line. "You get back there and have those wounds looked at! There might be poison involved!"

"Yeep! Y-yeah, sure thing…!" She hopped out of the line of battle with all the agility one would expect of harefolk. She almost rolled away, in fact, and Club Fighter leaped over her, letting his momentum carry him into a strike against the goblins. The sword and the club in his hands thudded against the goblins' rusty equipment.

"GOORG…!!"

"BGGGBGORG!!"

"You…stupid—" It might have looked cooler if he'd been able to come up with something more fitting—like, "This is for hurting my friend!" or something—but such is life.

He briefly locked weapons with one of them, but managed to shove the creature back. He had to think about both of the remaining goblins, though. He could smell their fetid breath, feel the warmth of it. Detect their disgusting body odor. Club Fighter was much stronger than they were in terms of brute force, but he couldn't let his attention waver. Couldn't afford to offer them the slightest opening.

"—stinking goblins!"

Club Fighter had barely learned everything there was to know about swordsmanship. He didn't think very hard, just pushed with his weapon, forcing his way through the goblins' own weapons.

"GROGB?!"

"GOOBBGG!!"

The goblins stumbled, but only for a second. Their eyes shone with a nasty light. Each one figured that while the other was being killed (they naturally assumed it *would* be the other goblin), he would jump on this human and kill him!

And it very nearly worked out that way.

"Hrrrahh!"

"GOROOGOG?!"

Club Fighter lashed out at the unlucky goblin with his club, adding the finishing blow with his sword. The other comparatively lucky monster screeched and made to move in on him…

"The fangs of the vorpal bunny take your life!" Harefolk Hunter, her face now bandaged, fired at him with all the anger of her wounds, and the modicum of luck ran out.

The goblin collapsed without even a scream. Club Fighter gave him a stab to be sure, and then it was done. He suddenly registered that he was standing among a room full of goblin corpses, his own labored breathing the only sound.

"...Is it over?" Supreme God's Cleric whispered, to which he replied, "I think so," and glanced around. It was too dark to see exactly what was in the shadows or hiding farther back in the interior of the cave. But he didn't think he felt anything. "I think so..." he repeated, and then he went on without much confidence: "I think it's over."

"Urgh...I'm *bushed*," Harefolk Hunter said, then sat down right where she was with an indecorousness that made one wonder if she was a girl or a boy.

"Nice work," Supreme God's Cleric said, passing the harefolk a waterskin, which she grasped with both hands and drank from lustily. After all, well-fed harefolk can keep going indefinitely, but without food they were paralyzed.

"I think we have some baked rations, too. All we have to do now is get home, so go ahead and eat them." Club Fighter took a swig of diluted grape wine from his own drinking pouch.

"Yahoo!" Harefolk Hunter exclaimed. "Gods, I'm just *starving*...!"

The tough baked goods were standard provisions for adventuring. Harefolk Hunter took them out of the item pouch with a big grin on her face, then started stuffing her face with them. Nibbling away with her cheeks full, she really did look like a rabbit, Club Fighter thought.

"Hey, not so fast," Supreme God's Cleric said. "You'll spill...or choke."

"I'm fine, I'm fine!"

"Gosh," Supreme God's Cleric added quietly, but she was smiling as she plucked a stray crumb off Harefolk Hunter's cheek. Club Fighter put his weapons away as he watched his two companions, making sure they were still all right. Then he repeated his conclusion to himself: *Goblins... Just small fry.*

Compared to the vampire, or the sasquatches they'd battled on the snowy mountain, goblins were nothing. Heck, they had taken care of this entire nest, just the three of them together. Including the battle to protect the farm on the outskirts of town—Club Fighter was sure that counted!—this made three times now. After fighting other monsters as well as goblins, there was no other conclusion: Goblins were real chumps.

"All right, let's catch a quick rest and then we'll scope out the inside of the cave. If there's no one else here, we head out."

"Sounds good," Supreme God's Cleric said with a nod. "I'm sure the villagers will want to know what's happened."

It was a classic—one might almost say cliché—quest. Some goblins had appeared near a village. The nest, it seemed, was in the mountains. Couldn't the adventurers do something about it?

And so these adventurers fought, cleaned things up, and that was the end of it. There were none of those "country" goblins—the big hobs they'd heard about—nor any spell casters, nor prisoners.

"Kinda makes you feel like they just now showed up here from somewhere, don't it?" Harefolk Hunter said, still wolfing down the food, her nose twitching. "Guess the stories do say that's how a lot of goblins get started."

"I know a certain strange adventurer who hunts goblins every single day who might disagree with you," Supreme God's Cleric shot back, and all three of them laughed.

Yes, this was how your average goblin hunt was supposed to go. They would head into the deepest parts of the cave together just to be sure, and then they would all go happily home. The reward was nothing to write home about, but it was another feather in their caps, and the villagers would be grateful, too.

They were feeling good. Downright happy, it must be said. But they didn't think that was any kind of mistake. They left the gloomy cave behind, and now they could smile up at the sun, which was getting lower, true, but the sky was still bright and blue.

All that was left was to work their way back through the forest and down the mountain, and back to the village. The adventure was over—no, wait.

"Hmm?"

"Huh?"

"Buh?"

The moment they stepped out of the cave, a shadow large enough to cover all three adventurers flew overhead.

"GYAAAAAAAAAAOSSSSSSS!!!!"

It turned out the adventure wasn't over at all.

§

He woke to a strange sensation; he felt warm, but his skin was clammy. His head was spinning, his mind thick. Deep in his nose and throat he detected blood, but it wasn't quite a smell, and it wasn't quite a taste.

He was caught unawares by a memory of when he was young. He had a friend who had fallen from a tree and hit their head. They'd laughed and said they were fine, but not long after, they developed a nosebleed and died. A blood vessel inside their head had burst, and they hadn't known.

Now Club Fighter forced himself to sit up, struggling dimly with the anxiety, the terror, that the same thing might happen to him. "Urr... Urgh...?" He felt dizzy, like he'd had too much to drink (though he had only ever experienced alcohol at the rare banquet). He quickly thrust out a hand to steady himself, and his fingers were met by a warm rock face. When he listened closely, he could hear both the crackle of a fire and the burbling of water.

Am I in a cave?

He blinked several times, trying to clear away the fog that seemed to muddy both his thoughts and his vision. After a moment, his eyes adjusted to the gloom, and the first thing he saw was the cheerful dancing of an orange fire. A hasty air trap had been devised from a piece of tent cloth or the like and hung over the fire to direct the smoke outside.

Yeah, otherwise you could suffocate, he thought distantly, letting out a breath. He realized his clothes had been stripped off. There was a blanket beneath his body, but he was still cold—and warm at the same time.

Okay, so I'm sleeping on the floor of a cave. And I have no clothes. Does that mean the others are all right?

As his mind finally began to sharpen, his first concern was for his friends...

"Ahh, y'awake now?" The voice that echoed through the cave was so cheerful that its joy was practically visible. "Yaaay!" A figure, soft curves outlined by the glow of the fire, clapped her hands. The long ears Club Fighter could make out bobbing above her head, and the poofy cotton tail, revealed that it was Harefolk Hunter. He could also tell that other than her mottled fur, her pale, healthy skin was covered by nothing at all. In fact, the fur on her hands and her most sensitive parts made the rest of her look even softer.

"Y-yikes—!" Club Fighter swallowed hard without meaning to, praying she wouldn't hear the noise—but who could blame him? The last female body he had seen was a quick glimpse of Supreme God's Cleric once, when they had been camping out together. And then, only at a distance, while she'd been changing. He hadn't meant to peek, of course. He would never. Although he might just admit to having the occasional impure thought.

"Birchwood burns even if the bark's a bit wet. Sure glad we brought some along!"

Harefolk Hunter's body was seemingly in constant motion, and paired with her unguarded smile, it was all the more alluring to him.

What was going on? What should he do? Club Fighter's mind felt literally frozen. He was well and truly gone, and wouldn't have come back if he'd been smacked on the head.

"Hold it!" came the voice that was his salvation. It was his childhood friend, wrapped in a blanket, her hair loose and her cheeks even redder than the fire. "Modesty! Clothes! Your clothes...!"

"Whazzat? Oh, I—ack!" Harefolk Hunter exclaimed as she realized what Supreme God's Cleric was saying. She hugged herself and shrank down, finally crouching on the ground. "P-please, dun' look at me... G-gee, that's humiliatin'. There's just so few boys in the village..."

She just hadn't thought of it. Now her accent was out in full force. The young man nodded. "Y-yeah. It's okay. Hey, I—I'm sorry..."

She pulled a blanket over herself with movements like a small animal, and he did likewise, grabbing the blanket out from under himself.

He seated himself with the blanket cowled over his head, certain that he was blushing just as hard as the girls. He was just glad that none of them could see well in the dark. It was best for all of them not to discover too many details about each other.

"...Hey," Supreme God's Cleric said, jabbing him gently through the blanket as though she could tell what he was thinking. "Keep your mind out of the gutter, okay...?"

"My mind isn't in the g-gutter...!" he protested, but he couldn't help his voice cracking. Her body was right there next to his. It was a challenging moment for a young man.

He stole a quick glance in her direction, taking in the fact that her hair, usually tied up, was loose; it was wet with water and gave off a faint aroma.

She's not a kid anymore, he thought. Back when they'd been children, playing together in the stream in their village, her body had been almost indistinguishable from his. So when had it started changing? When she had entered the Temple of the Supreme God? When they had set off on this journey together? Maybe when they had challenged the snowy mountain side by side?

The blanket covered her body, so he couldn't actually see anything, but the curves were all there. Combined with the glimpse he had gotten when she was changing, it was more than enough to let him imagine everything...

No, quit it! He desperately tried to fight back thoughts that made him want to split his own head open.

A young man alone with two nubile young ladies could hardly be oblivious to the situation. Yes, one sometimes heard of heroic men who could remain completely stoic at such moments, but Club Fighter didn't believe this for a second.

Still, it was a true hero who could step up at moments like this and say something sensitive. If you tried to pass everything off as a convenient accident, or if you mucked up your approach, your fate was sealed. And anyway, he didn't want the two of them to *like* him so much as he wanted them not to *dislike* him. But he was still too young to know whether this was pretension, longing, or desire.

For the first time, he found himself with renewed respect for that

Silver-ranked spearman. But Club Fighter didn't know how to handle his embarrassment over the girls without embarrassing them in the process.

That guy really must be something...

"Uh, um... A-anyway. I mean... Anyway." He tried to find the right words to say, noticing how dry the inside of his mouth was. "You're both okay?"

The two girls nodded, Supreme God's Cleric from beside him, and Harefolk Hunter from near the fire.

"What happened after...you know...?"

"W-we fell plumb into the river. And you...you got knocked out..."

"So the two of us brought you to this cave, got your clothes off, and started a fire so we could all dry out...and waited for you to wake up," Supreme God's Cleric said before whispering, "I thought you were dead." He wondered if he should be grateful for the note of sorrow in her voice. He offered a very quiet thank you, but heard only sniffling in response. Club Fighter smiled, just a little. "And our friend...?"

"Listen real close, and you'll hear him." Harefolk Hunter, on her part, had bent her ears down as if she weren't listening at all. Club Fighter soon understood why.

"...*ooooosssss.........*"

The wyvern's howl sounded like the wail of an enraged spirit screeching from the depths of hell.

"He... He's waiting for us...!" Club Fighter put his head in his hands and buried himself in the blanket.

§

"...Dragons breathe fire, right?" Club Fighter asked.

"Yeah, but some of 'em breathe poison or acid or ice or lightning; that's what they say," replied Harefolk Hunter.

"...Think wyverns breathe fire?"

"...Maybe. Could also be poison or acid or ice or lightning..."

"I don't know! I just don't know...!"

Outside the cave was a wyvern. And inside the cave were three novice adventurers. Their chances didn't look good.

Club Fighter almost thought he heard a voice in his head: *Alas, our adventure ends here.* He groaned, still wrapped in the blanket, trying desperately to come up with a plan.

"I don't suppose it's still too cramped out there for the wyvern to get in, is it?" he offered.

"I think it was pretty well open…," came the cleric's reply.

"Uh, okay, okay—maybe this cave leads somewhere else, then?!"

"There's water, right enough, but 's far as I can see, t'ain't no way to follow it."

They were cornered.

Club Fighter frankly wondered if he might be forgiven for simply throwing everything aside, curling up into a little ball, and crying. Of course, that wouldn't get them anywhere. It was possible nothing they did would get them anywhere.

If he'd been by himself, he might have simply huddled under the blanket and wept like a child who's made the biggest mistake of his life. He thought fondly of the tree hollow where he used to run when his mother had scolded him. Even if, admittedly, he had usually been dragged out of it when his mother found him. He'd hated that. He still hated it.

All this time, and it turns out nothing has changed. He couldn't suppress a smile at how pathetic he was.

That was when Harefolk Hunter twitched. "I'm hungry as all getout…" The words, deeply distraught, seemed to escape her almost involuntarily. Club Fighter looked over to see she had clasped her paws over her mouth in an *oops* gesture. Her eyes were wide and she was shaking her head, but a soft gurgle from her stomach gave her away. The harefolk girl blushed so hard it almost made him feel sorry for her, and she shrank even further down into her blanket.

"For goodness' sake…" The response came not from Club Fighter, but from Supreme God's Cleric beside him. "Just a second," she said, and grabbed her bag, which had been hanging from a rocky protrusion to dry. She produced baked rations wrapped in a cloth. The standard provisions. "…Here, eat this. I'm afraid it's a little damp."

"Er, but…" Harefolk Hunter shook her head when confronted with the hardtack, even as her nose twitched, enticed. "We dunno how long we'll all be in this cave…"

"But if you don't eat, you'll die, right? So eat."

"…Yes'm."

Harefolk Hunter took the food in both hands and obediently began nibbling. Supreme God's Cleric nodded. "Good," she murmured, then sat back down next to Club Fighter. She was still covered by her blanket. Club Fighter gritted his teeth, realizing that even the faint whisper of her breath was enough to set his pulse racing.

She glanced at him, not quite raising her head from where she had buried it in her blanket. "…What is it? You hungry, too?" She had her usual teasing tone, but her voice was weak, tired.

"Nah, just thinking," Club Fighter said. Then he added earnestly, "I'll eat later."

"Hmm…" Then his old friend fell silent. Harefolk Hunter continued eating, albeit apologetically.

All right, I need to calm down and think logically.

Club Fighter took a breath of the cave air, thick with the aromas of moss and smoke and the two young women, then let it out. It was thanks to his companions that he hadn't succumbed to his childish impulses. Neither of them was crying yet. It would be absurd for him to be the first.

I don't want to look bad. He didn't know if this was pretension, a sense of responsibility, or simple stubbornness, but…

"……Oh."

Suddenly it occurred to him that they might have already died long ago.

If that wyvern were able to spit out fire or poison or whatever crazy stuff like that…

Then wouldn't it have done so the moment they ran into the cave? Why waste its time waiting for them at the entrance?

Maybe because it couldn't eat us, then?

It couldn't get into the cave. If they died in the cave, it couldn't reach them to eat them. It was waiting for them to come out. But if they came out on the assumption that it had no breath weapon, was that when they would learn otherwise?

But wouldn't it have used it when we were running away, or when we jumped in the river?

OF WHEN YOU'RE RIGHT IN THE MIDDLE OF AN ADVENTURE AND A WYVERN SHOWS UP   23

Okay, so that thing didn't have a breath weapon. Most likely. He thought. Anyway, if it did, they were going to buy the farm. *So it's the claws, the fangs, and the tail we have to worry about.* Those three things. If they could just do something about them...

"...I'm sorry."

"Huh?" Club Fighter's surprised utterance sounded stupid even to his own ears. But that was how startled he was by Supreme God's Cleric's whisper, how totally he failed to comprehend it.

"...Can't help much..."

"Uh... What can't help?" he asked, genuinely not understanding, but his question only seemed to upset her. She glared at him, and the corners of her eyes seemed to glint ever so slightly in the firelight.

"Me!"

"Why?"

Even then, Club Fighter didn't quite grasp what his companion was trying to say. But he didn't want to leave the matter alone, either. Forcing down his embarrassment, he turned toward her decisively. She had to spell this out for him, or he wouldn't understand.

"I mean..." she started, subdued. "I've only been granted a single miracle. And I don't know anything useful or helpful... And, and..." Supreme God's Cleric narrowed her eyes and pinched her lips, speaking ever so quietly. "And you were looking at *her* earlier."

"What does that have to do with anything...?!"

He heard an odd little "yeep" from Harefolk Hunter. The two of them weren't trying to keep their voices down, and her ears could pick up a lot, anyway. Club Fighter and Supreme God's Cleric looked at each other, then smiled. It had been silly, they started to feel, to get so serious.

"Auuugh..." Thinking they were talking about having seen her so embarrassed, perhaps, Harefolk Hunter's ears drooped.

"Hey, sorry," Club Fighter said, then let out a big breath. "Anyway, I mean... I dunno, but... I don't think strong or weak, or...helpful or not helpful, I don't think that has anything to do with it."

He believed, with absolute sincerity, that he would never pick his party members, his friends, purely for such reasons. Yes, there might be places where it seemed too dangerous to take them. And each person was suited to different things, had different gifts, and so might be expected to take on particular roles. But that didn't mean they weren't able to help, or that they weren't a member of the party.

"So, uh, let's just… Yeah." The young man looked up through the gloom at the ceiling, trying to decide what to say to the two girls.

There was no response. Instead, there was only the howl of a monster waiting impatiently for its chance. And thus, what they had to do was clear.

"Let's just do something about that thing and go home."

Right. The girls nodded, and it was settled.

§

No matter what you were setting out to do, the first step was always to check your equipment; confirm the cards in your hand. This was an ironclad rule of adventuring that they'd learned well in the sewers.

"We've got our weapons and equipment, right?" Club Fighter asked. "Even if they are a little damp."

"That means your club and sword for you. Maybe you should wipe the sword down so it doesn't get rusty?"

"Oh, I've got oil!" Harefolk Hunter offered. "And pine resin, too. Lotsa stuff."

"Thanks, wouldn't mind borrowing that oil… But why pine resin?"

"Helps stick an arrowhead on an arrow, helps coat a bowstring, plus it's good for making poison bolts."

Huh. Club Fighter nodded. *Poison. Poison, eh?* Supreme God's Cleric leaned over. "Hey, do you *have* any poison?"

"Uh-huh," Harefolk Hunter replied. "Don't think a bit of wolfsbane would work on a wyvern, though."

"Yeah…" Supreme God's Cleric dipped her head in disappointment, though she probably hadn't been expecting much when she asked. But she promptly regained her good cheer and looked up, her hair bobbing and face shining. "Okay, we'd better make sure we've got everything!"

"Right," Club Fighter said. "Sword, club—check. And you two have your sword and scales, and your bow."

"Don't forget the slings. All our weapons are good to go. Right?" Supreme God's Cleric asked.

"Sure are!" Harefolk Hunter chirped, then the girls looked at each other and laughed. Club Fighter felt oddly left out, but nevertheless he nodded and said, "Good, then. Our clothes and armor are hanging over there to dry."

"Yeah, thanks to us," Supreme God's Cleric pointed out.

"I know, I know. Anyway…how's our potion supply?"

"Swallowed by the river. The bottles broke when we landed," Harefolk Hunter said despondently, shaking her head and causing her ears to flap back and forth.

Damn, and those were expensive, too. Club Fighter frowned, as did Supreme God's Cleric. How did other adventurers handle their potions? He would have to ask when they got back. *If* they got back.

"What do you think we should do with the shards?" Supreme God's Cleric asked.

"For now, take them out of the bag and set them aside," Club Fighter said. Then after a moment's thought, he added, "Don't throw them away, just keep them in a pile together."

"On it."

It was important to make the wisest choices, but at the moment they needed every advantage they could get. Later they might think, *If only we hadn't thrown away those shards…* In any event, since they couldn't get out of the cave, they couldn't really throw the shards away anyway.

"Then we need to know how many days' worth of food we have… And the Adventurer's Toolkit, is it here?"

"Never leave home without it, just like they say." Supreme God's Cleric said, echoing the words that the priestess—a girl about their age, perhaps the most notable of their cohorts—recited like a prayer.

The priestess might have felt humbled by the fact that she was in a party full of Silvers, but she had done a fair bit of growing herself. The three of them had seen it up close on their trip to the snowy mountain. It was clear why she was on the cusp of moving from Steel to Sapphire.

"We'd better do her proud," Supreme God's Cleric mumbled, checking over the contents of the Toolkit. "Let's see… Grappling hook, pitons, writing chalk... The torch is too wet to do any good, though..."

"We bought that thing because everyone claimed it was so important, but we ain't gotten a lot of use out of it," Harefolk Hunter said, gently smacking the bags that hung near the fire. With her minimal endurance, she didn't like having to carry any excess gear.

Club Fighter smiled. He felt the same way. After all, it wouldn't look cool to be hauling around too many bags. "Might still get a chance if we keep it with us. Okay... So, I guess the question is... What do we actually do?"

And then they were back to square one. Club Fighter understood that his sword and his club weren't going to help him against this enemy. Things might have been different if he could swing a broadsword like Heavy Warrior did—or maybe that weapon was magical?

Someday, sometime. The thought floated in his mind as he made himself focus on what was right in front of him. "That thing doesn't really track by scent, does it?"

"Think it's like a hawk or a kite—got good eyes," Harefolk Hunter said with a twitch of her nose. She knew the most of all of them about the beasts of the field.

"Okay, then how about we wait till night and sneak out?"

"It's a type of dragon, and you think it can't see at night?" Supreme God's Cleric said with a frown. "I really doubt that."

The three of them debated back and forth for a while, but sneaking seemed like a tall order. If a bit of hiding were all it took, they might have been able to get away when they'd fallen into the river. Much as they hated to think of it, they would have to go into this assuming they would need to fight.

"How about your divine miracle? Think it could reach a flying wyvern?"

"I... I think it would," Supreme God's Cleric replied guardedly, after careful contemplation of her friend's question. "But only if it isn't moving too fast. And even if I landed the hit, I don't think one blast would do it..."

"Okay—arrows, then?"

"Not if it gets too high up." Harefolk Hunter waved a furry white hand, concerned about altitude. "Think I can hit it, right enough, but I don't think I can get through those scales." Despondent again, she gave a subdued shrug and a shake of her head. Both gestures seemed very earnest.

Hmm. Club Fighter crossed his arms and tried to think strategically, something he wasn't used to. He began to think out loud. "Maybe if we could clip its wings so it couldn't fly, or cut off its tail to slow it down, or give it a good whack in the head and knock it out..."

"Impossible."

"Or at least darn hard."

"Yeah, you're right." Club Fighter gave a disappointed sigh. This was a tough one for a group that was only a step above novices. But of course, they knew that already. They weren't Spearman, or Heavy Warrior; they weren't even that guy who killed goblins. They didn't have enough strength or equipment or anything. But they would have to work with what they did have.

The three of them huddled together, debating and arguing and reassessing their limited options. They chewed on the hardtack when they were hungry, took sips of water when they were thirsty, and grimaced when the howl came from the entrance of the cave.

And somehow, long after they had lost track of how much time had passed, they managed to come up with something resembling a strategy. It wasn't a stroke of genius, a brilliant bit of turning the tables—of course not. It was a plan pieced together from their passing thoughts and half-formed ideas, and would have sent anyone who heard it into fits of laughter.

"If we can roll twin sixes, we might make it," said Club Fighter.

"Yeah," replied Supreme God's Cleric, "and if *he* rolls snake eyes."

"If we don't swing it, at least we'll all be together in his stomach...," added Harefolk Hunter.

Was that enough? Well, it might have to be. They looked at one another and started to giggle.

It would have been so easy just then to burst into tears, or cower in fear, or otherwise act absolutely pathetic. But they were full of the desire to do what they could, such as it was.

Better to die in the attempt than to die having done nothing at all.

§

In other words, a headlong charge ended up being their only option.
From the wyvern's perspective, they were just three tiny bipeds:
nothing special. Honestly, there wasn't even much value in eating
them. By the time it had chased the trio down, it would actually be
hungrier than when it had started.

Ah, but…

Imagine yourself confronted with three insects that you've chased
around your house until you're good and angry. Is there any choice
after that but to crush them? And if those three tiny bugs tried to run
away, squealing all the while, would there be any reason to let them?

For the wyvern, at least, there certainly wasn't. After the adventurers had dived into the river and then run into the cave, the wyvern
had set itself up just outside the entrance. That would have been the
height of stupidity had there been any other entrances or exits to this
cave, but happily for the wyvern, it knew there weren't. It needed only
to wait patiently, happily.

Sometimes such waiting can breed frustration, but in this case the
wyvern was delighted. The pipsqueaks who had fled into the cave
were afraid; shivering and panicked, they would soon come running
back out again. Nothing could satisfy the wyvern's evil dragon heart
so well as the tragic, defeated looks on their faces at that moment.

Wyverns, so-called "flying dragons," were less threatening than
full-fledged dragons in some ways, but in one respect they were the
same: Once they settled on their quarry, they would never give up on
it; they could wait for it if it took a decade or two decades. And if they
realized their chosen prey wouldn't live that long, they would let out a
great howl.

If its prey died there in that cave, what would it do to retrieve the
bodies? These were the pleasant thoughts that occupied the wyvern as
it eagerly waited for the bipeds to emerge.

"Y— Yahh— Ahhhhhh!!"

The creature did not miss its moment. One of the bipeds came
rushing out of the cave with a weapon in each hand, giving a comical

shout. The little creature seemed full of pathos and tragedy, but the wyvern could have fallen over laughing.

"GYAAAAAAAAAAOSSSSSSS!!!!"

Give the tiny creature what it wants, then. The wyvern turned toward the charging human, opening its jaws and baring its fangs. Start with the head, take two or three nips, and the human would be in its stomach, leaving only the arms and legs behind...

"The heart of the harefolk is in my arrow!!"

"OOOSOOS?!" The wyvern choked on its own roar. The arrow that came slicing through the air had flown straight down its throat.

Obviously, that wasn't enough to actually damage the wyvern. It was a bit like having a small bone stuck in its gullet. Thus, the creature hacked hideously once or twice, in great fetid coughs.

Vexing little beasts!

"GYAAAAAAAAAAOSS!!!"

With a scratchy, annoyed howl, the wyvern spread its wings and lofted itself into the air. There would be no more arrows flying down its throat.

An attack from above, then, raking the enemy with its claws. Just like a hawk catching a rabbit. Then it could drop them. Or break their necks in midair. Maybe not enough to kill them, just enough to make them suffer—that might take the sting out of this humiliation.

The sky was the wyvern's domain. Behold: The little boy with his two weapons, the tiny girl pawing at her bowstring—they couldn't reach the wyvern. It decided not to kill them in a single blow. The wyvern flapped its wings once more and—

"Lord of judgment, sword-prince, scale-bearer, show here your power!"

The flashing bolt from the heavens, though, came from beyond the sky itself. The sword and scales, brandished within the darkness of the cave in the name of the Supreme God, produced this blade of electricity.

"——?!?!?!"

This time the wyvern was rendered all but speechless. Of course, it didn't die from this attack; it wasn't even blinded. It blinked a few times, searching this way and that with its wavering vision for the fiend that had done this to it. This called for an even crueler death than the wyvern had originally planned. The boy, for example, whom the wyvern could see clearly even as the world seemed to tilt around it. It would pick him to pieces right in front of the two girls—that would make them regret their foolishness.

"GYYYYYYYYYAAAAAAAAAAAOSSSSSSSS!!!" The wyvern flapped its wings, trying to regain the altitude it had lost reeling from the thunderbolt, and howled out its rage. But the little boy—the adventurer—didn't stop charging. He was like an arrow flying toward a target.

And then, suddenly, wings appeared on his back—no, it was some kind of cloth tied to his sword and his club. Now the wyvern was beginning to understand. This was what he had been flourishing.

But it was still just cloth. What did he hope to accomplish with that? Did they think they could hide themselves from the wyvern that way? It would take the creature only a single turn to tear the cloth apart.

"Hrrrryyaahhhhhhh!"

The wyvern drove its head into the cloth, with neither the time nor the need to avoid it.

There was a sort of heavy *thunk*, and the creature bellowed as pain tore through its eyes.

§

"*That's* it, you big—!!"

"No time for cool wit, just run!"

Supreme God's Cleric, the sleeves of her vestments bound up, rushed past Club Fighter where he was giving a whoop of victory. A brave thing to do, considering there was a wyvern struggling to pull a cloth off its face right in front of him.

"Yeah, best we got going!"

"Hey, wait for me...!" Club Fighter cried, realizing Harefolk Hunter had passed him up, too. He rushed after the girls toward the riverbank, with his club and sword still hanging from his arms. He didn't want to put them in their sheaths just yet, lest the pine resin get all over everything. After some puzzlement, he finally used the thongs that secured them to his wrists to tie them to his belt. Very convenient.

"...Man! I can't believe that worked!"

"You're telling me...!"

"Yeah, no kiddin'!"

It wasn't anything that special. A childish prank, really. They'd daubed the tent with pine resin, mud, and wolfsbane, then laced it with the shards of glass from the potion bottles. If they put the stuff on thick enough, it would be hard to get the cloth off; it would cover the monster's mouth and maybe even get glass in its eyes—with the result as observed. Poison generally wasn't effective against dragons, but that didn't mean it was comfortable for them to get it in their eyes.

Of course, this was nothing more than a simple way to buy time. It would be foolish to think they had defeated the wyvern, or that they had won. They had, though, given up their tent and destroyed several potions; considering the average reward for a goblin hunt, they were going to take a major loss on this one.

They looked absolutely pathetic dashing for their lives along the river, and they were panting hard by the time they made it into the woods. But even as they fled, and despite the enraged monster behind them, the three of them had shared heartfelt smiles.

"Hey, that's at least one step closer, though!" Club Fighter said (it was all he could do to talk through the panting), wanting somehow to shout his lungs out.

Supreme God's Cleric caught up to him and Harefolk Hunter, exclaiming, "Closer to what?!"

"Slaying a dragon someday!"

That was the dream they'd shared since the day they'd left their sleepy village—in fact, long before that. Anyone they'd told would have laughed at them, made fun of them, told them to be realistic, and they wouldn't have been wrong.

But, the boy thought, *did you see that? Me—me, the guy who fled his village only to be chased around the sewers by rats and cockroaches—I just went toe to toe with a wyvern! I've done all sorts of things you'll never do, seen all sorts of things you'll never see!*

His murmured declaration of triumph might have been small, might have seemed silly to anyone else, but the harefolk girl clapped her hands. "Wow. That's really something...!"

The boy blushed at these simple but sincere words.

"Ooh, you're red up to your ears." Supreme God's Cleric cackled from behind him. "What are you so embarrassed about?"

"I'm not embarrassed!" he shot back—which was just about when the howl of a monster reached them from the direction of the river.

"'Kay, can't be chatting all day, unless we all want to be dinner...!" Harefolk Hunter said, starting out ahead of them with her ears bobbing. She held out a soft hand, and he took it.

"Hey, you two, not so fast...!" Even Supreme God's Cleric's face was red when Club Fighter looked back. She was stretching out her hand desperately, and he took hers, too.

"...All right, off we go!!"

It was a long way to town, even longer to their dreams, and the wyvern behind them was not that far away at all. Even so, the boy who had become an adventurer grasped what mattered most to him, his footsteps light as he ran.

His adventure—*their* adventure—wasn't over yet.

CHAPTER 2

Of How Girls Want to Go on Adventures, Too

"Yeah, this is how an adventure should be!" Never mind that it was a girl who was cutting down the wyvern in a single swipe as it flew over the castle walls; Female Knight was very pleased with herself.

Bereft of the use of its wings, the wyvern floundered through the air, screeching as it fell into the inner courtyard. The waiting soldiers jumped on it, stabbing it with spears and halberds and clubbing it with six-foot sticks, beating it to death.

Soldiers couldn't match adventurers when it came to facing monsters alone or in small groups, but a large band of soldiers would have the upper hand in combat. When a monster's claws and fangs and tail could each send a man flying, having ten or twenty together would see that the work got done. Such was the case with a wyvern at least, a so-called "flying dragon." If it had been a real dragon, it might have been a different story...

"I'm just sorry I didn't one-hit it," Female Knight said, "but I have to say, that's a gratifying sight!"

"That's for sure," High Elf Archer added with a nod, flicking her long ears. "All right, let me show you how it's done!" She pulled back the spider-silk string on her great yew bow, and let fly with a bud-tipped arrow. Her arms were thin as branches, but she drew the three-person bow as if it were light as a feather. She just laughed, though, and said, "My big brother's bow is way stronger!" That's high elves for you.

The arrow made a large arc, as if guided by a string. It was like the bolt was unconsciously joined with the wyvern's brain. The arrow ran flat sideways, pierced one eyeball and came out the other, then turned back in on the monster, piercing through its wing membrane and then stabbing it in the heart.

All this was nothing but a splotch in the distant sky, but High Elf Archer's jade-green eyes perceived it clearly. "Heh," she said, giving an elegant snort at her second catch of the day. "Next, to the west!"

"Hmph! You're still only ahead by one. Don't get too cocky!" Female Knight scoffed, but she was unable to suppress a smile. "Let's go!" She set off running along the ramparts at a speed that belied her full-body armor, large sword, and shield. It was impressive, but the high elf running along beside her looked as though she were traipsing through an empty field. They were obviously a breed apart: High Elf Archer moved without so much as a quiet footfall, like the wind.

The soldiers, though, hadn't a moment to admire the two lovely ladies.

Several robed figures were huddled beside the arrow ports along the castle's crenellated ramparts. They had been gathered from everywhere nearby: masters of the wind, readers of the sky, rain dancers. Mostly, what they did amounted to little more than parlor tricks. Maybe they could summon a breeze, forecast the weather, or even coax a little drizzle to fall, but that was generally it. Nonetheless, they wove words of true power desperately, shaving their souls away to do so, straining to cast spells of protection. And the soldiers incessantly firing from the tower needed all the help they could get.

Look overhead, and it was obvious: What you saw was seventh-tenths sky and three-tenths enemies. Maybe they could just be glad it wasn't the other way around. Down on the ground, it was no better. An army of monsters stretched all the way to the horizon, threatening the castle.

No, let's not indulge in hyperbole, here. A monster army of that size hasn't been seen since that battle years ago.

But if one wasn't accustomed to it, it was difficult to count the squirming shapes of the forces of Chaos emerging from the forest. Skeleton soldiers who would never tire populated the front line, their shields raised high, the hail of arrows all but meaningless to them. As for the undead warriors with their rotting flesh, they continued to press forward no matter how many shots pierced them. The only ways to stop them were cutting them down with swords, crushing them with maces, or smashing them with studded clubs.

But there was a reason the lord of the castle didn't sally forth, and why the Army of Darkness was allowed to lap at the castle walls: The castle simply didn't have the forces to scatter the enemy. If their tower should fall, the village it protected would lie open to this unholy horde.

The enemy was drawn to this tower, precisely because it offered a stout defense. The soldiers fired arrows at their enemies above and below, and if any of the invaders attempted to climb the walls, the soldiers dropped rocks on them, or poured burning oil down on them; and when they ran out of those things, they started throwing porridge.

When the undead—who, unlike the living, weren't bothered by the scalding heat—reached the top of the wall, they were greeted with swords and spears. Just because they couldn't die, didn't mean they couldn't be broken into pieces by a fall from a great height, and rendered physically unable to move.

A carefully constructed tower will have portals and openings for just this sort of defense. This was a human fortification, so humans were most prominent among its defenders, but everyone there, elves and dwarves, padfoots and rheas, fought relentlessly. Soldiers and knights, mercenaries and domestic servants, even the chefs and the prisoners from the jail battled as one. They brandished weapons at the monsters, cooked food, gave first aid, repaired the walls, offered water, did laundry.

They counted the money in the vault, checked how many provisions were left, recorded everything, played musical instruments, and sang songs. No one scoffed at even the smallest detail.

The battle here on the frontier of the Four-Cornered World was a microcosm of the struggle playing out between Chaos and Order. Fight to survive, fight for honor or friendship or love, for profit, for amnesty, or just to get home. It didn't matter the reason. The fact that all these people with their disparate motivations *could* fight together was what made it Order. Though some might deride it as naïveté, they felt like the last tower standing at the edge of the world.

"Um, I brought more arrows…!"

In the middle of it all, Priestess was likewise doing her utmost to help as best she could, rushing this way and that. Now she climbed a ladder with an armful of arrows, keeping low as she worked her way along the ramparts passing them out. Her quick footsteps sounded like the pattering of a little bird dancing along a branch.

Needless to say, there were wounded soldiers present, and Priestess would bite her lip each time she saw one. But she didn't use her healing miracle. She couldn't. These weren't life-threatening injuries.

She had several miracles, and could use three miracles per day. They were precious strategic resources.

It's really incredible to be able to use a fire spell twice in a day.

The girl had taken her first step into what could be called the middle levels, and she was learning well how to judge when to use her abilities. Thus, she said as cheerfully as she was able: "Food will be coming in a little bit! Hang in there!"

"Thanks, lass!"

"Yeah, it's a big help!"

The soldiers smiled tiredly at her, nodding their heads as they accepted the ammunition.

An army needs food and drink as much as it needs swords or shields or spears or arrows, in order to wage a battle. (Except, perhaps, the greatest lizardmen and the best martial artists.)

"They did a fine job thinning out that wyvern flock, too."

"Yeah, thought we were gonna be crushed under that. But I'm more worried about the zombies."

"The captain said he'd take care of them," another soldier interjected. "And anyway, I'm worried about them both."

"Got that right."

The soldiers spoke the truth: The wyverns didn't seem to *attack* so much as they seemed to come on like a herd of buffalo. Get in their way, and there was no hope for you. No one wanted to face them head-on.

Priestess knew that if she'd had to face any of this alone, she would have just run away, or stood frozen in terror. And yet the soldiers bantered and laughed with one another.

"Hey, what's the supply situation?" someone asked.

"The transport corps is supposed to be bringing supplies from the water town, I think..." Priestess replied. It wasn't a very certain or very specific answer, but the soldier looked pleased just the same. "Right," he murmured. "Got it." Priestess made the holy sign in front of her chest. "May the Earth Mother protect you..."

How much of a real comfort was that prayer to the soldiers gathered there? Maybe some of them followed another deity. But still, there was someone praying for them. Those who didn't understand what a joy that was would never know.

This was a battle for self-preservation. Surely the All-Merciful Earth Mother was with them. True, the dice of Fate and Chance could surprise even the gods, but still...

Praying that the soldiers would not be touched by the fangs and claws of the monsters, that the arrows of the skeleton soldiers would not strike them, Priestess descended the ladder. She let out a breath and looked for the next thing to do...

"Make sure you...rest a little...eh?" Witch's hand settled softly on Priestess's shoulder. The way she walked, with her generous hips swaying, made Witch an alluring flower to the defenders. With her magic, she might be the key to the defense of the castle at some desperate moment. She whispered to Priestess in her usual languid tone, "If you try too hard, you...won't last...you know?"

"Oh, y-yes! I'm sorry..." Priestess looked down, somewhat embarrassed. She felt like a child who had gotten too excited at a festival. Witch looked at her as if she knew exactly what Priestess was thinking, and the slightest smile edged onto her face. "But you're...used to it now...aren't you?"

Huh? Priestess looked at her in surprise, unable to understand, unsure what she was talking about.

"I thought...surely, you'd be more panicked, you see? More, afraid?"

Oh...

Now it made sense. Priestess nodded firmly, forcefully. "Yes, ma'am. At the temple… I mean, I've been doing what I can to help since I was a little girl." Priestess puffed out her small chest with confidence and pride (but always mindful not to let the latter become haughtiness). On a number of occasions, she'd helped tend to wounded adventurers and soldiers after a large hunt or battle. That incident with the Rock Eater, for example, had been particularly intense…

My goodness… That feels so long ago now. It's strange.

Not that much actual time had passed. Maybe it seemed like so much because she had been so young then. It wasn't a fond memory by any means, but there was a nostalgia in it, and Priestess smiled in spite of herself.

Shortly thereafter, the sounds emanating from beyond the tower began to ebb. Interestingly enough, even an army of the undead couldn't go forever without rest—at least, apparently. Perhaps the number of corpses had actually been reduced by that much, or perhaps the magical power of those controlling them was running short. Or were the skeletons knitting their bones back together, the undead wrapping their wounds with bandages…? (All right, it didn't seem likely.)

At any rate, this umpteenth wave of the attack had subsided. Priestess and the others, it seemed, had survived.

"Heh, I win!"

"I can't even touch them if they don't get close. You can't count those ones."

"You're a sore loser!"

The conversation that reached Priestess's ears, and quite clearly at that, was supremely inappropriate for the battlefield—or perhaps supremely appropriate.

High Elf Archer came down the ladder almost silently, and Female Knight followed behind her, creaking and heavy with armor. Female Knight, who had evidently lost the bringing-down-wyverns contest, seemed to regard the difference in the sound of their footsteps as just one more annoyance. Priestess thought she could hear her mumbling something about this being the reason why nobody liked elves as the knight turned and waved to Witch. Witch smiled a little wider and nodded, and something seemed to pass between the two old hands.

I wish I could be like that, Priestess found herself thinking, but she was too embarrassed to try to imitate them. Instead, she pattered up to High Elf Archer. "Good work out there," she said.

"If you can call this work," High Elf Archer replied, twitching her ears. "At least—unlike with Orcbolg—we've got a good, sturdy defense around here."

"Heh, couldn't let myself be outshone by some dainty cleric!" Female Knight, correctly perceiving High Elf Archer's remark for the compliment it was, sounded downright proud of herself, her beautiful face breaking into a smile. It was astounding that she was so gorgeous even when she was locked into her armor—though the content of her words was more gallant than gorgeous. Her lovely eyebrows slipped into a frown, however, and she let out a defeated sigh. "Never did take down a wyvern in one hit, though—just means I've still got some work to do."

"Hey, what cleric could possibly take down a wyvern in a single hit?" said High Elf Archer before adding, "You want to know your problem? It's this stuff." She was tapping Female Knight's armor, which resonated with the clear sound of good, solid workmanship. Had Dwarf Shaman been present, he might have been able to tell them how it had been made. And if Lizard Priest had been here, he would have been happy to analyze the girls' performance in battle.

And if Goblin Slayer were here...

"No, it really happened once, or so I've heard. There's a song about taking down a wyvern in a single swipe of the blade." Part of Priestess was trying to remember how it went, while another part of her was reflecting dejectedly on how much useless trivia she knew.

"Sounds like she was more *horrible* than *holy* to me!" High Elf Archer quipped.

"In any...event, shall we.........go back?" Witch said, chuckling at this exchange beneath her broad-brimmed hat.

Back into the tower for food and some rest. Even high elves didn't have infinite supplies of energy. High Elf Archer was actually starting to feel pretty tired; she just hadn't noticed until that moment.

"...Wait, what's that?"

Priestess was just reaching for the waterskin at her hip in a slight panic when she heard this sharp whisper from High Elf Archer. Apparently, the elf was tired, but not that tired. Priestess looked up to discover High Elf Archer watching the sky, her gaze steely. The sky was blue, and the sun was high and bright, although just starting to work its way down from the heights.

"I don't hear anything. But…something's coming…!"

Which happened first: the shadow passing overhead, or Female Knight wordlessly leaping into action? Either way, they both seemed a turn or two ahead of Priestess as she grabbed her sounding staff.

Female Knight kicked off the ground with such blinding speed that she might have been the wind itself, and jumped into the air. It was only by following her trajectory that Priestess finally saw it. "But… that's…"

At first, it looked like nothing more than a bit of fog in the air, but as she watched, it began to swell and expand. There were the huge wings and the sharp horns. A pale coldness about it.

"…a bird and…a deer…?" The monster resembled a madness-inducing combination of the two animals. It was unmistakably a creature of Chaos, and Female Knight went up, farther and farther, over its head. She jumped so high that she could have landed clear in the tower's inner courtyard, easily surpassing the monster. As she passed overhead, she aimed a blow downward, sure to end the life of any flying creature.

Priestess didn't know whether this was something Female Knight had come up with while fighting wyverns, or if it was some ancient swordfighting technique. But that fatal blow…

"Hngh?!"

The sword pierced the monster, true enough, but it continued with undiminished momentum, as if Female Knight had stabbed the sky itself. She grunted, twisting forcefully in midair, and landed neatly atop the ramparts. "Some kind of illusion…?!"

"It's like it's there, but—not!" High Elf Archer called back, her voice clear as a bell. She dropped to one knee in the courtyard, drawing her great bow with a creak—but she couldn't hide her concern. "It's like I can't *feel* it…! I won't be able to hit it!" she hissed through gritted teeth, but even these words, when spoken in the voice of a high elf, sounded pleasant.

There they were: the monster that had so suddenly appeared in the sky, Female Knight, who had made an attack against it, and High Elf Archer with her voice. The soldiers, too, who had been disturbed to the point of near terror, somehow managed to rise and prepare for battle with their weapons in their hands.

Priestess saw all of this at once, absorbed it in the space of a single heartbeat, and thought as hard as she could. What could she do? What *should* she do? Was this the time for a miracle? She started to pray...

"...Stop that...please." She felt Witch's hand slide firmly across her back and shoulder.

"Wha...?" She heard her voice scratch as the broken syllable slipped out, and she blushed in spite of herself. It turned out that one gentle stroke of Witch's hand had been more than enough to shatter her concentration on her supplication to heaven.

"When you don't...know...what...something is...then you must not touch it. Not yet." Witch looked up at the sky, but Priestess couldn't quite tell where she was looking. Nonetheless, she thought she understood what Witch was saying, if only distantly. The most wizardish of a wizard's pronouncements were always that way. The dwarves likewise had a certain gnomic streak.

Over the past year or two of accumulated adventuring experience, this was the conclusion Priestess had come to.

That's just the way it is, she thought. Lining up too-clever arguments would get no one anywhere. What they were working with, her and all of them, was *magic.*

"...All right." Priestess nodded, continuing to glare at the blue-black creature above. Witch had said "not yet." Priestess simply chose to trust her.

"Ah," Witch said, a hint of gratification in her whisper. "There's a good, girl..."

"Oh, stop that," Priestess mouthed in reply. She continued to stare straight at the enemy. If there was the remotest thing she could do to be prepared for when the moment came, she had to do it.

That's what he *would say, anyway.*

"I came to take the measure of you all, but you seem to be an apathetic lot."

Thus, although she was surprised by the husky voice, she immediately saw that it had emerged from the monster's throat. The creature, neither bird nor deer, moved its eyes—they reminded her of a dead fish—as it spoke.

"Excuse me?!" The response came immediately, and it came from Female Knight. Priestess heard her grumble, "*Gygax!*", a most unbecoming word for a servant of the Supreme God, before shouting, "You've got some mouth, you bastard! Get down from there! I'll knock your head off and roast you on a spit!!"

"As you wish, of course: I'll be here again tomorrow at the same time." Then the servant of Chaos laughed, a rattling noise that squeezed out of its throat. Just as it was about to disperse in a cloud of mist, the same way it had arrived, it declared: "Fear the hour, all of you! Bewail your powerlessness and die!"

And then, although it had not touched them, the soldiers beneath the unearthly ring the monster had drawn in the sky collapsed. The creature then vanished, leaving only its cruel parting words to pollute the air in its wake.

§

It wasn't want of money that drove adventurers to mercenary work. Adventurers typically didn't become mercenaries in the first place, even if the reverse sometimes happened. For one thing, trying to take enemy heads on the battlefield was a lot less lucrative than hunting down treasure chests in caves. Insofar as both professions involved risk to life and limb, adventurers had it better—at least, after they reached a certain rank.

If you wanted to make your fortune in the world, you could join the army as soon as possible, or else become an adventurer. If you made a name for yourself and were given a knighthood or noble title, land to govern and armies to lead, that was certainly one kind of fortune. One that involved being neither an adventurer, nor a mercenary.

There were two reasons why the military might hire adventurers: to defeat monsters in the enemy army, or else to infiltrate an enemy base and take out their leader. Or to steal some secret. Okay, three reasons. Monster hunting, assassination, information procurement, or to rescue a captured princess. So you see? Four reasons.

At any rate…

Priestess, for her part, wasn't on the ropes, and she wasn't there on some special mission. Put briefly, what had brought her here was… That's right. Reason five.

"What? Goblin Slayer isn't here today?"

Such was what she had asked, openly perplexed, at the Adventurers Guild several days before. It had been early in the morning; she had said her prayers and gotten dressed for the day, then headed for the Guild, only to be greeted by the distressed expression of Guild Girl.

"I'm afraid not. Or…he was, but he already— Well, he's been taken somewhere."

She told Priestess that Spearman and Heavy Warrior had arrived and dragged Goblin Slayer off without waiting for him to object. If it had been Spearman alone, a word or two from Guild Girl might have swayed him, but no.

"They said they needed a scout… I'm afraid I'm not the only one around here who handles quests, you see," Guild Girl said, then smiled apologetically. She could inquire with one of her colleagues as to what exactly was going on if she wanted to, but she was afraid they might think she was trying to horn in on their turf.

"I see…" Priestess replied, realizing she knew nothing about the internal politics of the Guild. She could hardly even imagine what they might be.

Whatever Guild Girl thought about Priestess's ambiguous expression, she smiled at her. "He's really changed."

"Huh?"

"I can't believe it's been two years already. He never used to do anything but solo, but first he joined up with you, and now he's got a whole party…" He was getting quests from big names that sent him to other countries, and sometimes other groups even asked him for help. "He's really changed," Guild Girl repeated fondly, shaking her head. Her bangs twitched silently, somehow giving an impression like a puppy's or a squirrel's tail. "I'm happy about that," she added. "But...a little sad somehow, too. You know what I mean?"

"Er... Hmm," Priestess said. She was embarrassed to deny it, but to affirm it felt childish, so she settled for an ambiguous shake of the head. "Me, I can't just tag along after him for the rest of my life."

"You've really come into your own, haven't you?" Guild Girl reached out her thin, lovely fingers with their neatly manicured nails, just brushing Priestess's chest. Or, more specifically, the status tag that dangled there, so new it still had its shine. Priestess wasn't used to it yet. "Just what we'd expect of a Sapphire-ranked adventurer."

"D-don't tease me like that..." Priestess returned, blushing. Guild Girl giggled at her.

Priestess puffed out her cheeks in annoyance, but quickly realized what a childish thing that was to do, and forced herself to stop. She wasn't used to receiving praise—that's what it came down to—she hardly even believed she deserved it.

Yes, it was true her rank had gone up. But an increase in rank doesn't always naturally accompany an increase in one's self-confidence. She was the same person who had up until yesterday been tirelessly accumulating experience; today she was just one level higher. They were a sequence, flowing one into the other, no difference between them—or so it felt to her.

She believed it would be very difficult, though perhaps not impossible, for her to do the things that she saw those adventurers who had come before her doing. In her own mind, she was still a novice, a rookie who didn't know her right from her left.

Admittedly, if I really think about it, I've learned to do a lot of different things, but still...

She'd even encountered a dragon and lived to tell the tale, which was no small accomplishment. If she'd met another adventurer who had done such a thing, she would certainly have considered them incredible. But when the achievement was her own, it somehow seemed smaller in her eyes.

Maybe if there was some way to tell how powerful a person was, what their level was, at a glance...

She couldn't hold back a sigh at the thought; such an idea was pure fantasy.

"What's wrong?" Guild Girl asked, but Priestess shook her head.

"Nothing. I'm just still getting used to the idea of being Sapphire…"

"Hee-hee. Well, don't worry, you'll settle into it. You just have to figure out how to behave like a Sapphire."

It sounded so easy when Guild Girl said it, but all Priestess could offer in return was a "Right" and a noncommittal look.

But what should I actually do? she thought. Lizard Priest was out on some quest from an old friend, taking Dwarf Shaman with him. So she'd thought Goblin Slayer, High Elf Archer, and she would go out, a three-person team, but the plans had fallen through at the last minute. Then again, calling them *plans* was a bit much—they'd only been their usual hazy ideas. They could each do what they liked.

Priestess wasn't necessarily averse to the idea of taking a day off, but maybe not this particular day. She'd woken up assuming she was going to work, and had dressed on that assumption. So what could she do?

Maybe I could study the Monster Manual. She could practice swinging with her staff or slinging with her slingshot as well, but she was in the mood to read a book today. After all, goblins weren't the only monsters in the world. You never knew when you might be on a goblin hunt and run into a completely different type of creature. *I know that from experience…*

Dragons weren't the sort of things you bumped into every day, and just knowing one's weak points didn't give you any guarantee of victory. And then, there were those stories of adventurers who encountered mantis men and found themselves killed before they knew what was happening…

Priestess was just scanning the Guild's bookshelves when a lovely, but clearly annoyed voice, said, "What, you got left behind, too?"

She turned to find Female Knight, gorgeous and gallant, standing behind her and making no effort to hide her frustration. Female Knight must have seemed a melancholy beauty to those who didn't really know her. Priestess heard several novice female adventurers squeal when they spotted her.

"Uh-huh. I...I've been *left behind*, I'm afraid." As for Priestess, she'd come into contact with Female Knight more than once. She could get away with mimicking her tone and annoyance (with a giggle).

"Gods above. Bunch of bastards. Toy with a woman's purity of heart, will they?" Female Knight snorted derisively, but finally shrugged. Priestess couldn't tell if she was being facetious.

"Boys...can be...so...selfish, yes?" an alluring voice broke in, sending a shiver down Priestess's spine. This was someone whose presence always made her feel even more novice than usual. "I've suffered the same...fate...as you two."

"Both of you?" Priestess asked, blinking. "Where's everyone else?"

"Our kids and our accountant got dragged off by that dwarf of yours in the name of seeing a bit more of the world." Female Knight fixed Priestess with a glare that caused her to squeak, "I'm very sorry..." Yes, the matter had been discussed and agreed to, but it could still sting.

Does this mean I'm starting to understand the unspoken rules of this world? Priestess wondered. She would have liked to think that her interpersonal skills had improved somewhat, but at the moment, it didn't really feel like it.

What a blessing it would be to have some way to grasp her own abilities and talents at a single glance.

"Hrm. Anyway, that still leaves your elf. Where's she?"

"Oh," Priestess said, her gaze briefly flitting to the ceiling. "Still sleeping, I think."

"In other words, you've got time to kill. Perfect, that settles it!" Female Knight announced, clapping her hands as if this decided everything. Then she called out "Hey!" in the direction of the reception desk.

"Yes ma'am," a Guild employee her party often worked with said, as if she understood exactly what Female Knight wanted. She quickly started going through some paperwork.

Priestess and (probably) Witch, for their part, still weren't sure what was going on. They looked at each other in surprise.

"C'mon, we've got a warrior—hell, a knight—and a wizard, cleric, and a ranger. Just one thing to do, right?" Female Knight smiled like a wild animal, baring her teeth, an expression Priestess recognized very well.

"Go on an adventure!"

§

"Why play by the rules? Why not just burst into the enemy encampment and start chopping off heads?"

"We can't do that."

"Sure, of course not.............. Are you *sure*?"

"I thought you were supposed to be a big, bad knight. You sound like a rank amateur..."

Thus it was, how Female Knight's invitation led them to the situation in which they now found themselves.

The scarlet sun of twilight played over the stronghold's mess hall—which was the fancy name they'd given to one of the big open spaces. Pelts had been laid on the ground and some long chests had been set out, some as chairs, some as tables. The soldiers ate restlessly.

Priestess, seated directly between High Elf Archer and Female Knight, laughed out loud at their conversation. The two of them seemed to work well together, somehow.

"I can tell I'm just not putting enough spirit into it, that's the problem. When I really get serious, I'll slice that flying pissant right out of the sky."

"Even elvish heroes can only execute a flying attack under absolutely ideal circumstances. There's no way a human could do it."

"Grrr..."

Priestess offered another empty "Ha-ha-ha!" It was good they weren't feeling too morose. Probably. She glanced in Witch's direction for help, but she only took a few elegant puffs of her pipe. Every time she brazenly uncrossed and recrossed her legs, the collective gaze of the soldiers was riveted to her thighs.

I'm sure she realizes... Right? Priestess looked at the ground, unable to stop her cheeks from blushing. She could feel her heart beat faster inside her modest chest, and her brain didn't seem to be working as well as usual.

How did we end up like this…? she asked herself. The stronghold was naturally under the command of the military, but soldiers wouldn't be the only ones there. After all, where the army went, priests and prostitutes followed, as well as caravans of merchants, and even battle-field scavengers. Businessmen who loaded their wares onto a cart and rolled it up to the door of a fortress weren't all that unusual. And to act as their bodyguard was an adventure—adventurer's work.

Priestess was open to it, but it wasn't for her alone to decide. She first had to consult with High Elf Archer, and picking her way through the elf's bedroom, where there was hardly a place to put her feet, had been a minor adventure in itself.

Naturally, she'd responded cheerfully that it sounded like a great idea. And so the four women formed a chattering, bantering envoy, accompanying the cart all the way to the stronghold—leading to the situation in which they now found themselves.

The merchant had been right in the middle of negotiations when the wyvern and the army of zombies had shown up, and they found them-selves in the middle of a siege. Of course, the quest Priestess and her friends had undertaken was only to see the merchant to the fortress, so they were free of their contract the moment they reached its gates.

They hadn't accepted a quest, wouldn't get any money, and had nothing to do with this—so in principle, they could simply turn around and go home. But this, in High Elf Archer's estimation, would have been to abandon their awesomeness as adventurers. They'd hap-pily chosen to come on the initial adventure, and if it happened to lead to more adventure still, they should go for it.

Because we're adventurers.

"…But still, what's going *on* here?" Priestess said to herself, taking a mouthful of a soup composed of beans, onions, and potatoes, with a modicum of meat. There was the blue shadow that refused to show its true form. The nightmare creature, half bird and half deer, that flew overhead. She'd never heard of nor seen such a thing before. She didn't recall them being in the Monster Manual, either. Just about all she knew about it was…

"…It's not a goblin."

"It's, a…peryton."

"A what?" The whispered word took Priestess by surprise. She discovered that Witch, who had been puffing idly on her pipe until that moment, was suddenly looking directly at her.

Priestess straightened up abruptly, earning a chuckle and a smile from Witch. "The beast…with the blue…shadow. A creature out of fantasy… It doesn't…exist." Her words—her explanation, such as it was—seemed to emerge from a haze. Priestess watched Witch closely, listening hard to catch every last thing she said. "So it's impossible…to defeat it, you see. To hunt a creature that…doesn't exist, can be done only within…a dream of…hunting."

"Within a dream…"

Witch often seemed elusive, but she didn't lie. Priestess furrowed her brow and thought hard, and after a moment she grimaced as she found her conclusion. "So this…thing that doesn't exist. It's…impossible to defeat?"

"Why, from…the very start. It was…never…there, you see?"

But… That still left one thing unexplained. If it didn't exist, how could it do anything to them? How could it attack people, kill soldiers, make proclamations of war, or command the undead?

"It doesn't exist, but…it does."

"That's, right." Witch nodded, exhaling sweet-smelling smoke. It left her full lips and floated off into the sky, forming mysterious letters. Priestess watched it go as if it might hold the answer to the riddle. After frowning for another moment, she grunted. "Urgh," Priestess said, sounding like a little girl, as she laid herself across the table. She probably would have mussed furiously at her own hair, if the Temple hadn't taught her better manners than that. "It just doesn't make any *sense…*"

Her mumble was overpowered by a pounding on the table. "Yeah, the girl's right! Talk sense, dammit!" Female Knight's face was bright red. She had either started listening in at some point, or else had been drinking the entire time. Judging by the mug in her hand, the latter seemed by far the more likely.

She slammed the mug on the table again, drawing looks from the surrounding soldiers. "I just want to know one thing: Can we take it down or can't we?! If it bleeds, then I can kill it!"

"…" Witch's eyes narrowed—whether she was put off or amused was hard to say. "…I should…think…so."

"That's all I needed to hear!" Female Knight shouted. Then she said, "Good!" and grabbed a bottle of wine that was lying on the ground by her feet. She didn't bother to pour, but drank directly from the bottle—which was still substantially full—draining it in a single long gulp. "The point is, we can win this thing! So listen up, everyone! Don't give that beast a second thought! Have some fun, drink your fill, eat what you want, and then get some sleep!" An audacious claim—a less generous soul might say baseless—but Female Knight proclaimed it with utmost conviction.

Priestess was somewhat taken aback, but the soldiers immediately exclaimed, "Huzzah!" Someone said, "If a Silver-ranked knight thinks we can do it, we can do it!"

"I'm more than just a knight!" Female Knight yelled, pouting. It was cute; the expression seemed quite at home on her gorgeous face. "I'm a paladin who serves none other than the Supreme God!"

"Yes! Yes!" came the response. There wasn't a soldier alive who would choose morosely contemplating a deadly enemy over a bit of rejoicing. If someone was willing to take a shot at raising their morale, that was enough for them.

The silence that had hung over the mess area a moment before had vanished, replaced by rather premature talk of a victory celebration. More wine was produced from the storehouses, along with the provisions they had been conserving until now—bacon and ham and bread. One might have expected the captain or the commander of the stronghold to stop them, but it was they who were bringing the provisions out.

Amidst the hubbub, Female Knight looked in Priestess's direction and winked. *She's really something…* Priestess thought. She didn't know whether Female Knight had planned this, or had simply been being honest, but she had managed to single-handedly change the mood in the stronghold. In fact, Priestess rued her earlier fuss about how things had made no sense. So many people had been watching and listening.

…I shouldn't do that.

She gave her head a shake and smacked herself on the cheeks.

It would do no one any good for her to get swallowed up in self-recrimination, become depressed and anxious, and finally stop doing anything at all. Instead, she needed to think, then think some more, and then finally act. That's what *he* would do.

"...All right!" With her thoughts working once again, Priestess didn't even notice Witch's limpid gaze on her.

That monster doesn't exist. And something that didn't exist couldn't be wiped out of existence. Because it hadn't been there in the first place.

"So I guess...that means...?"

"If you can hit it, that's all that matters, right?" That voice. It was so clear: High Elf Archer's words were working their way easily into Priestess's consciousness.

"Huh...?" She looked over to discover the elf had moved to the window. She was watching the celebrating soldiers happily as the wind played with her long hair. The sun was low in the sky now, dyeing the world red, but it seemed to be different, somehow, for a high elf. Those last beams of sunlight made her hair gleam golden.

Then the archer gave a wave of her hand and said easily, "You just have to hit it with something. Am I wrong?"

"Huh? Well..." Priestess tried to get ahold of her disorganized thoughts. "You really think so?!"

She craned her neck to look over at Witch, who didn't speak, but only tugged on the brim of her hat. Sometimes she was at her most eloquent when she said nothing at all.

"You're asking what something is that exists but doesn't exist. That's what it comes down to," High Elf Archer said nonchalantly. "If you can *hit* on an answer, then it exists." She gave a sort of hissing laugh, like a cat. "Simple, right?"

"I see! Then you could—"

Then you could take it down. Priestess, trying hard not to let go of the answer she'd finally got ahold of, clenched her fist and nodded.

The foe had said it would appear at noon the next day. They could set an ambush for it, then. Female Knight and High Elf Archer in the front row. In the back, Witch...and herself.

They couldn't expect the enemy to simply stand around now that they knew who and what it was. So offense would be paramount. It would be no time for the two on the front row to stand around solving riddles. And so it would be up to Witch—or Priestess herself.

When she reached this point in her thought process, though, Priestess furrowed her brow. "I can't possibly do it," she said despondently. This wasn't a matter of a lack of self-esteem, but, in her mind, a simple fact. The reality was that, to this point, she hadn't come up with anything approaching an answer. And out of the four women in her party at this moment, she was definitely not the most intelligent one. "Instead of me, how about…"

You? she was about to say, but before the word had left her mouth, she found a slim finger pressed to her lips to silence her.

"Wizards, you see…leave things ambiguous…and…use them… ambiguously." Priestess swallowed the word back down, and Witch went on melodically. "For if…a thing has one single meaning…then no other meaning can…exist… You see?"

Priestess, unfortunately, really didn't. She detected a faintly sweet aroma from Witch's finger that she thought must be the tobacco, and she quickly pulled herself away. No, she couldn't grasp the real meaning. It was literally shrouded in smoke.

But she did understand what it was Witch wanted to make understood. The proof was in how Witch smiled gently at her and said in a sweet whisper, "Just…try and take…a guess, eh…? From you yourself."

§

"…What, can't sleep?"

Of course not—how could she?

The cots in the garrison were simple but soft, decidedly more pleasant to sleep on than the beds at the temple. Probably even nicer than the economy rooms at the Adventurers Guild's inn. She'd wrapped herself in her blanket, stared at the ceiling, closed her eyes, turned over a few times, then opened her eyes again.

Cold light from the twin moons streamed in through the window. All around her, soldiers slept (this was the female dorm, of course), their measured breathing the only sound.

She'd tossed and turned a few more times, knowing she needed to sleep soon, unable to do so. What if she wasn't able to sleep at all, right through until morning? ....*No. Even if I did manage to sleep, I might be killed in my bed and never wake up again.*

Priestess was assaulted by sudden anxiety, but she let out a sigh. This was ridiculous. It was a cowardly thought, laughably so, and yet...

All this was what made the unexpected question such a relief to her.

"Um..." After a moment's thought, Priestess decided to own the fact. "...No, not a wink."

"Well, there it is," Female Knight whispered from a nearby cot. "Being able to fall right asleep is a talent all its own." She added how jealous she was of the elf. One heard that elves didn't really need to sleep, but could it be true? Maybe they were simply capable of sleeping when and as they wished, and being awake when it suited them. But whatever the case...

...*I agree. I'm jealous,* Priestess thought. She considered her friend— almost like a much older sister—sleeping on the cot across from hers. "Er, what about you...?"

"I was sleeping until a moment ago. Just happened to open my eyes." The cot on her other side creaked faintly. Priestess turned over again, and there she found a beauty bathed in the blue moonlight. Female Knight looked at her and smiled mischievously. "The night before a big battle's just like the night before an adventure. I get all excited and, well—here I am."

The moonlight fell on her lovely features, revealing the face of a child who was about to get up to no good.

Priestess was at a loss for how to respond. She looked up at the ceiling of the garrison, searching for the words. Finally, all she came up with was "That's really something." If nothing else, it had the virtue of being the truth. Female Knight was simply excited; she carried none of the anxiousness that burdened Priestess at that moment.

"Heh-heh," Female Knight said proudly, and her blanket (which bulged in more places than Priestess's did) shifted. "Still, I'm only at about eighty percent. Doesn't matter the fight—if you can handle it at sixty or eighty percent, that's ideal."

Priestess blinked once. Then she pulled the blanket up so it covered her mouth, and looked at Female Knight. "...Really?"

"Trust me. You can't go around fighting all your battles at full tilt."

"Er..." Well, she was right. "...I see, that's true."

"Yeah, right?" Female Knight laughed again, and then she went on, "Take tomorrow's battle, say. You can't help thinking about what you'll do, how you'll handle it."

Gulp. Priestess swallowed visibly, but nodded. She knew how childish the gesture must look.

"You picture yourself chopping up bad guys, taking out every enemy from here to the horizon."

"Uh...huh."

"Come on, admit it."

"Well, er... All right. Yes." Priestess couldn't bring herself to spell it out exactly, but this seemed to be enough for Female Knight.

"But that's the thing. When you get to the actual fight, you can only do—I dunno, it depends on the enemy, but let's say fifty bad guys." Sounding like a child complaining the dinner wasn't what she expected, the knight continued, "But that's fifty if you're a great warrior. If you *assume* you can take down fifty guys, the number you can probably kill is, say, three."

"Is that true?"

"Pretty much."

Priestess's interjection was feeble, Female Knight's response indifferent. But the knight's next words had a cutting edge.

"You afraid of getting too big for your britches?"

"Oh, uh, no, I..." Well, that was part of it. She couldn't deny it, and yet... Embarrassed, Priestess pulled the blanket even closer. "...It's more like, everyone else just seems so amazing. It makes me realize how far I've still got to go..."

She thought about how she had behaved during the battle that day, and at dinner that night. She hardly felt she had a leg to stand on in the presence of this knight. It was almost too humiliating even to compare the two of them. Such feelings were with her constantly.

She'd only just recently grown able to recognize that she was accomplishing anything at all.

"Nothing wrong with a little arrogance," Female Knight said, blowing away Priestess's ideals in a few words. Then she flopped back on her cot, which groaned again. Priestess took this as her cue to look back up at the ceiling. It was wooden, old and weathered, hard to call beautiful. Perhaps this was what ceilings should look like on a battlefield, she thought.

"So what if someone sasses you about it? They only see what they want to see."

"What they want to see?"

"They ignore all the effort we've put into getting where we are. Act like we're just full of ourselves because we're strong. Hrmph." Female Knight snorted, as if she were spitting out the sound along with the words.

Could it be? Priestess thought then. Could it be that Female Knight was actually talking to *her*?

She had thought something similar, hadn't she? She'd seen Female Knight's feats on the battlefield as nothing more than amazing. She hadn't considered everything Female Knight must have done to come to that point.

"Ah, who cares? You be as full of yourself as you want, until there's no room left for them." While others complained about her, she would keep moving forward.

The words Female Knight spoke seemed to Priestess as if they came from a dizzying height.

Of course they do. The two of them had become adventurers at such different times. They had walked different roads, gained different things along the way. And that wasn't just true of Priestess and Female Knight, but of her and the strange adventurer she was constantly chasing. It was the same with her other party members. And indeed with many people she had met.

So that must mean...

Maybe she could catch up. Maybe.

"...Gotta warn you, that's just how to become a *strong* adventurer. I don't know if it makes you a *good* adventurer."

"You don't know?" Priestess repeated, taken aback.

"Don't know what you don't know," Female Knight said, pursing her lips. "I know I'm pure and just and powerful, but whether that's good or bad, that's for other people to decide. I've got no way of saying what'll become of you."

"But you're teaching those kids, aren't you?" Priestess said, pouting a little herself. She wasn't really angry; she wasn't even really pouting. It might have been most accurate to say she was looking for a little comfort—although she would certainly have denied it.

"I take no responsibility for how that turns out—that's the whole idea," replied Female Knight. "No way to take responsibility, anyhow," she added gaily. "If they die, what am I supposed to do—take revenge? Quit adventuring? Kill myself? Will any of those things mean I've taken responsibility?" She could turn to a life of crime, but it wouldn't do any good. Female Knight announced this completely naturally, then snorted again. "The Supreme God tells us to think. Can't go blaming other people for *everything* that happens to me."

It wasn't that Priestess didn't understand this—indeed, she understood it very well. She still remembered her first adventure all too clearly. They could have avoided that tragic outcome—she could have avoided it—but she couldn't blame it on anyone else. If anyone had tried to claim that the failure of that adventure had been the fault of one of her other party members, she would have objected vociferously. At the very least, her own powerlessness, if nothing else, had put her at fault.

So what does that work out to?

There was the strong adventurer Female Knight talked about. The one that didn't necessarily mean being a good adventurer.

So what was a good adventurer?

Priestess felt sure that Female Knight, and High Elf Archer, Witch, and Goblin Slayer were all good adventurers. For that matter, what kind of adventurer did she even want to be…?

After what might have been one minute, or five, or possibly less than ten seconds, she sighed with resignation. "I think rather than worrying…it would be better to think about how to win."

"Bigger is always better," Female Knight said with a laugh. Then she gestured with her eyes, toward one of the other cots. Distracting snoring came from it. The blanket covered two large hills, and the graceful curves of a beautiful body were quite plain. It was Witch's bed.

Priestess whispered that she understood. And then she and Female Knight tried to keep themselves from laughing too loud.

Their giggles soon tapered off, and Priestess let her gaze drift from the ceiling to the window. The moonlight was still illuminating the night, a pale shimmer washing over the cots.

"Um," Priestess said, finally finding the courage to speak—but once the sound was out of her mouth, she found she had nowhere to go with it. "Why…?"

For a brief moment, there was no answer. Just as Priestess was starting to think Female Knight must have drifted off, her voice came whispering through the dark. "Why'd I become an adventurer, you mean?"

Yes. Priestess nodded under her covers, but didn't voice the word. "I don't have to know to talk to you. But I wouldn't want it to end without knowing the answer."

When she thought about it, she realized this might be the most she had ever spoken with Female Knight. You could certainly be someone's companion without knowing their past or their personal situation. You could even be friends. You could certainly fight alongside them. But sometimes it all ended and you never found out. Priestess thought she would regret that deeply.

"Huh, so that's your motivation. I thought it might come up some time, but… Well. Me, I…" Female Knight shifted under her covers, lapsing into silence. Maybe she was getting her thoughts together, or maybe she couldn't find the words. Finally, there was a resigned sigh. "Once upon a time…a certain country was engulfed in political strife. The prince killed his father, brothers, and sisters, and usurped the throne."

It was a story of something that had happened long ago. The only princess to survive the slaughter requested an adventurer—the illegitimate daughter of the crown prince's younger brother; in other words, her cousin—to get revenge. Priestess had heard that it wasn't so much a quest proper as it was that the adventurer had gone to help of his own accord. But Female Knight swore it had been nothing more than a quest, and that the adventurer had gone to do battle with the usurper.

He and the Princess had turned a group of would-be assassins to their cause, and ultimately destroyed the man who had stolen the throne. And then they vanished from history...

"Why do you bring them up?"

"It'd be cool to be able to say they were my parents or grandparents or something, but actually they're way further back than that. Don't even know if it's true." Female Knight closed her eyes and spoke like she was polishing a river stone she'd collected when she was a child. "But I like to think it's true."

And so she'd learned the sword arts passed down through her family, left home, and become an adventurer. Apparently, the story ended there—that was all there was to it.

Priestess thought for a moment, then a smile crept across her face. "...So you were a princess yourself."

"Ha-ha-ha. Guess so. If the world were a better place, I'd be a princess right now. A princess...a princess knight." Her voice sounded so immensely gentle. "We ought to get some shut-eye now. Tomorrow's a big day. Although believe me, I understand being too excited to sleep."

"...Right," Priestess said, then pulled the covers over herself once more. Just before she closed her eyes, she stole one last glance out the window. The two moons were still shining, but now they didn't seem quite so cold.

§

Soon enough, the sun was climbing into the sky. The stronghold filled with the sound of clashing swords, flying arrows, and the desperate recitation of magical chants. The soldiers were tired, but despite the fatigue and occasional anxious glances at the sky, morale was still good. There was every appearance that they would not break, that the fortress would not fall.

Priestess, for her part, was standing squarely in the stronghold's inner courtyard. Her sounding staff was proudly in her hand. She stood prepared—and yet she had to admit it felt uncomfortable not to be doing anything.

"...Why do you suppose the enemy is trying this?"

"Because they know they can't win in a straight fight, that's why!"

Priestess was happy to hear High Elf Archer's reply to the question that slipped out of her. The elf was crouched in the shadows, stringing her bow with spider's silk; her long ears twitched. "In war games, it's not the individual soldiers who make all the difference, it's the commanders," she said. So, she claimed, she'd heard from various elders.

High Elf Archer herself had no practical experience in pitched combat, but she was a close relation of some who had participated in the battles of the Age of the Gods. She might only have the knowledge she'd absorbed from them, but that put her understanding as far above Priestess's as the clouds were above the mud.

"You really think it's that big a difference?"

"Well, there's exceptions to every rule, and a really powerful hero can turn the tide... But basically, yeah."

But with adventurers, it was different. On an adventure, it was individual skill and power, each person's intelligence and courage, that meant the most.

"If this were an adventure, and the adventurer lost?" High Elf Archer said. "Then everyone would run away."

Priestess thought about that one. "Umm... You mean, like, if two knights had a duel?"

"Yeah, sort of," High Elf Archer replied with a wink. "It's a big responsibility. Can't let ourselves get beat—same as always!"

Priestess nodded, but she also looked up at the watchtower, where the captain was continuing to command the action. He hadn't registered very much with her; she'd hardly spoken to him. But she was sure his command was superb. Otherwise, she believed such a small stronghold could never have held out so long.

O Earth Mother, abounding in mercy... In her heart, Priestess offered up a prayer to bless him. *May that prayer be protected.*

"...Doing okay?"

Maybe Priestess's sudden silence had left High Elf Archer thinking she was anxious or upset. Priestess smiled to see her friend watching her so seriously, even though the expression looked out of place here on the battlefield. To be able to pray for someone's safety truly warmed the heart.

"Yes—we're going to do this!"

Yes, indeed. High Elf Archer waved a hand in acknowledgment. Her lips formed the words: *Give 'em hell.* It made Priestess happy. Then the high elf went quiet, as still as if she were moss growing on a stone in the forest; she gave no hint of her presence. Priestess was careful not to look around, but she was sure the others were just the same way. Female Knight and Witch were hidden right where they had planned to hide, she was certain of it.

That means I just have to do my part… I think.

She wondered if that strange, eccentric adventurer was worrying about her. She doubted it. But if he was, she wanted to be an adventurer worthy of his concern.

Priestess bit her lip with fresh conviction, then looked resolutely at the heavens. The sun was nearly at its zenith. And then, with no warning whatsoever, *it* appeared.

There was a gusting breeze, and a shadow swept among the ranks like a whirlwind. Several of the soldiers it touched fell writhing to the ground.

"Mm… So, girl, you found the fortitude not to run away." Just like the day before, the monster appeared—this time cloaked in a chilling pale white cold. To Priestess, it seemed to be the chill of death.

The way the creature mixed stag and bird almost arbitrarily was like something out of a nightmare. It was a blotch on the otherwise beautiful blue sky.

"…I did." Priestess grasped her sounding staff firmly, seeking sure footing as she turned toward the beast. Her hands did not shake. Her voice was steady. Her vision was clear, her footing firm.

"Then offer up to me your life!" The monster howled with pleasure. It was thinking only of how to shred the dignity of this poor, unfortunate cleric. "Let the feast of slaughter begin!"

Priestess's voice, though, rang out over the battlefield, refuting the creature's awful desire: "When you speak my name, I disappear. What am I?!"

§

"Hrk...?!" The peryton gulped audibly. The sapphire shadow had not realized that the battle had already begun.

Had this been any ordinary fight, the peryton would most likely have crushed the girl's skull in its talons. Or perhaps it would have torn off her limbs, and only then cracked her head like a walnut.

But this was not an ordinary fight. It was the peryton that had sought a deciding duel, and this small girl who had risen to the challenge. As such, the girl held her staff high, boldly facing the monster.

Riddles were more than a game for children. They were an important ritual, laid down by the gods from days of old, a way of settling matters. They constituted one of the highest forms of combat, permitted only to those who had words, who had intelligence. No one, be they a god or a wizard, dared to cheat at this game. If you doubt it, acquaint yourself with the tale of the rhea's adventures. Or else the riddles of the five dragons, or the battle with a dragon that lasted a solid two minutes.

Whichever you may choose, the peryton now had no way to back out of the riddle challenge. The upraised staff, the clear eyes that shone beyond it, and the prayer to the Earth Mother that radiated from them both.

"Arneson!" the creature cursed. The beast of Chaos could be as enraged as it wanted, but to try to nullify this would be to invite its own destruction.

It might curse the gods, but the module had been set into motion.

When you speak my name,
I disappear.
What am I?

The girl proclaimed the riddle at the top of her lungs, as if specifically wanting to agonize the monster.

"...I can tell you that. It's silence. It must be." The peryton was careful to make sure the irritation it felt emerged as no more than a slight undertone of mockery in its voice. "Life is beautiful, is it not, little girl?"

"Indeed, so it is," Priestess said. "I fully agree."

"I wonder if you'll sing the same song when I've brought you to the cusp of death."

The threat was not remotely subtle, and yet the young woman didn't so much as tremble. "It's your turn. Go ahead."

"Very well." The peryton's deer face smiled, a hideous rictus that would never have appeared on the face of any real deer. "There is more to this world than you would ever dream of."

It is yours, unquestionably,
yet you never use it.
Others use it, endlessly,
but at the end it's cast away like a stone.
What is it?

The peryton was getting its revenge with this question; the girl seemed uncertain. Her gaze wandered for a second and her lips opened and closed—but all that came out was a brief exhale, not an answer.

"What's the matter? If you can't tell me, then allow me to begin by crushing you under my talons." Yes, the peryton was convinced it was seeing terror in the girl's eyes, and added this taunt to fan the fires of fear. It had observed that humans, for whatever reason, were more intimidated by tone of voice than by an overwhelming presence.

The girl, however, looked straight at the peryton, squeezing out syllables one by one. "It's...a name. My name...... Isn't it?"

"...Indeed, indeed. The name that shall soon be carved on your tombstone." This time the peryton was unable to hide its displeasure; it nodded, speaking slowly and distinctly. It would not have been helpful to have the girl admit defeat so early in the game, but it was no less frustrating when she guessed the creature's riddle.

The monster glowered up at the shining midday sun and spat,

"Your turn, child." And then, unable to leave it at that, it added, "Best think of the most confounding riddle you can."

§

The riddle contest continued for two more rounds, then three, on and on. Priestess didn't serve the God of Knowledge, yet she endured the game admirably. Had anyone voiced this praise, though, she would certainly have merely blushed and said it was thanks to the teaching of her master.

She might not have been able to cause the peryton real distress, but neither did she give an inch. Her talk with Female Knight had convinced her of one thing: Riddles were the only way to discern this creature's true form. It was a battle she could take on alone, and one in which she could fight on equal terms with a monster she knew little or nothing about.

Of course, if she was facing an opponent whose intellect went beyond what she could imagine, then she might be inviting death in a matter of a few moments.

But that's always a possibility if I fail in battle. And when it came to a battle of wits, she was confident that she had every chance of victory.

The sun baked the two of them, their shadows lengthened, and she felt sweat dribble down her forehead and her cheeks. She blinked once, her long eyelashes fluttering. She wiped her brow to ensure the sweat didn't get in her eyes.

She wondered if the monster suffered from the sun in the same way she did. The blue-shrouded beast hovered in the air, flapping its wings, and occasionally glanced resentfully at the sky.

—...?

Priestess cocked her head. Something about the glance seemed odd to her. How much heat could the creature withstand?

"What's wrong—do you give up? If so, say 'I give up,' and then bow your head beneath my claws."

"Oh, ahem, no," Priestess said, the creature's triumphant boast bringing her to her senses. She shook her head. "As it eats, it grows. But the slightest drink—"

"Fire," the peryton said promptly. "Fire dies if it 'drinks' water."

Grrr... That hadn't been a very good riddle. Priestess exhaled. Her mind was starting to dull. This wouldn't do. She shook her head again, then brushed away the hair stuck to her cheeks. She was all too aware of the blue-shadowed creature watching her with disdain. And of the soldiers who observed the contest on tenterhooks, even as they continued their own battle. She was sure High Elf Archer, Female Knight, and that beautiful witch were watching, too.

It's...kind of nerve-racking.

The only thing she could do was conduct the fight in a way that would make her proud of herself. Do battle like she expected to win, even if she lost.

Priestess took a few quick, hard breaths to steady herself, and then managed to smile as she said, "Your next riddle, then."

"As you wish..." The peryton grimaced at the sky again, sulfurous breath coming out its nostrils as it ground its teeth and shook its head on its long neck. "I was just starting to think I might make things a little easier on you. Are you ready? Not that I would wait if you weren't..." And then the monster intoned the next terrible riddle.

In the morning, small on four legs,
at noon, tall on two.
But at eventide, a third leg is added.
What is this being I speak of?

"Go ahead. Solve my riddle, if you can." The creature spoke quickly, as if assured of its victory. Priestess smiled, ambiguous, almost awkward. She knew the answer to this one. Knew it very well. Could it be the creature was relenting a little?

Or is it just like me—getting tired?

Or again, could it be a trick question? If it was, though, no other answer came to her.

"Hmm, umm..." Priestess searched her mind, deeply unsettled, and then with all hesitation and trembling she said, "It's...a shapeshifter, right?"

§

"...What?"

"Well, of course, it must be...a shape-shifter." Was she wrong? Priestess was suddenly very anxious. She quickly added: "I mean, ahem, a mimic. It can turn itself into anything it wants. Like a treasure chest, or a door, or some loot..." She'd heard they could even come flying at you, and that they could creep along on four legs. That was the answer. It had to be. "Right...? Or, um, perhaps...you've never heard of this creature?"

"I know what a mimic is, you damnable fool!" the peryton howled, baring its teeth. It seemed Priestess's innocent question had touched the monster's pride. The eyes of the deer that was no deer flashed with rage, and it growled out: "Well, what does it matter? It was never an even fight between you and me. Give up now. *Man!* The answer is man. The 'morning' is its infancy—"

"Oh..." Priestess blinked, and then she pointed out simply, "You just said 'I give up.'"

"I said no such thing!" The peryton's temper finally snapped, and it landed angrily on the ground with its terrible claws. Priestess felt the *thump* in her belly when the creature came down to earth, and let out an involuntary squeak. She was only surprised, but she glanced around, worried it might have been taken for a sound of fear.

The peryton could say what it wished, but a human didn't grow and shrink throughout the hours of the day. In fact, no living creature that she knew of was taller or shorter depending on whether it was morning or night. Maybe a candle; that was the only thing she could think of, but then the rest of the riddle wouldn't make any sense...

"—!"

At that instant, there was a flash of insight, bright as lightning in her brain. Priestess seized upon it. She gripped her sounding staff tightly. It made a lonely rattle. There was no hesitation, no reluctance in her words, no fear at all. She held her staff high, brandishing it at the enraged monster, and unleashed the next words with a thunderous crash.

It shall appear by your side without fail,
at any time or place you might be!

You cannot flee from it!
Nor can you speak with it!
There it is, beside you!
Too bad for you! Best give up!

"Wha—?!" The peryton took another deep breath. The fire danced in its eyes. Priestess didn't hesitate.

"You're a shadow! A person's shade!!" She grasped the staff even harder, fanning the fires of her soul. Raising it so it would reach the gods in their high heaven. *"O Earth Mother, abounding in mercy, grant your sacred light to we who are lost in darkness!"*

There was a great flash of light. The sunlight combined with the Holy Light that Priestess produced, the two of them together eating away at the monster's flesh. The wind carried the pieces away like embers. The bizarre beast was just a shadow, one that was now stripped away in the twinkling of an eye.

"C—curse youuuu...!"

"Clavis...caliburnus...nodos. Key to steel, bind!"

As the creature tried launching itself off the ground and back into the air, a melodic incantation sounded words of true power. Witch stepped out of the darkness, her words clipping the creature's wings. They had looked so large shrouded in shadow, but now, revealed by the light, they were shown to be only some feathers.

Of course: How could a foul creature like this have truly grasped the arts the great sage once used to bring low a dragon?

"You're mine!" a voice like a bell called. Before the monster could pronounce a curse of death upon Priestess—the cause of all its trouble—a bud-tipped arrow pierced its jaw, pinning its tongue to the roof of its mouth, so it could form no words at all. As it reeled and fell to one side, the demon's vision fixed upon the high elf, who had climbed up and perched upon the tower without its ever noticing.

"DDDDAAAAAEEEEMOOOOOOOONN!!!!!!" The monster was not about to give up its quarrel so easily. As it fell, and then struck the ground, this creature from the nether realm set off running on its four powerful limbs. If this was how things were to end, then it could at least tear out that girl's throat before it went...

"Oh—" Priestess didn't seem to quite grasp what had happened. All she knew was that suddenly, Female Knight was in front of her, crouching and ready. In fact, she seemed to be bowed slightly forward. All Priestess thought she saw was this: Female Knight rushing past the demon at tremendous speed.

But that wasn't all that had happened.

"Hmph," Female Knight said, soft and low, the wind catching her beautiful golden hair. The platinum sword she gripped in her hand shone, even through the patina of demon blood that now stained it. It was only a moment later when somewhere, far behind Female Knight and Priestess, there came a sound of flesh splattering. Priestess looked back to discover the demon was now only a torso, where it had slammed against the wall. Its head, which had gone spiraling into the air, landed on the flagstones of the courtyard with a *thump*.

"A waste of my sword. That's what this foul creature gets for trying to play games with an innocent girl. These damned night stalkers." Female Knight shook the blood off her blade and returned it to its scabbard. Priestess realized that she had witnessed an ancient sword technique, one so long forgotten there were none left now to speak of it.

Everything Female Knight had said, every word of the story she had told, was true, Priestess realized.

"You're very...very strong."

"I know, right? Heh!" Female Knight puffed out her armor-clad chest, and Priestess's face softened into a smile.

"That's right!" she said.

Did she want to become a good adventurer, a strong adventurer, or neither? Priestess still didn't know. But then she saw Female Knight give a great war whoop, and the soldiers respond with shouting and cheering, following her forth into the enemy encampment. She saw Witch turn to her with a warm smile and call out, "You did it!"

And Priestess knew she wanted to be an adventurer who could hold her head high before them.

"...I did it!" she said, throwing her small fists in the air in celebration.

OF A GIFT FROM A YOUNGER SISTER

"Hmph! Some adventure this is. We're just running errands."

"Don't be rude!"

The grumbling Scout Boy found himself jabbed in the side by Druid Girl's elbow.

The vast winter sky spread out above them, as blue as if an upturned container of paint had spilled all over it. There was no cover on the wagon that rumbled down the road, and as long as you didn't mind the cold, it would have been very inviting to go to sleep.

Passersby kept glancing at the vehicle, probably on account of the hulking lizardman in the driver's seat. Or maybe it was the dwarf and the half-elf who rode with Scout Boy and Druid Girl. The crew might all too easily be taken for slave traders or kidnappers, but the sight of the children, relaxed and playful, dispelled this assumption. And anyway, the silver tag hanging from the lizardman's neck proved that he was a friend to humanity. A Porcelain or Obsidian rank might not have inspired the same confidence, but Silver—that would overcome even prejudice about his appearance or race.

Though, for all things there were exceptions...

"Ha-ha-ha, somethin' wrong with that, kiddo? Don't like doing deliveries?" The dwarf, a shaman, laughed uproariously at him. He seemed to consider the winter-blue sky a perfect drinking companion, and was indulging accordingly.

Dwarves, who lived underground, were untroubled by either heat or cold. Or maybe it was thanks to the wine he was consuming so liberally—the young scout wasn't sure.

"I mean, y'know. I finally get to leave town, go all the way to the fortress on the border, and then they just hand us a single scroll and tell us to drop it off," the boy grumbled, clearly vexed by this turn of events.

"But how often do they let you into a fortress?" Druid Girl said pointedly, dangling her bare feet off the edge of the wagon. A border fortress was sure to be crucial to the nation's defense, not the sort of place people from town could just wander into. Even the area they had been shown was only the small part of it considered safe to reveal to outsiders. "And anyway, it was really interesting."

This time it was Scout Boy who jabbed Druid Girl as she prattled on. "You're just happy we got to try out all that great eastern-border food."

"Wh-what's wrong with that?!" Druid Girl retorted hotly, her face flushed. "We each have our own interests, don't we?"

"Gods, rheas are such gluttons."

"What?!" Druid Girl said, her voice cracking. "We are *not* gluttons!"

Rheas were famous for eating four or five meals in a day. Druid Girl most likely objected to the terminology because, as a young woman of a certain age, it made her feel self-conscious.

"Ah, yes, in any event, we had a contact," the lizard priest said merrily as he listened to the two youngsters bicker behind him. "Some resent this way of doing things, but the simplest way to ascertain someone's stature is by family and friendship."

"You think?" the boy asked in surprise.

"There is, simply put, no reliable way to judge a person's abilities and intellect at a simple glance," Lizard Priest replied, nodding his head on his long neck. "However, if someone comes from a prominent family background, we may assume they're likely to have been educated, and if you happen to know someone who knows them…"

"…then they might just trust you." The half-elf fighter lounging beside Lizard Priest on the driver's bench finished the sentence. He was looking up at the sky. He had a young leaf in his mouth (where had he gotten that?), which he had formed into a grass whistle that he was now blowing on idly. He sat up abruptly, then turned toward Lizard Priest, bowing his head with an elegance and decorum that emphasized the elvish blood flowing in his veins. "And you have my thanks for the introduction."

"Think nothing of it."

"Scaly's right. We'd nothing else to do."

Lizard Priest and Dwarf Shaman, both experienced adventurers, waved away the thanks as if what they had done didn't really matter. But to Half-Elf Light Warrior, it mattered quite a bit. It would normally have been his own party that would have had to introduce this boy and girl to powerful people. Perhaps it was luck, or perhaps simple kindness. But whatever the case, it remained that he had incurred a debt of gratitude.

"Hrm... I mean, I get being grateful and all, but still..." Scout Boy, still looking like it didn't make perfect sense to him, leaned off the wagon, so far it looked like he might fall.

"Be careful!" Druid Girl chided from beside him, but he ignored her, gazing up at the sky. He squinted against the sharp blue, so bright it hurt.

"Is it as great as all that?" he asked.

"Someday, when you two discover some plot of Chaos, and bring it to that esteemed woman..." *Then you'll understand*, Half-Elf Light Warrior didn't add aloud. So long as the youngsters didn't die, they would presumably continue their steady climb up the ranks.

"The point is, you have to be able to get them to listen to you, and not just dismiss what you say out of hand as the babbling of an inexperienced adventurer," Half-Elf Light Warrior said.

"You mean like those nobles and stuff who are gracious enough to listen to anyone, even commoners?"

"Not really. Most people in the world—and I include myself—will say anything they've convinced themselves of, no matter how baseless it may be."

It was important to gather information, yes, but it was too often forgotten that it was just as important to check and verify that information. One might be sent an important communiqué, but then it would be buried in a mountain of papers on a desk somewhere, and not discovered until after it was too late. Chances were that happened all the time; and sadly, it would mostly be covered up as the negligence of some bureaucrat or other.

"If you've really got something important, then you have to have a way of *showing* people that it's important," Half-Elf Light Warrior went on.

"Huh…" Scout Boy still didn't sound wholly convinced.

Half-Elf Light Warrior smiled slightly and added, "That person's honored younger sister is supposed to be quite the mage. Never undervalue someone who knows their way around the magical arts." Deciding it wouldn't do any good to explain further, he went back to blowing on his grass whistle. He glanced to one side (barely; his peripheral vision was excellent) and saw Lizard Priest opening his jaws.

"It's the way of the world for there to be much that we do not understand. Proceed along the path of learning one step at a time, and your neck will one day stretch to reach the leaves."

"But I'm just a rhea," Druid Girl mumbled.

"And I'm a dwarf!" Dwarf Shaman boomed with laughter.

I don't know… Rheas very rarely even left their villages. Everyone knew the story of the eccentric old man who had come back with a hoard of treasure once, long, long ago, but for the most part, they preferred to stay safely inside. A long day relaxing in a sunny house was their idea of paradise. Thus, it was only infrequently that they spared a thought for the "way" of the wide world beyond.

What would they think if they met that scarred, yet somehow resolute—beautiful—female general?

I see—it's the seed for bigger adventures. That was about as much as the rhea girl could comprehend. Difficult things were difficult. So she would go one step at a time.

Then there was this scroll the woman had handed them. "A little something from my younger sister," she'd said. It bore a label, seemingly applied at some later date, with a legend in a hasty hand. Druid Girl was literate, so she could discern that it read "Wyvern's Roost."

Well, even if this was a simple delivery, they should focus on delivering it. She was sure it was the seed of someone else's adventure. "…And that's good enough for me."

"___?"

The boy beside her shot her a questioning look, but she shook her head and said, "It's nothing." Then she, too, gazed at the sky. The vista above their heads seemed impossibly huge, as if they really could follow it to every corner of the world.

CHAPTER 3

HIT AND RUN

He'd never seen an assassin walking around *dressed* like an assassin.

No, scratch that—he had seen one, once, shortly before that person had been spotted by the guards and apprehended. So maybe he should say he'd never seen a *professional* assassin do it. Anyone who did was an idiot, an amateur, an ass, or maybe all three.

Needless to say, he was a pro.

§

Not that he really thought of himself as a pro killer for hire. The notion nagged at him as he sat up slowly in his bed. Outside the window, the sun was high; it was already past noon. To go to bed at nearly dawn and wake up after noon wasn't healthy—he knew that, but still...

"I've become a certified night owl."

He'd started talking to himself more, too.

He was in a cheap room, with nothing more than a bed and a wardrobe to keep him company. The floor was in bad shape, too, and threatened to creak when he walked. His movements were light, but his body was still flesh and blood, still had weight. He got delicately out of bed and put a hand on the floor. He stretched out his fingers, stiffened his spine, and pulled himself forward using the same arm.

After his usual number of reps, he switched arms. It wasn't about quantity or speed; it was precision he was after. The whole point was not to make the floor creak.

Once he had done both arms, he stood on one leg and tried to repeat the exercise using only leg strength.

Right arm, then left arm; right leg, then left leg. He'd exercised and warmed up all four limbs, a good start. Ideally, he would have liked to do some pull-ups using a rafter or a crossbeam, but he feared to think what would happen if he accidentally broke something.

How much good this isometric training did him wasn't entirely clear, but it was unquestionably better than doing nothing. If nothing else, he felt it was far more trustworthy than relying on gimmicks or gear or magic. Of course, if he made the mistake of saying so out loud, his partner would have launched into an endless lecture on the virtues of spell casting.

He understood one thing, at least: Without the spells carved into his arms and legs, he would never move an inch.

"...Hrm." The water carafe he'd grabbed turned out to be empty, and there was no food to speak of, either. That was nothing new, and so, cursing his carelessness of the day before, he decided to go out to eat. It wasn't so bad; he'd been planning to go out today anyway. His favorite team had lost at Wizball yesterday, and when that happened, it was better to go out and look for work than to mope around in his room.

He wiped himself down with a rag, then headed over to the wardrobe and opened the double doors. It was full of clothes on hangers, but he shoved them aside, looking for the hidden lock in one corner. With a *click*, the back of the wardrobe opened, revealing a second, secret compartment.

"Heh!" No matter how many times he did this, no matter how well he knew what was in there, it always made him grin. There weren't many furnishings in his room, but he'd put an awful lot of work into this one—enough to drive his friends nuts.

It was more than just leather armor and military caps stashed away in the compartment. He had his pistol in there, his repeating cross-bow, all sorts of things that weren't technically allowed. Things that had to be kept away from prying eyes.

He'd seen a play ages ago where a king's spy had hidden his gear this way. Ever since then, he'd wanted to do the same thing—although, given that the spy was killed at the end of the play, maybe it was bad luck.

"...Mm. Perfect. All in order." He took out the pistol, worked the crossbow, checked everything over to make sure it was functioning properly, then put them neatly back on the shelf. He wasn't entirely certain of what good this inspection did, but again...better than nothing.

Then, with his routine complete, he pulled on a shirt and jacket. Obviously, he wasn't going to put on a military cap or a trench coat. He wasn't even going to be walking around with his pistol or crossbow on him. Because if you saw anyone traipsing around town *looking* like an assassin, you knew they were an amateur.

§

In the hours before dark, a breeze blew through the water town, carrying the damp aroma of the river. Bathed in golden sunlight, the town seemed sluggish and slow.

A dwarf expertly poled a gondola along a canal. The assassin who wasn't an amateur watched him for a lazy moment, then set off walking upriver. A rhea led a gaggle of kids who ran past him, shouting and jabbering. The rhea was nearly thirty; he had the worst kids in town eating out of his hand. He was probably planning a heist or something.

Speaking of how old people were, what about that elf listlessly scrubbing a cloth against the washing board? Elves stayed beautiful no matter how old they got, and anyway, it would be boorish to ask the age of one of these flowers of the night, even a human one—let alone an elf.

The woman eyeballed him, and he returned an embarrassed smile and a friendly dip of the head.

Doesn't matter, he thought. Good little boys and girls didn't join the Guild, and they weren't out wandering around town this late in the evening. *I'll have to hit the employment agency pretty soon to get hooked up as a night watchman or a bodyguard or something.*

He, after all, was not like run-of-the-mill adventurers, who either went out on quests or rambled around town. The fake rank tags were convenient, but they came with the caveat that if you went too long without going on an adventure, people would start to ask questions. And when a man with no obvious employment or source of income was hanging around, people started to suspect him of being behind whatever crooked things happened in their area.

He didn't mind being blamed for things he'd actually done, but he didn't want people coming after him because some dimwit had gone and caused trouble in the neighborhood. Having an alibi ready at all times was part of the game.

For a while he walked in such a way as not to stand out on the relatively empty streets—in other words, straight ahead, like he knew where he was going, but not in any hurry. Then, pretending he'd just had a thought, he ducked down a side street, then another, then another, working his way through the maze of alleys.

Beyond the bustling town center, it was startlingly quiet; neat and tidy. Somewhere back there was an unremarkable entryway that looked like the back door to some restaurant or other, and which led downstairs to a basement. It had a sign that made him think of the Silver Moon or the Grim Reaper. He glanced at the sign, then took the stairs in a single graceful leap.

He was faced with a wall covered in graffiti that looked like it had been there for eons. Written where a human would have to crouch to read it were some unfavorable remarks about elves. Up where a human would have to stretch to see it were some derogatory things about dwarves. And right smack at human eye level were two lines of very nasty stuff about humans.

He grinned, as he always did, and brushed the words *Longshanks* and *Strider* with his hand. Then he opened the lowest door down—the entrance to the speakeasy.

He passed the counter, where the bartender was doing a coded opium deal with one of the regulars.

"Gimme three peanuts."

"Two ought to be enough for you."

"Naw, three. Two plus one—three."

"Order a drink every once in a while."

"That dog piss?"

"Try to see things from my perspective..."

It might seem like a vulgar place at first glance, but inside, you realized it had a certain class all its own. The rug was soft; the counters, tables, bottles, and glasses were all kept sparkling. There was the billiard table, surrounded by people losing themselves in the game, and En Garde, a fighting game, that people were enjoying with glasses of wine in one hand. There were elves, rheas, dwarves, and padfoots. And that woman having the tête-à-tête with the lizardman over in the corner looked like she might be a dark elf.

If they'd been squatting somewhere in town, they would have been nothing more than a collection of ruffians, but somehow, here in this establishment, they were something more. There was a quality to the clientele here that you didn't find in every dive on the street. If he had to put a name to it, he'd probably say it was...

Style, goddammit!

Anyone unfortunate enough not to have it was quickly and violently shown the door. They certainly wouldn't be admitted into the establishment's innermost sanctum.

He wove among the seats until he saw the door he was looking for. Thick, made of metal.

Yes, everything else about this place looked more or less like a normal tavern. But not what was on the other side of that door.

It was a cave, some people thought. But not him. To him, it was an ocean.

An open space bathed in cold blue light, the lamps dim but present, utterly different from real darkness. Bartenders and barmaids in perfectly tailored vests swam through the room, taking orders and delivering drinks. A hired band set up a melody of degungs that pressed on his ears like the roar of the sea. How could they produce such sounds with instruments that only seemed to rattle and shake? He had no idea, just like he couldn't tell the difference between waiter, bartender, or garçon.

But hey, guess it doesn't matter, he thought.

This was the ocean. And when it came to swimming in the ocean, the barmaids—the mermaids—were his preference, he decided as he found his usual seat.

"Oh, you're here!" The red-haired girl looked up at him eagerly and smiled, clearly at least a little bit pleased to see him. As for his "eye," he could see through this ocean, too. He let his cheeks relax into the slightest of smiles.

"Yeah, figured there'd be work afoot soon. You thought so too, eh?"

"Well, I either want to work or I want to bitch." The red-haired elf looked awkwardly at the table. He sat down beside her as naturally as anything, then looked around again, spotting another girl laid out across the table.

"Mahh... Urgh..." The inarticulate groans hardly seemed suited to a cleric who served the God of Knowledge.

The assassin pulled a face. "What's with her?"

"Just ignore her," their brawny driver whispered—he was already here, too. He was happily sipping some fruit juice—staying sober so he could take the reins, presumably.

"Says she's out of money."

"What? We were loaded after the desert thing." He looked more exasperated than he'd meant to. Granted he'd been trying to keep a low profile until the fuss died down, but even so, it was a little soon to be running short of cash.

"It's the books' fault! They're so expensive..." the cleric grumbled, in a voice that wasn't quite a sob and wasn't quite a curse.

"Yeah, books cost," the red-haired girl said with a half-smile. "Believe me, I deal with enough magic to know it can hurt."

"That's why I have to take on these nasty jobs. It's all in pursuit of the truth." The cleric's head lolled to one side, and she giggled, sounding for once like a girl her age. Maybe she felt better now, having gotten her complaint off her chest. If nothing else, he was pretty sure it wasn't alcohol—only an idiot drank before a job.

Hrm...

The thought reminded him that he still hadn't had anything to eat.

"Shove over. I'm starving."

"Yep, yep. *Hup.*" The cleric girl sat up so the table was clear. The assassin called over one of the barmaids—she really did look like a mermaid—and ordered without even looking at the menu.

"Three burgers. Skip the buns. And some carbonated water." He flipped her a gold coin, and the barmaid left with a smile.

"Well, at least *you're* not out of cash." The red-haired elf grinned, her smile turning into laughter. "Trying to act like a gunslinger?"

"Nah, just overslept," he said simply. He had never liked that handle; it made him uneasy. "Lost yesterday."

"Wizball," the red-haired girl said softly. "…Is it really worth getting that depressed over?"

"I tell you, it's all because the captain got hauled in by the city guard the other day."

Even as he spoke, the barmaid, admirably quick at her work, returned with his order and set it silently on the table. The metal hot plate crackled with jumping fat from the three still-red meat patties on top of it. He grabbed a pinch of salt from a nearby jar, added plenty of peppers, and then began cutting into the patties with his knife. Finally, he brought a bite to his mouth. He wasn't after flavor so much as quantity, nor nutrition so much as heat. The feeling was distinct. Anyway, he knew where he was. He was confident it would taste great.

"I mean, wouldn't be the first time some dwarves got drunk and high and messed up a tavern after a match," he said, finally catching up with his own thoughts as he swished some of the carbonated water around in his mouth. Finally, he added, "Stuff seems to be everywhere these days."

The driver took up the subject from another angle. "The city watch caught this centaur, one of the aurigae—the runners from the Quadriga competition—just the other day."

"Yeah? What for?"

"Dope," the driver said disinterestedly. He was a big fan of the Quadriga competition held at the arena. "Guy said it was asthma medication, but I guess it was *illegal* asthma medication."

The assassin had just a couple of choice words for this: "Bullshit story." He stabbed the last bit of meat on his plate as if it had killed his parents, then popped it into his mouth.

The red-haired elf watched him with amusement, then contributed a question of her own to the conversation. "Okay, okay. But is the 'demon chief' of the town guard really as terrible as they say?"

"I hear he used to be part of the underworld, so he's been known to turn a blind eye." The cleric of the God of Knowledge flagged down a passing employee, having been swayed by the smell of the meat to order something for herself. "I'd like a lemon water. And something to eat—the cheapest stuff you have in the cheapest possible quantity. Don't care how much you have to water it down."

"I'll get a cured-meat sandwich," the red-haired elf said with a grin, pulled along by her friend's display. "Want to split it with me?"

"An elf eating meat. Will wonders never cease?"

"There are no wonders in this world."

It was a good feeling to see a couple of young ladies joking and giggling together. If nothing else, he felt a lot better than he had last night, both physically and mentally. For him, that was enough. So, when the unidentifiable white creature scampered out of the shadows, he was even able to smile at it.

"Hrm, are you sure that's the way to treat a friend? I think I must object." The familiar bapped his hand, but he didn't even care, just patted an empty seat.

"Oh, you're here," the red-haired girl said, reaching out a hand, and the cleric added, "Work! We want work!"

"You all saw that, didn't you? The way he treated me just now. Awful, wasn't it? Grabbing a person by the neck! Gods above." Their companion—wherever its true body was—licked its fur in between bouts of bellyaching.

He just shrugged. "You brought it on yourself, sneaking out of the shadows like that."

"That's right, you have the Bat-Eye, don't you? Suppose I should have expected it, then."

They were only needling each other, anyway. He even forgave the white creature for making off with a slice of a guy's meat.

Shortly thereafter, the red-haired elf's sandwich arrived, and the innocuous conversation among friends continued. Mostly about the book the cleric had purchased (succumbing to her thirst for knowledge), and about the swindle that had taken place in town the other day. When the food and drink had finally been cleared away...

"All right, everybody here?" their friend said gaily, approaching their seats. It had probably been there for a few moments before it showed itself. This wizard only ever appeared via her familiar; she herself was probably somewhere far away. Otherwise, she could never have timed her entrance so perfectly, for the exact moment when there was a lull in the conversation. That much was easy to pick up in even a short time working with her.

The rest of them, including the assassin, frowned when they saw the fixer with his little grin. It was time for the cloak and dagger: running through the shadows of the great city. Spy's work.

In other words, it was time for a run.

§

"This job comes from someone I trust, but I haven't been able to get any intel on it myself," the fixer told them.

"Man, swap those around, would you?" the spy said sarcastically. "It'd inspire more confidence, at least."

"I haven't been able to get any intel on this job myself, but it comes from someone I trust!"

"It's the same thing!" the driver spat, annoyed.

"Yes, but we'll do anything. For the right price," the cleric said blandly.

"Quit that, would you?" the red-haired elf interjected, slightly amused.

"Well, it sounds like a milk run, so I wouldn't get myself in a twist over it," the white creature remarked, summing up the situation, and thus their briefing began.

It really wasn't a very difficult assignment, the fixer reiterated. A quick night's work.

Quick *and* easy *ain't the same thing*, the spy thought. Maybe they should make that a saying on the backstreets, he reflected.

"Anyway, tonight's target is a little girl somewhere who made a big mistake."

They'd told him, the fixer said—now, this was just what he'd heard—that it was the sort of thing that happened all the time. A riff-raff girl, a beggar, the type you might take for a prostitute. But hey, when you walk around with squared shoulders and a knife in your bag, people are likely to think you're a lawless ruffian. She was just an errand girl for one of the street gangs, but...

"Then she started hawking the dope on the side, screwing up the territories, diluting the draw."

Common story, the spy felt. And oddly admirable. When you didn't have any money, you were always cringing and hiding. When you had money, you got to walk around like you owned the place. That extra confidence was important.

The driver, though, appeared to have a different view of things. He spat out, "What a damn idiot!"

"A fat cat forgets that a rat can bite."

"Sounds more like a rat who thought she could beat the cat by biting it..." The red-haired elf somehow looked both dismissive and sympathetic at once. "So, what's the job? We're intimidating her? Grabbing her and bringing her back here?"

"No, this is a hit."

The red-haired girl fell silent. After a second she said, "Oh."

This sort of thing happened virtually every day in the great city. The street gangs survived by their reputations. Look at them the wrong way today, and you could expect to die tomorrow. Drug dealers never lived long to begin with. One might not expect runners to even need to get involved.

But for them, it went the other way around. Trouble meant business. If they could get in on it, they could make money from it. It was the fixer's job to find the most profitable trouble of all. And the smirking man in front of them discussing this assassination was very, very good at his job.

"So, give me a verdict. Do it or don't."

The group went quiet, trading thoughtful glances—or perhaps consulting one another with their eyes. Only the spy was prepared to immediately open his mouth. "You didn't tell us the most important thing."

"Oh? What's that?"

"The reward," he said sharply, annoyed with the man for trying to play dumb. "We need ammo, spells—that shit ain't free, y'know. Money in advance—that's the way it's done."

"What do you take me for?! Of course there's a reward. Here." He tossed four heavy, jangling bags of coins onto the table, right where the spy's meal had been a few minutes before. Half the amount provided by the quest giver—the "johnson"—would remain in the fixer's pocket. Half of the rest would be paid to the runners in advance, and the remainder held until the job was finished. That was the etiquette in these things. Chances were, the wizard, the familiar's master, had already received her portion as well.

The spy weighed the payment in his hand—just half the total he would get. *Hmm...* Quite a bit of money for a quick night's work.

The spy watched the fixer with his inhuman eye. The man's expression didn't shift.

I know this guy. Must have been a whole group of gangs, or some other collective, that came knocking. But the spy didn't complain. He would get money. Money could help beautify the city. That meant good karma for him. Even just a little bit at a time.

He only had one thing to say about it, just two words. "I'm in."

"Me, too."

"I do want that money."

"All right, you've got me."

"There," the white creature said, pleased to see everyone's hand in the air to volunteer. "That wasn't so hard." The creature jumped down from the fixer's knees (when had she gotten there?), and then up onto the table. "I've already got a bead on where the target is, and everything else we need to know. Only thing left to do is to head over and scope it out for ourselves."

If it was a fixer's job to bring them work, it was she who did all the research before they set out. *She*—that was how the spy thought of the wizard who controlled the familiar. He *thought* that was right.

The red-haired girl and the cleric got along well. They were thoughtful, on the same wavelength. Not easy to pull the wool over their eyes. That's why the spy was willing to trust what this woman (that's what he felt her to be) said. There was no room in this world for insisting that your friends had to have all the proper credentials.

"Not that far away," the driver said when he heard the place. Naturally, he already knew how to get there. "But we'll want something more than our own feet to carry us. I'll get the carriage."

"Sounds great. Thanks." The red-haired girl smiled and stood. She pulled on a cloak and grabbed her staff, and she was ready to go. The cleric followed suit. She, like the elf, needed no more than the vestments draped over her slight frame, along with her holy sigil, to be completely prepared.

The driver only needed a vehicle, and there were plenty of sprites everywhere in the city. When he saw the three of them ready for the run, and so promptly, the spy also stood. Then he gave a dramatic frown. "Maybe we could stop by my place first."

"Why would we do that?" the red-haired girl said, a bit concerned. The way she tilted her head, puzzled, partially revealed one of the long ears normally hidden in her hair.

"Gotta get my stuff."

Okay, so there hadn't been a job when he'd left that morning. Still, it wasn't a good look.

§

Even by a circuitous route, the destination wasn't that far. Along the edges of the water town, somewhere among the chaotic sprawl, was a den of drug dealers.

Squatters hovered around fires among the abandoned buildings, empty houses, and trash piles. There were no maps of this area to speak of. Even maps of the city itself weren't easy to come by. They were tough enough to get in proper walled towns, but most places didn't have the money to spend on such things.

When it came to sprawl like this, there was no planning, no rhyme or reason. It just spread out, and people who wanted to live there showed up and fashioned the place to their liking. Whoever was there yesterday would be gone today, the town itself seeming to change from moment to moment.

Properly speaking, they were beyond the bounds of the water town here, on the fringes of law and order. If they wanted to get around, they would need to rely on one of the local squatters for guidance, or otherwise...

"Mm. Info was basically spot-on, more or less."

Or otherwise, on their sweet young lady with her gifts given by the God of Knowledge. She had been meditating in the rocking carriage until she opened her eyes and spoke those words.

The God of Knowledge didn't actually provide knowledge directly, but gave help to seekers thereof. Untrustworthy sources were as bad as a Dark God, or so the cleric often complained.

"I'm sure about the location, anyway. And I'm *fairly* sure she's still there. Even if she might be gone tomorrow."

"Only question is the situation on the ground, then." The spy nodded slightly, playing with an object in his hands. The pistol was a complicated weapon, the crossbow even more so. You didn't want them to go off accidentally. It was *deathly* important. Such was the thought occupying the spy's mind as he rapped the gun stock against the side of the carriage.

"Don't do that. You'll scratch it," snapped the driver. That was what he always said. Whacking the side of the carriage was the quickest way to get his attention.

"I'm gonna have a look. Stop here."

"Tell me with your *words*," the driver grumbled, but he pulled the reins, and the horse—or rather, the kelpie—came to a halt. The best thing about the spirit-horse was that it made no hoofbeats. And the damp patches it left in its wake swiftly disappeared.

The spy reflected on the benefits of their animal as he tucked the pistol in his bag and put a ball cartridge in his pocket.

"Counting on you."

"Uh-huh. Take care of my shoes."

He always kept his words at a minimum, and her response was no less restrained. There was no hesitation and no doubt.

The red-haired wizard closed her eyes and slumped against the spy's shoulder like a puppet with her strings cut. She'd told him this was what happened when she projected her soul into the astral realm, traveling free of her body. As pure spirit, she could travel many miles in an instant, enabling her to see whatever was out there. Of course, she was traveling on the astral plane, not the physical one, so she wasn't seeing exactly what he would see when he showed up. Nonetheless, she could tell if things felt off, or roughly how many people there would be, and that was worth a lot.

The spy, of course, hadn't the slightest idea what the world was like that she was seeing. But then, he didn't know what world the cleric was seeing, either, or the driver, or the white creature, or the fixer. In the whole party, the only "mundane"—the only non-magic-user—was the spy.

But so what? That was what it meant to play different roles. He knew what his position was.

The spy gently laid the girl's body down, folding up a blanket for a pillow. Then he took the crossbow he had just checked so carefully and watched from the carriage with perfect vigilance. He was the meat shield, and he had no questions about that. The spy knew whose pound of flesh was worth more, a patchwork's or a wizard's. He knew very well.

Night had already enveloped this trash pile of a city, but the darkness was no impediment to his vision. His forbidden eye perceived the world in wire frame, much like the infamous Dungeon of the Dead was said to have looked.

"Hey, question…" The voice came unexpectedly from the direction of the luggage. The white creature, their means of communicating with the wizard, came slithering out. The spy asked what she wanted without ever looking at her—of course he didn't—and the creature swished her tail interestedly. "I know I asked you already, but that eye of yours, it can see through things, right? I mean, the Evil Eye isn't my specialty, but…"

"Only sort of. Thin walls, I might be able to get a glimpse of what's on the other side." Shadows hovering around rotting barrels. The crossbow's crosshairs. A giant rat. *Fine. Let the thing eat some leftovers if it wanted.* "I don't really know how it works, but it lets me see in the dark."

"I just thought of something!" the familiar said, her voice going up

an octave, like she was bouncing on a keyboard. It sounded like she
had, in fact, been thinking about this for some time. "That would be
a great way to sneak a little peek at an elf's lovely body—perfect for a
young man like yourself!"

The spy didn't respond immediately. Instead, he spent a good two
seconds on a sigh before he said, "...Yeah, I could. But I don't, eh?"

"Wow, you admitted it," the familiar said with a very un-familiar-
esque tilt of her head. It made her look more like a small, confused
animal. "That merchant lady the other day—she was awfully pretty,
too. Those feet. Just lovely!"

"With that rapier and the dagger at her hip, too," the cleric girl
added quietly. "Toned and trained."

The spy cast a suspicious look at her, but only for an instant. Then
he said in a deliberately dutiful voice, "Someone asked a question, and
I answered, that's all. That's my job, isn't it?"

"Gosh, and here I thought you had a thing for elves. The way you
laid her down there was so gentlemanly, too. Am I right?"

"You're right."

They aren't listening to me, the spy thought. He was about to give a
click of his tongue, but thought better of it. Best not to let them know
they had gotten to him. But even his self-restraint seemed to amuse the
creature—or at least the magician somewhere behind her. And she
wasn't the only one. The cleric girl was smirking at him; he didn't
have to look at her to know.

"So, not interested in her at all?"

The spy gave up the act and let out another very long sigh. "I'm not
saying that."

"He's *not saying that*!!"

"But listen, she trusts me, and I'm never going to betray that." The
spy reached back with one hand and mussed the creature's white fur
in an effort to quiet her (her voice had risen another key in the meantime). She squealed in a way that sounded genuinely girlish to him,
though he didn't say so.

He had her trust. He wasn't going to betray that.

"Stop getting weird ideas." That was all he said, and then he
straightened up. He moved his limbs, with their magically attached

flesh, like a panther preparing for the hunt. "I'm going to patrol outside," he said, then spared a glance at the red-haired girl. "Tell me when she gets back."

"Yep, sure thing. After all, you've been *very* informative!"

The spy jumped down off the carriage with a click of his tongue, added purely for the benefit of the gratified familiar.

As soon as he dropped off the carriage and into the darkness of night, he heard another voice, this time from the driver. "How is it these days?"

"Decent." The huge driver looked like an ox, but he was quick-witted. The spy's lip curled slightly. "The joints do ache when it gets cold, though."

"Not saving up any money?"

"Not enough for real flesh." The spy shrugged. "Might be Wizball for me one day. How about you?"

"Going well enough," the driver responded blandly. "Enough to cover the carriage, and enough to keep the woman paid up."

"Veritable contributing member of society, you are."

"I didn't say she was *my* woman. *Hmph!*" the driver snorted, but that was all.

The spy shook his head and stood by the carriage. His crossbow dangled in one hand. He needed to patrol. But there was a time to focus all his energy, use it up. That time wasn't now.

A bit of banter in the middle of the run was a good thing. At least for this party, it was. If you couldn't even afford to crack a joke, that meant you were really up against it...

The passengers fell silent once more when the spy left the carriage behind. The white creature and the cleric of the God of Knowledge looked at each other and giggled like two very old friends.

"You heard him, didn't you?"

"He's not *not* interested!"

"........."

They couldn't help but notice that the pointed ears that emerged ever so slightly from under the red hair were trembling. But they would wait for her to get back from her travels. It was the friendly thing to do.

§

"…Thanks for waiting." The red-haired wizard hopped down from the carriage about five minutes later. Some fine wit had concocted a proverb that went something like: "Do it in two minutes! Now do it in two seconds!" But what really mattered in this line of work was precision, not speed. In that sense, the spy had no qualms with the woman. How could he?

The spy slung the crossbow over his shoulder by the cord, took a quick look around, then said, "How was it? …Something the matter?"

"Nothing," she said quickly. "Just wondering why they'd ask so many questions right here." She looked put out. Most likely because of the blathering women. If that accounted for eighty or ninety percent of her annoyance, another ten percent might be the driver, and the last ten, him.

"Well, speed's of the essence when it comes to information."

"I know that…" The red-haired girl heaved a long sigh, then said slowly: "I saw her. She's there."

Huh. The spy nodded. Looked like their drug dealer was out of luck tonight. If she hadn't been there, might she have lived to see another dawn?

Dunno about that.

He wasn't sure how long it was really possible for her to survive. Running headlong toward a cliffside wasn't something smart people did.

"The place reeks of patrols and drugs. Several others there besides her. They didn't shine very brightly, though."

"Squatters living in the insula, maybe."

"Couldn't say," the red-haired wizard replied with a shake of her head. She pulled up the hood of her cloak. "Sorry."

"All good," the spy whispered, then he pulled his pistol out of his bag, spinning it idly in his hand. Playing with a gun makes a person unlucky. Apparently. He tried to remember who had said that.

Didn't matter who it was. He tore open the ball cartridge from his pocket and loaded the weapon. Then he smacked the stock into place, wadded up the empty packet, and he was ready to go.

"Best case scenario, we're runners. Worst case scenario, we're still runners."

§

When the spy and the girl started walking, the driver slowly rolled the carriage away, just as planned. An unfamiliar vehicle stopping for too long would attract unwanted attention, and stick in people's memories. Not to mention that such a nice carriage in such a nasty neighborhood would become a temptation before long. Before starting a run, they always settled on an innocuous route for the driver to amble around.

"……"

"……"

The spy and the red-haired girl stuck close as they made their way toward the insula, a sort of apartment complex. They appeared to look into the far distance because they were each observing different worlds, one of sound, one of magic. The only thing they shared was that they each had blind spots. The way they each looked out for the other was the natural thing to do when operating as a two-person cell.

When he thought about it, the spy realized it had been no short time that they'd known each other. He so rarely ran through the shadows alone anymore.

"…First floor empty?" he asked.

"Looks like it," the red-haired girl whispered back. He could hardly see the light of her life. It was quiet indeed. Unfortunately, the walls and floor were made of stone, which dampened sound. You really couldn't expect x-ray vision from the Bat-Eye.

Probably used to be an eatery, way back when, he thought. Decaying tables and chairs sat around, forgotten even by the scavengers. The windows and doors had been taken out to fit more customers in, so there was too much breeze in here. If you were going to live in this building, you'd want to start on the second floor, just like their intel and the reconnaissance sweep had suggested.

"Moving up," he said.

"I'll watch our backs."

With that quick, whispered conversation, they started forward, feet moving as if in a dance, starting up the stairs. His own footsteps sounded heavy. Hers seemed so light. Between the two of them, it worked out to simply sounding like two people on the stairs.

The spy kept his crossbow ready at all times, making sure he was always checking the angle of fire. Suddenly, he found himself remembering the idle conversation with his party back in the shop.

Drugs, drugs, drugs. Three strikes and you're out.

Was it chance? Fate? It didn't make any difference. What he had to hit, he would hit.

Thus, when he gained the top of the stairs, he noticed the inky shadow floating in the hallway.

"That's unusual," the red-haired girl with her astral vision said before the spy could speak; she must have noticed it, too. "It's more tense than before. And I don't know if there's any light of life."

"Trouble?"

"Maybe."

"If we could go home and still get the reward, I'd do it right now," he mumbled.

"And I'd go with you," she said with a chuckle, adjusting her hood. They proceeded down the hallway.

Their goal was a room on the far end of the second floor. No windows, as far as they had been able to tell from outside. If the place had some preparations, though, they would like that. Surely the room had one or two escape routes...

Then the spy was standing in front of the door. Traps—very likely. Didn't even have to ask whether it was locked. They weren't sneaking into some company HQ or big merchant's shop. Speed would matter more than caution.

He and his partner exchanged a knowing glance. They got in rhythm. One, and two, and...three.

"......!"

One good kick from the spy's magically augmented leg smashed the door open. He slipped inside without a sound, whipping his crossbow this way and that as he checked the room.

A woman—there she was. The first thing he noticed was the sickly sweet smell of opium; he hated it. The heavy aroma surrounded the bed on which the woman lay, her arms and legs sprawled in a slovenly manner. Maybe she'd just been washing up, because her thick chestnut hair was soaking, sitting in waves on her head, long ears peeking out from under it. Her body, covered by only the barest excuse for undergarments, was preternaturally delicate, slim, and light. That didn't necessarily mean she didn't have meat on her bones, though, as he knew from having to heft his partner.

Huh. Maybe he *did* have a thing for elves...

At least, when they aren't lying there with their eyes wide open, their tongues hanging out, and a knife buried up to the hilt in their chest.

"Sh-she's dead?!"

"...Well, she ain't alive."

The red-haired girl squeaked, just short of a scream, while the spy went over to the bed. It'd be no laughing matter if it turned out she was only playing dead. But there was no heartbeat, and you couldn't fake that.

"She's still warm," the wizard whispered, placing a hand on the woman. She reached up and closed the woman's eyes.

That takes care of the open eyes—now she'd look great if it weren't for the knife. It was a ridiculous thing to think, but the spy was trying to get his confused brain to form some coherent thoughts. "So she must have been killed just recently, then?"

"Yeah—I mean, she was alive when I projected from outside."

Okay, let's think this through.

When? Just a moment ago.

Where? Right here.

Who? Not us.

How? Knife to the chest.

Why? That, we don't know.

No windows. No one came out while we were watching. Haven't passed anyone since we came in. All of which adds up to...

"...Whoever did it is still here?"

"That's not funny..." the red-haired wizard said.

No, it wasn't. The spy didn't know exactly what was going on, but it wasn't good news.

One thing seemed obvious: They would want to get out of this building posthaste. The spy started backing up, one sliding step at a time, trying to keep himself between the body and the red-haired girl, to cover her.

Hurry. Had he missed anything? Wouldn't get another chance to look. Would they even get their money for this?

"Let's go. We'll join up with the others. We have to figure out what's going on, or—"

"...!"

He heard his partner suck in a breath. That was enough. He spun, his crossbow at the ready.

From the doorway came the last thing in the world he wanted to hear. "*Stoooooooooooooooop!*"

"Guard...!" He wasted only enough time to curse the gods. Standing in the doorway of the room was a town guard—he could tell from the sword-and-scales symbol branded on the leather helmet. He gritted his teeth, wrapped his left arm around the red-haired girl, and ran straight ahead.

"Eep?!" she cried, but he didn't even register it as he picked up speed. He was looking at the sword the guard had drawn, ready to stab him.

"Hrrahhh!" The spy slammed his right arm against it.

"Wha?!" Not expecting such a firm impact, the guard tumbled backward, the voice strangely high-pitched. A woman?

The strike knocked the guard's helmet off, revealing brown hair tied high on the head. But the spy didn't have time to hang around. He swung his left arm away from the guard, protecting his partner, and dealt his opponent another blow with his right arm. There was a screech of metal as his arm bounced off the sword. The blade filled his vision. He let his momentum carry him forward, slipping out of the room.

He covered the hallway in three great bounds, his legs groaning, then grabbed the railing of the stairway with his free hand.

"Counting on you!"

"Uh-huh!"

There was no need to even discuss it. He just jumped. Gravity grasped his body. He began to fall.

"*Falsa...umbra...oriens.* Arise, false shadow!" From her perch on his shoulders, she flourished her staff and intoned words of true power. He felt a shock run through both his legs, then the shadows began to bubble up from the ground, filling the stairwell.

"Ahhhh?!" He heard the woman shout in confusion. So it *was* a woman. The Vision spell was no doubt wreaking havoc with her sight right now. If that was enough to make the guards give up, though, they wouldn't have been the object of so much anger...

"Damn Lawful Goods...!" the spy growled when he heard the woman blow a sharp whistle. He didn't spare a backward glance as he rushed through the shop-turned-abandoned-building, faster than the speed of sound. So what if there was a little junk lying around? With his limbs in overdrive, the place might as well have been empty.

"Should I cast Transparent, too?!"

"No, it'll be okay!" he responded to the voice over his shoulders. Her judgment was always spot-on. Every time. Stun spells like Sleep were useful in a pinch, but if you screwed them up they were a waste of a turn. The spy knew it worked better to confuse targets with an illusion, after which it was his job to handle things.

He was really glad his friend wasn't so fatally stupid as to try to launch offensive magic at the guard. If, by any chance, a court mage with a black staff showed up, it would be too terrible to contemplate. Above all...

Offing a guard is bad news!

There it was. The guards might overlook someone pinching an apple, but if you killed one of their own, they would hunt you to the ends of the earth. He happened to want to keep living in this town, so it was well-advised not to murder local law enforcement.

Yes, he could see sound, but that didn't make him a daredevil, heedless of his life. Which meant he had one option here—run away—and one way to do it—on his own two feet. The whistle would summon other guards, but they wouldn't appear and attack instantly. He had time. They would go to the whistle first. They would only set off in pursuit after that.

That just meant he had to escape the cordon before they banded together and got underway. Time, that was what mattered most now.

Time and speed. He leaned forward, running, running. Running like a tiger.

"I have to wonder—was this a setup?"

"Yeah, maybe we were tricked." She reached out, holding onto the spy's cap so it wouldn't be blown away by the wind. "He's never made any mistakes in that department before, but... Hey, why are you laughing?"

Well, that was because neither of them actually thought for a second that the fixer had sold them out. The spy just ran faster, through the streets of the slums, around corner after corner. He had the driver's route in his head, of course. But to go straight to him would have been absurd. The squatters weren't his friends. They would sell any info to anybody for some money. So the spy ran a convoluted route, keeping the time in mind, and when he jumped out into the main thoroughfare...

"All aboard!" The carriage came barreling into view, moving so fast the kelpie barely had time to whinny.

The spy gave the driver an affirmative shout, and as he passed by the vehicle, he shoved the red-haired wizard through the door. "Ack!" she exclaimed, but naturally, he ignored her. He felt guilty, but this was an emergency.

He grabbed onto the back of the racing vehicle, pulling himself aboard by sheer arm strength. He held his cap to his head against the buffeting wind with one hand as he scrambled onto the roof. The vehicle the driver had requisitioned for this particular job had a sky-light. The spy shoved himself halfway through it, then finally brought his crossbow to bear, twisting around and facing backward.

Not gonna chase us?

The slums receded in the distance. He didn't sense any enemies. Their target was dead. They were being pursued.

In other words, this isn't over.

He let out a breath, then slid the rest of the way into the carriage.

§

"Target status?"

"Not alive."

The question came from the cleric girl, a brief interrogation over the sound of the clattering wheels. The red-haired girl, amused by the spy's diffident tone, added, "He means she was killed."

There was a *thunk*, and the carriage jumped. Probably riding over some rubble, something the springs couldn't absorb. The cleric's eyes burned with curiosity. She leaned in close. "There were no windows in that room, were there? Was the door locked?"

"Used the master key," the spy said laconically, by which he meant he had kicked it down. He felt floaty, hot. He needed some time to cool down. He put a cigarette between his lips.

It was always like this after he had been in overdrive. His brain felt like it was on fire, and he had to let it cool off or it would stop working entirely. "No time to look to close or use an unlocking spell." He searched in his pocket for a flint, but didn't find anything; the red-haired girl saw there was nothing for it but to reach into her bag. She produced a palm-sized cylinder with an attached straw, both made of water buffalo horn.

She brought them together with a practiced motion, driving the straw smartly into the cylinder. There was a rush of air, and when she pulled the straw out, the flint on the end was glowing merrily.

"Here," she said, holding it out, and the spy leaned forward with a "Thanks" to light his antipyretic. His dried wolfberry caught, sending up sweet smoke that filled the cabin.

When had she started to carry around that fire-starting thing, again? He didn't seem to remember her having it when they'd first met...

"So, we don't know whether it was a locked-room murder or not," the cleric mumbled in annoyance, resuming her original position.

There was another *thump* and the carriage jumped again; the driver gave a low click of his tongue. "Guess they'll figure it out when they do the inquest, not that it matters. We're hitting the sewers."

"Got it."

"And open the windows. Don't want the smell to stick."

"Yeah, sure."

The spy nodded and calmly opened the carriage windows. This wasn't a point he was going to argue.

If you were going to get involved in smuggling, you had better know the best ways to get discreetly out of town. In other words, this called for a specialist. The fight was over, and now he had no choice but to place himself in someone else's hands.

The carriage leaned precariously as it slid off the dock and into the river. The kelpie's hooves made stippled patterns on the water, and the spinning of the wheels gave way to a gentle burbling.

"...Gotta wonder, though—what was a city guard doing there?" the spy said, exhaling the smoke of the antipyretic out of his lungs. The red-haired girl shot him a look to ask if he was all right; he nodded and pinched out the end of the cigarette with his fingertips.

"Don't drop it in the cabin and don't throw it out the window," the driver growled.

"I know, I know." The spy stuffed the butt in his pocket.

"Good," the driver said, seemingly able to sense this. Then he said, "Got a better question. How'd a small-time punk living in a shithole like that get their hands on enough dope to sell?"

"A backer's everything in that business... Milk run, my ass."

That was the one grievance he could have held against the fixer. The thought lingered in his head. Well, they would deal with that after they had solved their other problems. Trying to apportion blame in the middle of a run was as good as signing your own death warrant.

"Sorry," the white creature said, and she sounded like she genuinely meant it. "The two of us will try to get a handle on what happened. But it's not a betrayal by the johnson, I guarantee it."

"I know that. So does everyone." The red-haired girl laughed softly and patted the creature on the head. Not the way you would an animal, but like a friend. "But who do you think did it? If it got to the point where we got a quest for it, then almost anyone could've killed her..."

"Huh? It's simple, right?" the cleric of the God of Knowledge said, sounding like the answer should have been the most obvious thing in the world. From her spot in the corner of the carriage, she said, "Let's review. There were at least three people at the scene. You, him, and one more."

"..."

"You didn't kill her. *He* didn't kill her. So...?"

The spy groaned softly. No assassin ever looked like an assassin.

"The guard..."

"Bingo." The cleric leered at him. He wasn't sure he had ever seen quite that expression on her face before.

§

"If they killed her, I think we can assume killing her was of some benefit to them." In the quiet confines of the underground sewer, the cleric's words sounded strikingly forceful. The carriage had floated this way and that through the maze of waterways, finally coming to a rest gods knew where. Well, the gods and the driver—the spy was sure *he* knew where they were, even if the spy for one couldn't have begun to guess. He wasn't worried.

He could hear water rushing around them in the dark; it hardly even felt to him like there were any other living things around. But the spy's eye *heard* it. Things that hid in the dark; literal bringers of death. Things that squirmed in the shadows. Things that made their homes here, under the city.

Ghouls.

They had snouts from what he could tell, but maybe that was to be expected from those calling themselves ghouls. Ghouls were monsters that emerged from burial mounds and ate only corpses. At least that stuff about them being denizens of the dream world had to be a lie. What happened to the rat that was caught just after skittering past his feet, though, that was reality.

"Lively, aren't they?" said the driver, who had evidently made contact with the ghouls after the fracas the party had been mixed up in with those goblins. These ghouls might eat humans, but they didn't want to be destroyed wholesale along with the goblins that had once attacked people in town in the night. That had been a year or two ago now, and it had been a pretty payday for their group...

Carefully, the driver pulled down a hempen bag sitting by him on the bench, and kicked it into the darkness. A veritable army of beasts lunged at it and tore it apart, the sound of feasting briefly echoing around before everything went silent again.

"Give 'em a little something to eat and they want to attack you—might even help you."

"It's all good, as long as they don't invite us to dinner," the spy said. He pulled himself back into the carriage—he had been leaning out the window to keep an eye on things—and urged the cleric to continue. "So what? Maybe someone snapped and did it in a fit of rage."

"In which case it would at least yield emotional satisfaction. That's reason enough to kill *some* people." The cleric sounded like she was explaining things to a particularly dim pupil—and then she threw in a pop quiz for good measure. "Dope's been showing up more and more these days, right?"

"Far as we know, yeah."

"Then it has to be starting somewhere," the cleric said quietly. "A supply depot where it all comes from."

"...And where's that?" the red-haired girl asked with a tilt of her head. She spoke softly, even though it was unlikely anyone was listening to them.

"The city guard garrison," the cleric replied flatly, narrowing her eyes. The other young woman sucked in a breath. "They take the opium they've confiscated and let it slip to suppliers, make themselves a little pocket change. Simple enough, right?"

The red-haired wizard was the only one who looked like she was having trouble believing this. The driver, who had gone silent, and the white creature, who was probably deep in conversation with the fixer, both seemed to accept the likelihood. But the red-haired girl, sounding like she still didn't want it to be true, asked, "Would servants of the Supreme God really do that?"

"They would," the cleric told her friend confidently. "After all, it's not the gods who decide what's good and evil—it's us."

The gods in heaven didn't demand that people act a certain way. They didn't give miracles in exchange for faith. People didn't believe in the gods because there was profit in it.

"Sometimes you hear someone say that great people are beloved by the gods, or that if you're unhappy, it's the gods' fault," the cleric said. "But that's because people only look at outcomes. The process matters, too," she continued in a whisper. "Those people just don't want to take responsibility for losing out—they want to foist it on the gods."

"...Guess it's not that hard to guess what happened," the spy said, largely ignoring the girls' conversation. He could think about good and evil all day and all night, but he wouldn't have anything useful to contribute. They were killers who killed when they needed the money. No more and no less.

The driver flicked the bill of his hat with one finger, saying blandly, "If a dope dealer's in trouble with her supplier, that means there was an argument during negotiations—market couldn't decide what it wanted."

"And then they killed her," the spy murmured.

The driver nodded. "Then they figured they might as well at least get something out of it."

"The money she'd earned."

When you got rid of the fancy titles, that was what it came down to. That was all: a completely, disarmingly ordinary case. Fate or Chance, or both, had simply coincided with their run with uncanny timing. It was as simple as that. But...

"Knowing the truth doesn't mean anything's finished," the driver added; exactly what the spy was thinking. "They catch us, they've got their scapegoats—everything works out for them."

"I'm sure they'd love it if they caught us because of their own screwup." The spy laughed. But there was no hint of hesitation as he said, "Gotta take 'em out. Only choice."

"...I don't like bein' in the business of killing city guards," the driver mumbled.

"Yeah, well, that's why *I'm* the one who's gonna do the killing."

The driver pulled the brim of his cap down over his eyes. The red-haired girl was giving the spy a reproving look, but he ignored all of them. He knew his position. As an asset, he was replaceable. And, more importantly, deniable.

"Well, you *are* the man in charge of violence around here. And it sounds like it's about to get violent," the cleric of the God of Knowledge said in her usual calm tone. Maybe none of this interested her. Maybe there was something else that drew her attention more.

The cleric opened the door of the carriage and then—*vwip*—with the particular gracelessness of someone who wasn't a gifted acrobat, she jumped out of the vehicle. "There's something else we have to do first, right?" she said more forcefully than usual, in order to hide the way she was reeling from the landing. "What part of town is this? I hope it's close to the God of Knowledge's temple."

"Mm... Well, it's not too far," the driver said.

"Hmm," the spy grunted, taking up the crossbow from over his shoulder. "You going back to the temple?"

"Obviously. Have you lot never researched anything?" The sweet young cleric sounded absolutely exasperated. But her eyes sparkled as she said to them, "If you're going to really investigate something, books are the place to start."

§

What does "the man in charge of violence" do during the research phase? Commit violence, of course.

It might consist of nothing more than guarding a "face"—a negotiator—or a spell user. If he could be of help just by standing around, then standing around was what he would do.

"The reality is that the amount of knowledge any one person possesses is minimal. You have to either ask around, or you have to do research."

"I know we've been to the Temple of the God of Knowledge before, but it never fails to impress me..."

The spy followed the girls and their whispered conversation up to a bookrest, thinking about his role. There wasn't a sound in the temple, which housed rows of bookshelves that stretched up to the ceiling, a forest unto themselves. The moonlight that filtered in through the windows wasn't enough to see by; candles burned by several of the bookrests, suggesting they weren't the only ones flipping pages in the middle of the night in pursuit of knowledge.

Can't say any of it makes much sense to me, the spy thought. "Reading,

writing, and 'rithmetic? As long as I can add up the points in a game
of Wizball and follow the rules all right, that's enough for me."

"Then that's your truth. That's all you'll ever have in your life…
Ah, here it is. Take this."

"Yeah, sure."

The cleric girl tugged a book out with her fingertips, and he grabbed
it off the shelf. It was a thick book with a metal cover; it would have
been an imposing weight for a flesh-and-blood person, but the spy held
it as lightly as anything. The weight was supposedly intended to dis-
courage thievery, but it was also quite a piece of work in and of itself.
And it was brand-new.

"…The heck is this?"

"Book of heraldry," the cleric responded. "It describes the history of
the nobility, their roles—it's all in there."

"Oh, it's this year's edition… I didn't know it was out already."
The red-haired girl sounded like she was seeing a seasonal flower in
bloom. Apparently, the spy was the only one who didn't recognize it.
He groaned. Even in the darkness, he could guess that the cleric was
doing that thing she did, where she managed to look self-important
while maintaining a neutral expression.

Sometimes it's better not being able to see, he thought. It would only make
him seem sore to actually say anything, though, so instead he headed
promptly for the bookrest. Clerics with their slight builds could hardly
carry these books, let alone hold them to read them; that's why they
needed the bookrests. The book could sit there while they flipped the
parchment pages.

"This is a good publisher. Bit on the expensive side, though… Oh, is
that why you don't have any money?"

"Uh-uh. There was this song going around, 'The Wolf of Hell'…
No, we're staying on task. Who did you encounter? Did they have a
family crest of any kind?"

"Let's see… I got a quick look at the embroidery on her clothes.
There was a lozenge-shaped escutcheon, and the crest—"

From the spy's perspective, the girls might as well have been talking in code. He didn't know about heraldry or whatever, and he didn't

know why they wouldn't just write their names—"I am such and such of the house of so-and-so!"

Guess I'm not one to talk, the spy thought. The red-haired girl had a better memory than he did. And she was an elf, so she could see in the dark. He would just stand there quietly, scanning the area, until he was asked to do something else. If that was enough to be of help, then that was what he would do.

They might be in the Temple of the God of Knowledge, but they were still on a run, and still fugitives. And what was he supposed to do—leave the spell users to their own devices while he stood guard back at the carriage? *That would be ridiculous.* The spy had no interest in such role divisions, which were little more than excuses to stop thinking.

"Do you need help with anything?"

Look, just like that. Someone approached holding a candle, their face hidden deep within a hood. If this was the enemy trying to feel them out, the girls would have had to deal with it all by themselves.

"Oh, uh…" The spy tried to stall for time as he thought quickly, appraising the situation. The person's voice was low and calm. Not sure if it was a man or a woman. But probably a cleric. In other words, not an enemy. The spy relaxed his tensed muscles and allowed a smile onto his face. "…I think we'll have it worked out soon," he said. "My friends here are very good at finding things…even in books."

"I see." The hooded person's words were brief, but gentle. He thought he heard a smile in them. "Possibilities are indeed plentiful in the library. A place of habit for those on the hunt."

"Er, right…"

The woman—was it?—bowed her head in the flickering candle-light. *"Fall not, darkness."*

"F-fall not, darkness…" The spy vaguely remembered that these were the words of a prayer of the God of Knowledge. A wish for their success, probably.

Almost as suddenly as they had appeared, the person with the bowed head vanished among the stacks, into the dark. Only a few twinkling stars, far in the distance, seemed to remain.

At that moment, the cleric spoke up. "…Found it. I think this is her."

"Yeah, looks right," the red-haired wizard said. The spy glanced over his shoulder at the gloom and noted that he no longer saw the candlelight, but he didn't let it bother him. He glanced over the shoulders of his two friends (it wasn't hard; neither of them was very tall), but found the hasty hand in which the book was written too difficult to read.

"So who was it?" he asked instead.

"We were right. It was a woman." Then the cleric of the God of Knowledge reeled off a name as long and complicated as a magical spell. Daughter of Mister Big Important Count This of Clan That who had lots of land.

"Girl comes from serious money, then." Nothing about the name meant anything to the spy. He didn't know a duke from a marquis from a count from a viscount from a baron. When he'd once asked if a margrave was the overseer of a cemetery, he'd received only crushing looks of pity. In his mind, anyone who held such a title simply fell under the category of "noble," and most nobles, in his mind, had it good.

The red-haired girl ran her finger over the page several more times, making sure of the name, then nodded. "Yeah, I know this person. She used to come buy drugs—medicine—from my mentor sometimes."

"Drugs?" Again with the drugs. The spy looked at her searchingly, and for some reason the red-haired girl blushed and looked at the ground.

"Well, ahem…" She shuffled uneasily. Finally, she took a breath and mustered, "S-some elves become, uh, concubines, I guess? And so, she, uh…"

"She wanted something to help her have more kids?" the cleric asked bluntly. "Or fewer?"

"F— Fewer."

"A fish's air bladder, honey, acacia wood, and pine sap, maybe. Of course, the best plan is not to get pregnant in the first place."

Don't say that, the elf seemed to be thinking, but the cleric refrained from acknowledging it, and shut the book. "So, what do we do?"

"Hmm?" The spy cocked his head. He didn't really follow. The cleric continued as if reading from a dinner menu, "We know who we're dealing with now."

"I guess that means a run, then," he said, trying to sound as detached as she did. "Whatever you've found out, the fixer ought to know how to make money from it."

§

The nighttime sprawl was as silent as an abandoned building. The denizens of this part of the city typically either spent their nights engaged in unspeakable deeds, or else sleeping the sleep of the dead. All the more so when there had been a killing just hours before.

The body had already been removed from the insula where it had been found, and there was no longer any sign of the city guard. After all, the criminals, the MO, and the motive were already fairly clear. Leave it to the rank and file to catch the bad guys, then; no need to sniff around the scene like dogs.

"…Hmph."

That makes it the perfect time to do a little investigating.

There was a quiet rustling, and although there was no need to hide her footsteps, the woman guard snorted with annoyance over them as she entered the abandoned shop. Perhaps the interlopers had been a thorn in her side. Or perhaps they had been a gift from heaven.

Were the pips on the dice of Fate and Chance good and evil? It was beyond the powers of a pawn like her even to imagine an answer, and thus she silently climbed the stairs. She didn't hesitate for a moment when she reached the room on the next floor, blocked off only by a rope since the door had been kicked down—she went right in.

The door was gone, as was the half-elf woman's body; nothing else in the room had changed.

Damned Devil. The guardswoman's lip curled into a sneer. The guard captain, who went by the sobriquet of the Devil, had pressed her relentlessly about the state of the scene of the crime. Including preservation.

If you weren't part of the Devil's clique, then you might as well have been smoke on the wind. But it was also the Devil's modus operandi that allowed the woman to find what she was hoping for. It was a good roll of the dice.

Better than the seven I needed, at least.

The guardswoman crouched, one knee on the floor. The blood that had dribbled from the bed stained the rug underneath, leaving a large spot. She was just pulling up the carpet when she stopped.

Is it just me, or does something feel off...?

She couldn't explain it—it wasn't quite her sixth sense, nor any of her ordinary senses, but her brain picked up on it all the same. Was the stain on the rug and the stain on the floorboards slightly... misaligned?

"That was intentional. We needed someone to do some excellent detective work, or there would've been trouble." The voice caught her by surprise. It was cold as an icicle, sending a shiver down her spine. "It was a toss-up whether we should do this at home or at the office."

Her hand was already on her sword as she jumped up like a spring-loaded doll. She cast her eyes to the right, then the left in the dim room. The corner. The bed. No windows. The storage container—the space where the door had been. Right behind her...!

"Wouldn't want to miss you, after all. But I guess the criminal really does return to the scene of the crime."

There was a shape there. A nameless living thing that ran through the shadows. The woman could just make out a leather trench coat; a military-style cap obscuring the figure's face. The only thing she saw was an uncanny light emanating from the person's eyes.

"Best way to avoid a search cordon is to go back inside it after the cordon's expanded." The guardswoman took a few steps backward, trying to put some distance between herself and the shadowed figure. She might not see well in the dark, but she could see the person—the spy—was holding a pistol.

The spy chuckled that this was the reverse of earlier, but the guards-woman didn't dignify him with an answer. The spy just gave a little shrug and reached into his breast pocket with his free hand. "We already found the hidden cash store you're looking for. I've got some friends who are very good at finding things."

He produced a small parqueted wooden box, the kind that might be used to hold papers, and one that looked far nicer than anything else in this room. It had been hidden under the floorboards, under the rug, under the bed. She'd worried the city guard might have gotten ahold of it, but this, she could work with. After all, she was the one who was going to be in trouble if the guards found that box.

Eight or nine out of ten, she figured this was a slam dunk. She could usually expect to roll a three or four at least. And if all went well, then what need was there to fret about what she would do if she failed—which she wouldn't?

"I'll thank you to give that back this minute." The guardswoman sounded like she might snap at any moment. The spy realized this was the first time she'd unequivocally sounded like a woman, and the thought made him smile. She went on, "Accept your arrest quietly. I'm certain our Lord, the Supreme God, will be merciful."

"You mean this is yours? Wow, color me surprised." The spy's smile never slipped as he produced the contents of the wooden box. The accumulated harvest of selling drugs, presumably: a bag of gold coins, with a few bronze and silver pieces mixed in. And then there was the envelope with a wax seal depicting a green eye. It had been opened. The contents: an order, and a detailed map of the city.

"I don't know how much you planned to wring out of the cultists for this thing, but I *know* this map isn't your work."

"…"

If looks could kill, the spy would have been dead five or six times already. He snapped the lid of the box shut, then squeezed it into a pocket of his overcoat. He traded it for something else in the pocket, which he tossed to her as if it were a ball. "*This* is yours, right?"

Shing. The object lodged in the floor with a sharp sound. It was a striking—but at this moment, thoroughly gore-stained—dagger. The one which, until a few hours before, had been sticking out of the half-elf woman's chest.

The owner of the knife didn't move to retrieve it—and after he had been so nice as to give it back to her. Not that the spy had been expecting some dramatic reaction. He'd just brought the knife along because it would be helpful to him to be able to mention it.

"I knew it was weird that you only had your sword. They always issue the sword and the dagger as a pair."

The guardswoman fixed the spy with a glare, breathing hard, as she finally managed to squeeze out, "But how...?"

"Aw, don't ask."

In reality, it had been simple: pose as a squatter, swear to the guards he was one of her people (and throw in a few coins to convince them), and walk off with it. After all, what guard worth their salt *wouldn't* trade material evidence for some pocket change? There were plenty of people who wanted such things as—the spy didn't know—mementos or something. He'd figured it would work out.

To be fair, he'd heard the guard captain these days was a real devil. The rabbit-faced guard would probably get a dressing-down for her trouble. But it wasn't his job to spell out the details for her. And he didn't have time.

"——!!" The woman gave the knife a kick, simultaneously drawing her rapier and leaping at him. He considered whether she was more like a tiger or a lion. The sword could strike like lightning, and he wouldn't have time to dodge both it and the dagger.

The spy gritted his teeth. Power coursed through his limbs. He saw the tip of the knife approaching with his dulled vision...

"At this distance, a knife's not as fast as a pistol." The finger on his right hand was already pulling the trigger. There was a *boom* and the lead slug blew the rapier out of the woman's hand.

"*Clavis...caliburnus...nodos!*"

At the same time, there was a click of iron sabbatons fixing in place, and the woman pitched forward. Almost before she had a chance to shout, the spy was catching her dagger out of the air. With his accelerated consciousness, the entire thing took hardly the blink of an eye.

"A spell caster...!" the guardswoman exclaimed.

As she tried to get up, the spy walked over and placed a foot firmly on her back. "Two-person cell, don't you know." He grinned. "She's reliable. A lot more than me."

If you were pro enough to fight in the dark, you couldn't also afford to be a daredevil, risking your life all the time—but with two of you, well, you might get away with it.

The spy crouched to look the woman in the eye; her breath came in strangled gasps as she tried to get air into one functioning and one crushed lung. Nobody who knew the spy could have stood up under that gaze for long. Now, he just shrugged. "Lots of people think a pistol is just a distance weapon, but it's really a way of getting through armor at point-blank range."

He pressed a pillow against the guardswoman's face. Then he grasped the barrel of the gun, raising the butt. The place already had the drug dealer's blood all over. No harm in a little more. And besides, dealing the blow through something soft was the best way to make sure he didn't damage his weapon.

"Killing a city guard is bad for business. Word's gonna be, you grabbed the money and took off."

"Wait—we can make a deal!" the guardswoman cried, somewhat unexpectedly, cringing and looking like a cooked shrimp. The spy wasn't particularly interested in hearing what she had to say, but he was having trouble pinning her down, and his response was a beat too late. "Maybe instead of killing for money, you'd like to…to help make the world a better place!"

"Hmm?"

"After all, if you wanted to kill me, you'd have done it already. There's something you want."

"Usually is."

"Money. And glory. You want to do great deeds. I'm sure of it." The woman seemed to have taken the spy's offhand response in the most favorable possible way, for she started speaking rapidly. "You're human too, aren't you? You must understand, then. You must see that this town is being invaded!"

"Yeah, I guess it is."

"Just look around—you can see them everywhere. Elves, dwarves— the padfoots and rheas. Whole swarms of them…"

He could feel her shifting under the pillow. He wasn't sure if she was trying to escape, or if she was simply shuddering.

"We need to be rid of the demis, depose the foolish king who tolerates them, and take our country back. It's the only just and right thing to do!" The woman showed no compunction as she spoke, gave no

sense that it ever occurred to her that she might be in the wrong. That
was the whole reason she'd put the confiscated goods out on the street,
spread the drugs around, killed her client, tried to frame the party,
and was now begging for her life.

"'Demis.' So it's come to that, huh?" The spy spat out each word
like the seed of a fruit.

"Am I wrong?" the guardswoman spat back. It was like there was a
fire in her belly and she wanted to get it all out. "An elf born from the
loins of a human is a disgusting thing."

"Guess everyone's entitled to their opinion."

So the squatters, slaves, and sinners of the slums had wasted themselves on drugs and been killed. No particular reason to get mad
about that. He himself took money, sometimes to do a good deed,
sometimes to kill someone. All the same. What the johnson in front
of him wanted, was a city that was beautiful and pure in accordance
with her ideals. The reward: money and fame. It would be to humanity's benefit, the good of the world. A beautification project that he
could contribute to.

For that purpose, he would kill. He would kill elves who had come
forth from the loins of humans. All the same.

The spy shrugged.

"Like trying to spot a shadow at night."

"...What?"

"It ain't my job."

The guardswoman didn't respond immediately. She forced her
head up, pushing aside the pillow, and looked at him as if she couldn't
quite comprehend what she was seeing. "...In that case," she said
finally, "what *do* you want?"

"Good question," the spy replied. He gave it some thought, then
grinned like a shark. "Guess I want my team to win."

§

By the time they had delivered the sack full of meat bits down to the
sewers, the first soft rays of dawn were beginning to appear. Some

would call the dark purple of the clouds beautiful; others might call it terrifying.

As for the spy, now that all the heavy lifting was done, he could only call it dizzying.

He emerged from underground and stood for a moment, listening to the flowing water. He and his friends could at least have themselves some hearty meals for the next couple of days.

The rabbit-faced guard would probably be taking her scolding pretty soon, and the guards would be going back to the scene of the crime. They might notice a new stain. All they would find, though, would be the empty wooden box. The guardswoman would be missing. One obvious conclusion. The guardswoman who had been supplying the drugs had gotten into a disagreement with the seller, offered her the money, and then stolen it and run—to where, nobody knew. That would be it; case closed. Nothing for the Four-Cornered World to worry about.

The spy slowly began to walk away from the entrance (or was that the exit?) of the sewer. But his body just wouldn't relax. In the faint light spreading over the city, he saw someone he didn't recognize standing next to a carriage that he did. The spy felt for the reassuring weight of his pistol at the breast of his trench coat as he walked. The repeating crossbow had a better rate of fire, but for ease of use and sheer power, it was the pistol every time. No question.

Then, though, he stopped walking. He couldn't believe what—or rather, who—he was seeing.

"Is that you? The maid?"

"The representative of the johnson, if you please." It was the silver-haired girl (she could easily have been taken for a child)—although she almost didn't seem to be there, like a shadow.

Representative? the spy thought. Then the outfit was either a disguise or a personal proclivity. There was no way she was actually a maid.

The spy looked up doubtfully at his friend the driver. In response, the driver pulled his cap down as if to say it was no business of his, and shook his head in mild annoyance.

"Looks like you're done with the job. How'd it go?" the maid asked.

"…" Still being careful, the spy slowly undid the buttons of his trench coat to reveal what was within. The pistol hung near his chest. He reached past it, pulled out the opened letter and the map, and tossed them to her. The silver-haired maid grabbed them in midair and looked at them with an interested noise. "Did you happen to look into what this map depicts?"

"No," the spy said, shaking his head. "Too busy."

"That's fine, then." The maid folded the map neatly and put it in the envelope, then put the envelope in her pocket. "That ought to be the end of the drug problem in the water town. Your quest giver is very happy, I assure you." The words sounded scripted, almost silly. "The quest is now over. Your reward is with the fixer."

"Aye-aye," the spy said, nodding. "Think of us the next time you need to do business."

"I will." The silver-haired maid murmured, "Good-bye, then," and started off down an alleyway. She might have been going to buy breakfast—but then she lost herself among the shadows and disappeared from view.

The spy watched her go, not saying anything. His head—his brain—burned.

"…Looks like it's over," said the white-furred creature, poking her head out from the driver's bench. She let out a breath she seemed to have been holding. Maybe she knew who the silver-haired maid really was. "Excellent work."

"Yeah, thanks," the spy replied shortly. It really felt like work, too—he was tired.

The creature seemed to notice this. She cocked her head as if listening to something far away, then sniffed and said, "She says… 'Sorry to put you to all this trouble every time.'"

"All good."

Actually, it wasn't remotely good. There was the one who did the negotiating, the one who did the research, the one who gave support, and the one who got them around. And then there was the one beside him, casting spells. All of which boiled down to… "My role is to do the hit and get everyone home safely."

"Heh! They can swap out all your meaty bits, but they can't change your personality." The white-furred creature laughed. The fixer was probably laughing, too. So the spy added a chuckle of his own. It wasn't such a bad feeling, to be praised by his friends.

"I'm heading back," the creature said. "Have to check in with the fixer."

"Isn't he right there in the room with you?" came the teasing voice of the cleric from inside the carriage, along with a giggle.

"Hmm," the familiar said evasively, but she found herself plucked up by the scruff of the neck and placed on the cleric's knees.

"I'll be going back to the temple today, myself. I feel like I've been asleep for three solid days." It was, in fact, the cleric girl who had been keeping watch on their surroundings, using the abilities gifted to her by the God of Knowledge.

"Sure, good work," the spy said softly.

"Hrmph," the driver grunted. "How about it—you want a ride back?"

"Nah," the spy answered after a moment, shaking his head. "I'll walk."

"Suit yourself." The slightest of smiles came over the driver's normally impassive face, and then he gripped the reins of his animal. *"Go now, kelpie, it's time to get busy! Earth to river and sea to sky, turn all a-tizzy!"* The kelpie raced off pulling the carriage, its mane of froth flying, leaving behind it only hoofbeats like raindrops and neighing like the burble of a river.

The spy watched them go. He stood there alone in the street, staring vacantly after them. Finally, unable to stand the pale light of dawn any longer, he started to trudge away.

It's all over now. Got a chance to think.

Imagine what the guardswoman must have been feeling, maybe that was the thing to do. If it was all ghoul shit, all just the way the world had to work, then maybe no one could complain.

Now, to piece together fragments of random information like they meant something, just because you thought you saw a pattern in them—that was simple paranoia. But say—just say...

What if the half-elf drug dealer had been the guard's older sister, or maybe her younger sister? Maybe the child of a lover. At any rate, the illegitimate spawn of some noble family. Mixed blood. Chased out of the house of her birth, but still financially dependent on them. She turns to a life of crime, even to opium, taking advantage of the fact that she's the blood relation of a member of the city watch to get her hands on confiscated goods.

If it all comes to light, it could undermine the honor of the guards. Or even worse, her own family. And the other daughter, the guardswoman— think what that would mean to her.

Human supremacy. She was willing to do anything for it. Even ally herself with the forces of Chaos.

Suggests the johnson was the girl's parents. Maybe they just wanted to make sure things didn't get out of control. Or maybe it was more than that.

But the drug dealing had already been discovered. Someone had gotten ahold of the secret messages between the women, whether by chance or through treachery. Maybe they'd blackmailed the women— or maybe they'd wanted to stop *her.*

Whichever it was, there were plenty of things in the world one was better off not knowing. And plenty of things one had no way of knowing.

So, the squatters, slaves, and sinners of the slums wasted themselves on drugs and were killed—would anyone mourn them? Why jabber about such negligence to the common classes—there would be no point disturbing them with it. Only the hopelessly stupid or the most heedless daredevils would insist on exposing it, and he was neither.

"…Hmph."

He would prefer if it had been blackmail. It was easiest if no one was really good. If there was no real way to be saved.

Karma feels a little bit lighter that way.

The spy was buckling under heat that was starting to burn; he searched in the pocket of his trench coat. He pulled out a slim cigarette. Now he just needed to light it…

"…Here." He heard the cylinder straw striking, and then there was a glow of flame before his eyes. "…'lo." The red-haired girl— the changeling elf-daughter—was standing there with a shy smile. The spy silently accepted, taking in a deep lungful of the smoke of his

antipyretic, and when his brain was a little cooler, he asked, "…What, didn't go back with the carriage?"

"Nah," she said. "Just sorta felt like walking home."

"Huh."

Wreathed by faintly sweet smoke, the two of them set off walking at an easy pace. He had a head's height on her. Elves were tall, but she was slim, delicate, and light. Maybe it was because her parents were humans. He didn't know. The spy didn't know any other changeling elves.

The spy was careful to shorten his long strides, the red-haired girl jogging to catch up and then walking beside him. They didn't know much about each other's backgrounds. He was a failed Wizball player who'd lost his arms and legs in an accident, who now went into the world of shadows looking for money. She was a merchant's daughter, targeted by slavers because she was a changeling, who was after revenge for a friend who'd got caught in the middle.

It wasn't a question of good and evil, of high principles or low motives, of Order or Chaos.

"Hey," she whispered. "Next time you're gonna go see some Wizball…take me with you."

"Never seen it before, right?"

"Not really."

"Huh." The spy nodded. "I'll buy you some peanuts and crackers, then."

"Is that what you eat when you're watching a game?" She giggled as if this were funny.

It was about time for the water town to be waking up. The streets filled with people, shop signs were flipped to the OPEN side, and the city filled with footsteps and the hum of crowds. Rhea chefs were preparing their utensils, dwarf smiths were banking their fires, and elf troubadours were tuning their instruments. Soon, everywhere would be packed with human kids and padfoot children tumbling and playing.

What must the two of them have looked like as they walked through it all? The spy briefly wondered as the idle conversation went on, but it didn't take him long to decide it didn't matter. He laughed; just because he was an assassin didn't mean he had to go around looking like one.

CHAPTER 4

OF WINTERTIME PREPARATIONS

"Hrrgh…"

It was fiendishly difficult to get out from under the blankets that morning. The sun wasn't even peeking through the window yet, and the chill was cold enough to sneak through the walls to freeze her skin. Frankly, Cow Girl wanted to just burrow under the covers and stay there forever. And until a few years before, that was exactly what she sometimes did in the mornings. (Looking back now, it seemed dissolute in the extreme.)

Really, though, I guess I didn't have the energy to get up and tackle the day, she thought. She had a lot more energy now, although the days when *he* wasn't there were always a little tough.

Afraid that if she just lay around she would go back to old habits, she decided to put her foot down with herself.

"…Okay……… Okay… One, two—!"

She took a deep breath, then flung herself out from under the covers. The freezing cold immediately clung to her skin, and she shivered helplessly. She pulled the blanket around her shoulders and trotted over to her chest of clothes as quickly as she could. She had to get dressed.

She pulled her underwear over her well-rounded body and took a breath. Next, she picked up a padded wool undershirt, weighing it in her hand.

I was thinking it was too soon, but maybe not?

The question was directed at no one in particular. Bested by the cold, she decided to put the thing on. She shoved her head and arms into the shirt, then started to squirm into it...

"...Hrgh...?"

It was a little tight.

Or is that my imagination? she wondered. She raised her arms, shimmied her hips, and spun around, her bare feet moving in little *tap-tap-taps* on the chilly floor, as she tried to figure out exactly how bad it was. Everything else fled her mind. For a girl of her age, this was of utmost importance.

Did I gain weight...? No...I couldn't have. Right?

Right. Definitely not. Definitely probably not.

Now that she thought about it, she realized it was quite a long time ago that she'd knitted this sweater.

That's growing up...I guess.

"Suppose I'll need a new one soon..." She exhaled, then pulled on her work overalls, hanging them off one shoulder as she pulled on her socks and shoes.

That would do the trick. Now...

"...Hee-hee-hee." She did this every morning recently, yet for some reason, it always made her smile. She thought she understood now where expressions like "a smile blossomed on her face" came from.

Last, Cow Girl took out a ruby-colored scale that glimmered even in the predawn darkness. She wore it as a necklace; the scale had defied her best efforts to bore a hole in it, so instead she'd wrapped a string around it. *He* had gifted it to her as a souvenir after his recent trip to the desert in the east.

I wonder if there really was a dragon.

She doubted it was untrue. But—a dragon! It sounded like something out of a fairy tale, incredible to hear. And this was one of its scales—the very idea seemed dreamlike; and that he had actually brought it to *her*, more dreamlike still. That she was wearing it around her neck felt virtually beyond belief.

It had become her habit to study the scale as the first rays of dawn

©Noboru Kannatuki

appeared and glinted off it. She wasn't sure if he remembered that moment—they had been so young then...

"Hee-hee." Cow Girl was unable to hold back another giggle, then hung the dragon scale around her neck. She tucked it under her shirt so she wouldn't drop it or lose it.

"All right, time for another day...!'"

§

The biggest disadvantage to being the first one in the kitchen was that it was so cold—but the biggest advantage was that you got to enjoy it as it warmed up. Cow Girl put the last of yesterday's embers, which had been covered and set aside, in the oven and started a flame going. The crackling fire gradually began chasing the cold away. Soon the morning sun would get brighter, and the room would become noticeably warm.

"You don't like the cold either, do you?" Cow Girl said to the canary in the birdcage hanging in the kitchen; it twittered politely back at her. She knew the bird couldn't take too much of the chill, and she wished she could put it right up next to the oven with its fire, but she was equally concerned the smoke would poison it. After agonizing over it a bit, she'd put cotton inside the cage, a cover outside, and warm stones tucked in cloth pockets nearby.

Sadly, she didn't speak the language of the birds, but as far as she could tell, the canary looked energetic, and that was what mattered.

"Today... What should I do today?" she said to herself, but the reality was the food at the farm didn't change much from day to day. It was almost always a stew of boiled vegetables. Thankfully, her family were yeomen, independent farmers, and they had it better than the denizens of some desolate village. But even so, it would have been nice to be able to save something in the way of cured meat for the winter.

As for fish, you had to soften it up with a mallet before you could eat it, and that sounded like too much trouble today. If *he* was here, she might have pushed a little to make the best possible stew for him, but when he wasn't, she went with more ordinary fare.

"Well, maybe we could use a bit of bacon. And some cheese, and... Hmm..."

They had beans. And bread. And a few potatoes. So, if she were to boil some cow bones...

"We'll have soup!"

With that decided, she got started right away. First, she braved the cold and the chill, and got water from the well to fill the jar in the kitchen. Then she poured some of it into a stewpot that she placed on the fire, before tossing the bones and the scraps of last night's vegetables into it. It would be a while before the broth was ready, obviously, so in the meantime she grabbed a potato from one of the hempen bags hanging around the kitchen and began to peel it.

"We'll have to boil this...then mash and strain it!"

Kitchen work was its own kind of physical labor. Gathering the water and preparing the ingredients took real effort.

I wonder if that's why restaurants so often employ padfoots? Cow Girl thought as she mashed the boiled potato. That's when she heard footsteps coming toward the kitchen.

"G'morning, Uncle," she said without turning around. "It'll be ready soon!"

"Mm, morning... My word, but it does get cold in here." Cow Girl heard her uncle pull out a chair and sit down.

"Sure does," she agreed with as much vigor as she could muster. It really was very cold this morning.

"I guess that lumpy donkey of yours is doing all right in the cold. I'm glad to see it—thing's a help."

"It's called a camel, Uncle."

"Ah, that's right. A camel... A camel... Kind of a nonsensical creature."

The strange animal living in the barn—the camel—was another souvenir from *his* trip to the east. And as glad as she was that he'd managed to remember their little chat before he left...

Of all the things to bring back...

But there was no helping it. She smiled in spite of herself at the thought of the luxurious gift. Thankfully, both she and her uncle could read and write, so they had somehow managed to figure out how to take care of the thing.

It's actually pretty cute, when you're right up close to it, Cow Girl thought.

This was the second animal he had brought her, after the canary. Soon she'd have a regular flock...or was that a herd? Well, whatever; the more the merrier.

"It does make good milk, though." That was her uncle, ever the professional. He had been trying to find a good way to put the camel to work on the farm. This would also be the second time her uncle had tried to incorporate something *he* had brought back into the farm's business model, after the ice treats.

She couldn't deny that it made her happy.

"Not enough of it. But the flavor isn't bad," her uncle continued.

"You think we'll be able to sell it?"

"Only one way to find out, but I think it should make a decent cheese. If we can't produce it in quantity, we'll just have to position it as something rare and unusual."

"I see. That's good."

And it really, truly was.

Cow Girl, smiling from ear to ear, continued working on breakfast. She strained the potato just as the soup was coming to a boil.

I wonder if it's really true that at castles, they spend all day boiling soup, she thought. But then, she and her uncle were not royalty, and this was quite enough for their daily sustenance.

She extracted the bones and vegetable bits. This soup base could keep for several days in the cold. Finally, she added the strained potato, mixed in some milk, beans, and bacon, and let it boil again.

"There, ready!" She thanked her uncle for his patience and brought over a bowl of the stuff for each of them, then sat down across from him, and breakfast was on. They gave thanks to the Earth Mother for their daily food, and then they commenced eating.

The harvest had been good this year, also thanks to the goddess. Cow Girl hoped next year would be as fruitful...

"...Huh?" She stopped with her spoon halfway to her mouth.

"What's wrong?" uncle asked, but she shook her head. Her uncle was wearing a handmade cotton overshirt, but it was starting to show its age.

I guess I made that for him quite a while ago, Cow Girl thought. She wondered if she'd made a shirt for *him* back then, too. She couldn't remember. Her own shirt, though, was getting small, and her uncle's was getting old. So even if she had made him one...

"...Well, I guess that settles it."

She hadn't quite meant to say it out loud. Her uncle looked at her again, but she shook her head once more.

Maybe after today's work is done. I'll make one for everyone. But still.

The one she would *really* be knitting that sweater for was him.

§

"...Oh, shoot." It was only after she had finished her work, gone back to her room, and pulled out her wool and knitting needles, all fired up to go, that Cow Girl realized her mistake. She almost put her head in her hands.

I don't have any idea what size to make it for him...!

Obviously, she knew her own size. And her uncle, well, she could come close enough. But *him*—she hadn't a clue.

It's his fault for wearing that armor all the time, she thought. Yes, he occasionally removed it after he got home, but he kept it on *practically* all the time.

Disappointed to have the wind taken out of her sails, Cow Girl puffed out her cheeks sullenly. She could just imagine what *he* would say about it—"I see," and nothing more—and that annoyed her, too. She couldn't admit that this was effectively a way of denying responsibility, of venting her anger.

"Hrm... Maybe I could...take a look at his clothes...?"

Cow Girl quietly left her room and snuck (for no good reason) down the hall to his room. She frequently popped in while he was away to clean or straighten, but today it felt a little different. Unlike her usual household chores, this time she was coming in to help herself with something she was doing in secret.

Er... Well, I guess there's no need to knit in secret, but...

But, well, somehow that was what it worked out to. Yep.

"Sorry to...intrude..." she mumbled as she opened the door. Of course, there was no answer.

He'd been out of the house the last several days on an urgent adventure or something. She knew that perfectly well. This wasn't a problem of etiquette so much as it was a conflict in her own heart.

"…Hmm. No more possessions than usual, I see. Very spare room you keep…" She smiled to herself. There was an oblong chest that held his smattering of personal effects, and then there were a spare helmet, sword, shield, and so on. This was really just a place for him to sleep; that shed was closer to being his "room" in the meaningful sense.

If I'd left him to his own devices, he'd probably have just stayed in there forever… It's like a cave, she thought. A secret hideout. She remembered running around near the village when they were small, making secret bases like that. The thought filled her with a fondness and a longing that constricted her chest at the same time as it warmed her heart. It showed up on her face as a small smile.

She knew now that her parents must have been aware of those hideouts. Then again, maybe they hadn't—and she was still the only one, both then and now, who really knew them inside out.

"…Hee-hee."

Unsure if that was a happy thought, or a rather sad one, Cow Girl sat down on the bed. It didn't smell like him; how could it? Even when he was gone, she faithfully changed the sheets. Still, she sat there staring distantly up at the ceiling, wondering where he was now and what he was doing…

"No, no, stop that. Now's not the time." She smacked herself on the cheeks and stood up aggressively in hopes of shaking herself out of it. If she didn't do something when she had determined to do it, then she never would. She was just too lazy.

Let's see, now… She lifted the heavy lid of the chest and pulled out one of his shirts. *What did he call this? A gambeson?* She seemed to recall it was a type of under armor. It was made of thick padded cotton, pillowy for the most part but reinforced in certain places. An aroma drifted from it—his smell.

"It kind of stinks…" she said, and smiled wanly. The odor was a mixture of mud, sweat, blood. Not exactly a fragrance to stir a young maiden's heart. But this jacket was something that kept him alive. She couldn't just go trying to clean it. She didn't even know how.

When he comes back, I'll ask him to teach me, she resolved to herself, and then she spread the gambeson on the bed and started measuring it.

"Hmm…"

What exactly was going on here? To reiterate, the gambeson was stuffed with cotton and reinforced in places. It even had some puffy spots, maybe because of the expectation that armor would be worn on top of it. If she tried to knit something on the basis of these measurements—well, it wouldn't be a total disaster, but it didn't seem likely to fit quite right. Maybe one of the master craftspeople of the Knitters Guild would be able to do it, but not her.

"What to do…" She put her chin in her hand with another "Hmm."

Normally, someone trying to answer a question like this would ask her friends, but the only person Cow Girl could think of was Guild Girl. *And I'm not entirely comfortable going to her about this…*

So, what else could she do?

§

"A sweater, huh… Come to think of it, I've never worn one myself." They'd initially tried chatting out behind the Guild building like they usually did, but a gust of northern wind sent them scurrying into the dining hall. The padfoot waitress, who was on her break, sat rocking her chair back and forth (most unladylike). "After all, I've never needed to. I've got my own fur!"

"Yeah, you're very fluffy," Cow Girl said to her friend (who was quite close to her in age). "May I touch it?" she asked, and then she ran her hand through the soft fur. The waitress had large pads on her hands surrounded by fur. Cow Girl pressed gently on them, and Padfoot Waitress let out a breath. "See? My winter coat's in!"

"That's really nice. I'm kind of jealous."

"Right?" Padfoot Waitress flicked her ears. "But shedding in spring *sucks.*"

Parting the fur gently revealed distinct under- and overcoats. So as soft as it was, Cow Girl could see how getting rid of it would be an ordeal. "Everyone's got their own struggles, huh?" she said.

"True that. You know, sometimes I wish I could wear all sorts of different outfits, like humans do." Padfoot Waitress rested her chin in her hands, her generous chest settling on the table. Her big ears, her big hands, and her tail, all covered in fur, dictated the sort of clothing she could wear. It got in the way of hats and handbags, and there was always the risk that a revealing skirt could come off entirely. And no matter what she wore, the color of her outfit had to coordinate with the color of her hair.

"Guess the grass is always greener on the other side," Cow Girl said, sighing. Nothing ever went quite exactly the way one would hope. "So, uh, about the sizing…"

"Oh, yeah." Padfoot Waitress nodded. "Clothes for that goblin-slaying guy. Heck, I dunno. Wouldn't you of all people know that stuff?" Padfoot Waitress looked at her skeptically.

"Ha-ha-ha," Cow Girl laughed. "You think the person who makes his armor and helmets might know, though?"

"Oh, you mean the boss at the workshop." Padfoot Waitress crossed her arms and nodded quickly. Cow Girl knew the waitress was close to the young man apprenticed to the shop master. "I guess it's possible he might," Padfoot Waitress said.

"Could you maybe ask him for me?"

"Hmm… I dunno, he seems pretty busy right now…"

"Really?" Cow Girl cocked her head, and Padfoot Waitress said "Yep" and nodded as if she wasn't thrilled about it herself. Apparently, there was some kind of unrest in the country to the east, while right around here there were plenty of wyverns and demons and the like. That meant lots of adventurers who wanted new equipment, and *that* meant lots of work at the armory.

"So, they're doing well for themselves; that's great."

"Yeah, it's fine. But I hardly ever see him these days…," Padfoot Waitress said in annoyance, leaning on the table in a way that seemed to threaten to crush her chest.

True, Cow Girl was treating this all as if the talk had nothing to do with her—but what else was she supposed to do? They were always separated from war by the thinnest of margins—but that was enough for them to think of it as somewhere else. Cow Girl surely wasn't completely removed from what was happening. She hadn't been in the past, and wasn't now.

The adventures *he* undertook were goblin hunts, and however much or little, that influenced the scales of Order and Chaos.

"So, I propose a trade!" Padfoot Waitress announced, sitting up abruptly. Cow Girl was grateful for her light touch.

"Oh-ho," Cow Girl said with an almost comical air of sagacity. "And what is it you wish for?"

"Teach me to knit a sweater, too! Since I've got you here and everything!"

"That's not easy," Cow Girl said, but she found herself smiling as she said it. There was no need to play coy. "Hah, I don't mind. But you've never needed one before, have you?"

"I bought some gloves once, because my little paws were getting cold. Back when I was a kid. My mom gave me two bronze coins for it." Padfoot Waitress smiled.

Cow Girl suddenly found herself trying to remember her mother. Her face was already hazy with emotion. "You won't be able to make anything if you don't know the sizing," she said. "That's my problem right now."

"Aw, it'll be fine. I already know every inch!"

"What?" Cow Girl said, blinking. Then she blushed a little. *No. She can't mean...*

"...You're using your own measurements?"

"Uh-huh," Padfoot Waitress said blandly, even with a hint of pride. "Anyway, even if I screw up, I'll still foist it off on him!"

Doesn't seem like much of a gift, Cow Girl thought. She felt a little bad for the young man in question, but decided it was his fault for not being assertive enough. Cow Girl pressed a hand to her own significant chest—and to the red scale tucked there—and giggled.

A girl couldn't be kept waiting forever, after all.

§

They had their materials, and they had their plan. All that was left was action.

"So tell me, tell me, what are we gonna do?! Start with the collar?!"

"Well, uh, there's a number of possibilities..."

Padfoot Waitress had successfully obtained the requested information ("He's a soft touch," she said), and they were back in their corner of the dining area. The two young women sat side by side, deep in conversation. Failure wasn't really a possibility in their minds.

Cow Girl had managed to get ahold of knitting needles and a variety of yarn, but now she smiled in spite of herself. "I guess we'll start with the front, then the back, then the sleeves, then sew them all together... Maybe that would be simplest?"

"Right, right!"

"The front's nice and big, so that's a good starting point for your first time."

"Start with the part that takes the longest, got it." Padfoot Waitress nodded fervently, leaning forward in her seat, and an unexpected sparkle came into her eyes. "In other words, it's just like cooking!"

"Ha-ha, uh, I guess so... Yeah, just follow the recipe and you'll be fine."

"Don't worry! I'm not gonna try striking out in my own weird, stylistic direction on my very first attempt." She waved her paw as if to dismiss the notion and laughed uproariously. "Just gotta take it one thing at a time. Awesome, let's go!"

"Right, it's not something you'll pick up in a day, so don't sweat it."

"That's just like learning to cook, too..."

As they talked, the young women started making delicate movements with their hands, beginning to knit.

There was nothing particularly unusual about it. Fall and winter afternoons were long. It was the way of the world for farm girls to spend those interminable stretches working by the hearth. Sewing, embroidering, doing lacework, and so on... And of course, chatter blossomed like a flower between the two women.

"Hmm, your guy off somewhere again?"

"Uh-huh." Cow Girl nodded as she pulled on one of her knitting needles. "He's an adventurer. That's what he does, right?"

"More goblin slaying?"

"Didn't sound like it. He didn't really give me the details, though."

"Huh…"

Padfoot Waitress seemed to be substantially better at talking than she was at knitting. But the fact that she didn't simply throw the project aside, despite her obvious struggle, was evidence of how serious she was. Scrunching up her adorable face in concentration, she tried to manipulate the needles with her ungainly paws. If someone saw her who didn't know any better, they might well think that she was simply playing with some string.

I guess maybe I could give her some pointers or lend a hand, but… Cow Girl had the distinct feeling that that wasn't the right thing to do. It was so dispiriting, when you were working hard on something, to have someone simply pluck it away from you. And words would be no different. It would get annoying to be constantly bombarded with "tips."

If Padfoot Waitress looked to her for help, asked her a question—or if she was completely defeated and in danger of giving up, then Cow Girl might have to intervene.

Yeah, that's a good policy, she told herself.

"Like I said, don't sweat it too much," she advised, and that was all. She wasn't communicating about the specific process so much as from what mindset to approach it. "If you make a mistake, you can always just undo it and try again. You really don't have to worry."

"Y-yeah, sure… There's more than one round to this fight…" Padfoot Waitress looked like she'd dodged the end of the world. "Thank the gods. I thought if I screwed this up, it was all over!"

"That's one of the nice things about knitting. You can always take it back." Cow Girl really believed that. She wished everything were that way. There were so many things in this world that couldn't be redone, that couldn't be taken back…

"My, what's going on here?"

"Ooh, knitting! Wow, I guess it's that time of year already, isn't it?"

Just as Cow Girl was in danger of getting lost in her lonely thoughts, the two voices snapped her out of it. She looked up to see Guild Girl and Inspector, both stylishly dressed. Cow Girl was always a little jealous of them. She wished she had a slim, curvy body like they had.

Guild Girl, apparently taking Cow Girl's look to be asking what they were doing here, smiled softly. "Hee-hee-hee, it's getting into the afternoon. That means it's time for tea!"

"Oh, want me to go ask the chef to get you something?" Padfoot Waitress said, seeing an opportunity for a quick change of pace. She jumped up, her ears and tail almost fully upright, and tossed her knitting onto the table. Then she bounded off just as energetically, leaving Cow Girl smiling to herself in her wake.

Still... She wasn't sure how she felt bringing *that* thought up while knitting something for him. Cow Girl stared into space for a moment, hoping to find a topic of conversation there, and then latched onto the most innocuous thing she could think of. "How are things these days? It sounds like it's been awfully busy..."

"Hmm, busy... Well, I guess so." Guild Girl grasped her chin thoughtfully in her delicate fingers. Then she sat down at the round table with the most natural of motions, her beautiful hips swaying as she seated herself. Inspector followed suit.

Every employee of the Guild moved in a careful and practiced manner that drew the eye. It wasn't the same effortless elegance that high elf exuded; it was unmistakably a way of moving aimed at other humans.

"But not unusually so," Guild Girl said.

"Plus, the war in the east looks like it's settling down. Besides, the forces of Chaos running rampant is nothing new." Inspector nodded as if to emphasize her own statement.

The scales of Order and Chaos were forever swinging back and forth. They would never tilt completely to one side or the other. There was always some greater or lesser unrest occurring; that was simply the way of the Four-Cornered World.

Indeed, it was to be expected. It was hardly possible to imagine a situation in which no trouble occurred anywhere in the world. Instead, Cow Girl thought, if things were quiet around her, that was peace enough.

So she asked, "Things are okay, then?"

"Yeah, I don't think the effects should reach us," Inspector said with a nod. The symbol of the sword and scales hanging at her neck jingled with the motion. "I guess the princess rose up to stop the prime minister before he could take complete control or something. Simple enough affair."

"I heard there was a dashing young knight at the princess's side," Guild Girl added with a girlish sigh. A knight who saved a princess. It was like something out of a storybook. A tale of heroism being played out in some far-off country.

Cow Girl, swept away by the thought, found herself murmuring, "How wonderful..."

"Wish that was your story?" Guild Girl said, giving Cow Girl a teasing look. Cow Girl felt heat come into her face. She looked this way and that and finally gazed at the floor.

At last she simply admitted it: "...Yeah, a little." Saying it out loud, she found the words were lighter and came more easily than she'd expected.

"I can see why..." Resting her chin in her hands, Guild Girl let out another sigh.

I guess even the daughters of nobility fantasize about being princesses with their knights, Cow Girl thought. She felt she could hardly imagine how the pampered children of elite families passed the time.

"You two ladies can have your knights. I think I'll pass," Inspector, who was presumably the daughter of a respectable household herself, said with a wave of her hand. "I'm not keen on having anyone around me twenty-four-seven, whether it's a knight or a husband."

"Huh, you're a cold one."

"I'd prefer you to say realistic."

I wonder if she's right, Cow Girl thought. Another thing she didn't know much about was what it meant to have time to yourself to do exactly what you wanted. Looking at it this way, she started to see that she was lucky enough to have met quite a few different people. It was thanks to her parents in her youth, and then her uncle, and *him*, and her friends.

"Aaaaand here ya go!" one of that handful of friends exclaimed, bounding up to the table. The tray was just barely balanced on her hand, but amazingly, nothing spilled or fell off. She set the tray on the table and with a "Have some!" she began pouring everyone...*something*.

"This…isn't tea, is it?" Guild Girl asked, eyeballing the drink. One could see why: It was a viscous brown liquid. Cow Girl brought it to her nose and sniffed politely to discover it gave off a sweet aroma.

"It smells good, anyway," she said. "It's kind of like…"

"Wait, is this—" Inspector clapped her hands as the other two girls pondered. "—that stuff made from the nut of the gods?"

"Bingo!" Padfoot Waitress clapped her big, padded paws.

Cow Girl still didn't understand what that meant, though. "Nut of the gods?" She cocked her head, then added, "Does it literally come from heaven?"

"I don't know much about it myself, but I guess it's called 'cacao' or something…" Padfoot Waitress circled her paw in the air. "The chef said it's some kinda bean they get from the south. I guess you boil it and then add sugar?"

"I'm not sure if it's a bean so much as a seed," Inspector said. "It's supposed to be popular at the capital these days, but I've never seen it before, myself. Hmm, hmm…" She studied the contents of her cup with real interest.

Hmm… Well, sure, I guess so, thought Cow Girl.

The stuff had the consistency of barley soup, but the smell was quite pleasant. She didn't know what the gods ate, but it seemed they were at least capable of eating.

"The south—there's lots of lizardmen there, aren't there?" Guild Girl said, likewise studying the dark drink. (At least, she thought it was a drink; it was in her cup, after all.)

"There are supposed to be lots of unusual foods down there," Cow Girl said. Like tomatoes, and maize, and even the potato she'd had that morning. The potato grew happily here, so maybe some of the other vegetables would as well—just like that camel.

"Anyway, since we've got it here," Cow Girl said, nodding toward her cup, "we should try a sip."

"Totally. I'm so excited!"

All right, then. They all looked at one another, then brought their cups to their lips.

First, a sip.

"…Wow."

It was bitter. But definitely sweet. Those seemed like completely contradictory flavors, but there they were, mingling in her mouth. Cow Girl blinked, then took another sip, enjoying the experience. This was a taste you could get hooked on.

"Mmm…" Guild Girl licked some droplets off her lips and closed her eyes as if savoring the aroma of a fine black tea. "I think you could afford to put some pepper in here. It would give it a nice little kick."

"Sounds like that's how most people do it," Inspector said. Then she added "Mmm," relishing the bittersweet flavor. "Adding sugar is something we thought up here, it sounds like. There's lots of ways to do it."

"Maybe we could try some milk. Just like how you can take sugar and milk in your tea."

Two of the women, though, didn't speak. They were Cow Girl, silently luxuriating in the flavor, and Padfoot Waitress, who was looking at the floor, red-faced.

"You know, I've heard something else, too," Inspector said with a sly look at her two silent tablemates. "They say this is an excellent aphrodisiac."

"Huh…?!" Cow Girl yelped, her hand freezing in midair. She was lucky she didn't reflexively spit out the stuff in her mouth.

Inspector laughed uproariously; it had all been a naughty tease on her part. "Ha-ha-ha! I'm joking, I'm joking!"

"U-urgh…" The clarification seemed to come too late for Padfoot Waitress. She started growling like an actual animal, then suddenly jumped up out of her chair. "My…my heart is racing! I'm getting dizzy…!"

"What?!" Cow Girl looked up in a hurry. She asked if Padfoot Waitress was okay, but the waitress didn't seem to hear. Her face was bright red, her eyes unfocused as she clung to her cup.

"It'd be a waste, though… I'mma go make *him* try it!" And then she went rushing off—to where? Well, even to imagine it might be a little much.

She's gone…

The three women left behind looked at one another, then burst out giggling.

"They say padfoots are especially sensitive to fragrant herbs—I wonder if she didn't like it?" Guild Girl questioned.

"They definitely seem to have different tastes than we do," Inspector agreed. "There was this cat-eared girl the other day..." She smirked and took another sip from her cup. "She got completely soused on one mouthful of beer—ended up shoving her head in a water jar and singing about how thankful she was for it."

"Huh," Cow Girl said. "I guess you have to take that sort of thing into account when you're coming up with a new dish." She decided to make sure she informed her uncle later, but for the moment she enjoyed another sip of the brown drink. It was both sweet and bitter. Not that she intended to take any of that stuff about aphrodisiacs at face value.

Still, maybe she should have *him* try some of it when he got home? Ha-ha...

"Oh..."

No wonder she was cold.

Flecks of white were starting to drift through the air outside the window. Winter had come to the town on the frontier.

Of a Council with the King and His Advisers

"All right, I understand the situation now." The young king of the land leaned wearily on the arm of his throne and sighed deeply. He had an office (separate from his throne room) with a perfectly good chair in it; the throne was all elegant and cushy. He thought it would be more efficient simply to shut himself up in his office and work, but somehow he didn't think he could get away with that.

What, are they afraid I'll just abandon my duties?

He glanced to the side, where a red-haired cardinal was standing. The cardinal snapped, "Your Majesty."

"Yes, yes," the king replied, and looked down at the papers in his hand. Even in the royal family there were many who could not read or write—one need only hire a scribe to help them—but it was none-theless a useful skill to have. He wished he could funnel a little more money into proselytization for the God of Knowledge, but... Well, best focus on the task at hand.

"So just when we thought the real action was the unrest in the east, we find out the army of evil had their base in our own territory all along."

"A most ordinary occurrence, I daresay."

"Hence, why we never seem to have enough money or resources."

It seemed like the most common thing in the world. No country existed that had limitless amounts of everything at all times. Collect too many taxes, and there would be a rebellion. Fail to collect enough taxes, and the national coffers would run dry. Without money in the treasury, it would be impossible to implement policy, and then there would be more grumbling. No part of the running of the nation could be neglected, and yet one was only given so many cards to play. One had to use them thoughtfully, one turn at a time.

Frankly, it's a lot easier running a party of six people, the king thought. The red-haired cardinal snickered softly, and smiled as if reading the king's mind. "In all history, the only flawless nation-states have existed in the imagination."

"And is that a reason I shouldn't aim to have the first real one?"

As if they hadn't had this discussion before. The king shrugged in a gesture not unlike a lion. The cardinal nodded. "At least the ideals of the country may have their feet on the ground, and be more than peasants dreaming in between the jobs on their farms."

"That's the idea."

The king nearly sighed—he had lost count of how many times this was—but managed to hold it back in deference to the cardinal, who was looking at him as if to say that all he ever did was complain. He coughed once to cover himself, then pointedly rolled up a sheet of sheepskin parchment.

"It looks like we're maintaining the battle line," he said. "The soldiers are holding out well. Make sure they have all the supplies they need." It wasn't that the national treasury had much to spare. But only a fool would begrudge his troops the provisions they needed. "The last thing I want to do is shoot our people in the back."

"Very true." The cardinal nodded without even looking at the paper. "Also, we have reports that a unique monster has appeared…"

"And been dispatched by adventurers, I see." For the first time that day, the king looked genuinely pleased as he studied the paperwork.

"Your Majesty."

"I didn't say anything……… Ahh, shit." The king scowled again, for a reason altogether unrelated to the cardinal's scolding.

A silver-haired attendant, standing in one corner of the room, gave a proud thumbs-up, even though her studiously neutral expression never changed.

"…So, there was someone on the inside. That would explain how they knew what to do." The king took a quick look at the report of the disturbance in the water town. "Sounds like those bastards were hoping to get to the capital."

"Well, it *is* the hinge upon which the entire country turns," the cardinal said lightly. "A map of the capital city, and of the castle grounds. Get ahold of those and who knows where your thoughts might go."

"Heh! If they took me too lightly, they'd have another think coming!"

"I'd say it's exactly *because* you're so light that they thought they could just sweep you aside," the silver-haired lady mumbled, entirely disrespectfully.

"The point is, the plot failed—we can worry about the legalities later," the cardinal continued, not precisely acting proper either, and the king snorted, not the least amused. He passed the letter to the cardinal, who glanced over it again and then promptly threw it into the fire in the hearth.

"Waste of good parchment," the silver-haired attendant commented, her tone just this side of sarcastic. But the cardinal had known the lady a long time, and was well acquainted with her barbs. He shook his head firmly and said, "Couldn't have the report destroying itself automatically."

"When you plan to deny all knowledge of me and my hired help if we're captured or killed."

"*You* were the one who decided that royal orders were to be fulfilled even at the cost of your life, and even if there were none to retrieve your corpses," the king rejoined.

"True enough," she said disinterestedly. That was what it meant to be a deniable asset. If that was the sort of thing you complained about, then you weren't cut out for the job. The attendant knew perfectly well that her life was disposable. Instead, she turned girlish eyes on the king and said, "So, what are you going to do?"

"There's nothing so pointless as a game in which all the cards are faceup," the cardinal answered, seemingly intuiting what the king was thinking.

"That's right," he said, nodding. "I don't have to lower myself to playing along with their little tricks. Did you see what we received from the esteemed lady from the frontier?"

The responses were immediate:

"Ah, you mean the scroll, sire."

"Awfully convenient timing."

The king grinned as if seeing his plans come to fruition. "The Gate spell. Hmph... Chaos sons of bitches aren't the only ones who can go chasing after maps."

"I never realized we knew someone who dealt in such things," the silver-haired lady said; she sounded impressed, but her expression changed not at all. "Color me surprised."

"Many are the secret sages in this world, the great magicians of scant renown, spell casters of skill unknown, and hermits," the cardinal said.

"Nobody knows what lies in the deck, though many purport to." The king crossed his arms and grinned like a wild beast, as if he were staring down the forces of Chaos even then. "So, all we can do is cut the deck. Find some excellent cards, something powerful, with which to put an end to the game."

"Hrm." The young, silver-haired lady crossed her arms in front of her chest, a most unladylike gesture, and added with the conviction of a veteran soldier, "Then we'll need a diversion."

"Yes, I should think so."

"An entire army? A small unit?"

"Small numbers," the king said promptly. "I'll leave the personnel decisions to you. But well-known people, if possible."

"You got it." The attendant nodded and worked her way gracefully out of the throne room. Or perhaps it was only because they were accustomed to the way she moved that they could discern the grace. To someone not so accustomed, it would have seemed she simply vanished, like a shadow.

"Get the army underway, too. This is a major battle. We need to draw the enemy forces out of their base, as many of them as possible."

"As you command," the cardinal said with a respectful bow of his head.

That ought to do the trick. Use the army as a distraction, while a picked force struck the vital point. The enemy would be expecting that, no doubt, so the small force would have to split up to attack. One ought to strike where a wild card was expected—but not letting your enemy know which one *was* the wild card; that was the key to strategy.

Committing one military force after another was to throw good after bad—but only if things didn't work out for you. To commit your forces when you knew what the enemy strength was—that, was in fact, good strategy. This had been the immovable principle ever since the hero in shining chain mail had changed the war game forever.

Good after bad; that, they told you, was what you had to avoid.

But maybe they should have said, "unless the time is right." The thought came upon the king quite suddenly, and he found it very congenial. To leave everything to his subordinates and advisers would itself have been the behavior of a foolish ruler.

"And who will we send on the job, Your Majesty?"

"Let's see, here…"

Distinguished adventurers would be ideal. Silver, at least.

They were looking to infiltrate an enemy base and topple their leader. So some dungeon-delving experience would be a must. And it wouldn't be feasible to get in and out of this situation with the sword alone; some magical ability was called for. Then, too, the infiltration party couldn't be discovered. Absolutely no more than six people could go.

Adaptability was another requirement. The enemy might bring any number of ploys to bear, so the members of this mission should have experience with a wide variety of monsters and combat situations. It wasn't just about who went and what level they were, either. They would need a panoply of items and gear at the ready.

All of which was to say, the leader would have to be someone capable of bringing and holding together such a guerrilla force. And above all, they would have to be able to act immediately.

"All right, then…!"

"Majesty…"

When the king jumped up from his throne, the red-haired cardinal greeted him with a tone of complete resignation. The young ruler, of course, was not the least bit interested in listening to him.

Perhaps the best thing that could be said of this king was that he would always decide for himself whether to heed any exhortations. Let them call him a throne-warmer who spent all his time mulling over how to make his lands more peaceful. If they wished to say he was a good-for-nothing who'd come up from being an adventurer, let them see if they could stand up to a good punch from him. If he told those people, fine, *they* could run the country—they would turn tail and run. Such people were simply full of themselves, convinced that they were smarter and more accomplished than anyone else.

But what did he care? If it was an honor even to be punished by the king, it must surely be a *dis*honor to be brought low by the third son of some poor knight.

"Summon the captain of the royal guard. And the palace wizard, too. They must be getting bored."

"*Majesty.*"

"Oh, don't worry," the king said, and smiled in what he thought was a reassuring manner. "You get your stuff together, too. Your fire staff, and the ice chain mail. Maybe I should call the others, as well. Biggest thing to happen to us in a while."

"…" For the first time that day, the red-haired cardinal let out a sigh. It seemed the report from the water town was the way the king intended to deal with all his built-up frustration. Now, what to do about it…

"Excuse me…," a probing voice broke in from a corner of the throne room.

There she stood, her posture erect, her clothing perfectly fitted to the shape of her body, the aluminum sword at her belt—Female Merchant.

"Hrm," the king grunted, upset of course to have someone rain on his parade. Those two words were the first thing this woman had said since she arrived; she had otherwise been completely and diligently silent. He knew there was no reason not to listen to her; he stilled his hand, which had been reaching for the vacuum sword at his hip. "What is it? You know you're welcome to speak your mind at any time."

"May I indeed, Your Majesty?"

"I've never known your counsel to be ill-considered."

"...But I have done my share of very foolish things." The slightest of rueful smiles seemed to creep over Female Merchant's face, barely a twitch of her lips. She let her gaze drop to the ground for a mere second, then she raised her head and looked straight at the king. "My mind, then. There is a report I must bring to Your Majesty."

"What would that be?"

"I thought you might ask that, sire," Female Merchant said, "so I took the liberty of summoning them already."

That was when the door flew open with a *bang*, and a voice as refreshing as a spring breeze came flying through the room: "Maaa-jeestyyy! We're heeere!" The sound of two sets of footsteps followed, and his little sister came tumbling into the room.

"Manners!" scolded a black-haired woman, but she quickly tried to compose herself in the presence of the king.

One ought to strike where a wild card was expected—but not letting your enemy know which one was *the wild card...*

The king groaned softly and tried to find the words. Finally, he said the only thing that came to his mind: "...A fine strategy."

"My thanks, sire." Female Merchant smiled with just a hint of pride, but the king slumped back onto his throne with a sigh.

CHAPTER 5

OF WHAT PROBLEM THERE COULD POSSIBLY BE WITH A MALE HUMAN FIGHTER

"Urgh… It's so…slimy…"

"You just won't shut up about that. Put on some shoes, if it bothers you so much!"

"I'm a rhea, you know that's the one thing I can't do! Why, if my dear, departed grandfather found out, he'd spank me silly!"

Shlip, shlip. Tok, tak. One pair of bare feet, one shod, echoed through the sewers.

It felt as if they might be the only living things down there in the gloom. The red-haired boy held his staff aloft, the end shimmering with magical light; he was aware of his own nerves fraying.

I wonder if this is what a city looks like after it starts to go to dust…

It reeked. The water that flowed past them was murky with pollutants. The rats, and even the bugs, were nowhere to be found anymore.

The boy didn't know how long it had been since the city had fallen. Less than a month, he supposed. And the decay had already reached the sewers underground. The wizard boy shivered, praying that the girl beside him wouldn't notice. He didn't have the courage to look and see whether the thing he'd just stepped on was a corpse or not.

"Yeek?! I just stepped on something squooshy! Squooshy and… soft…!"

"Shut up! Be quiet…!"

Despite the boy's scolding, the rhea girl with him—a warrior with a sword strapped across her back—continued to squeak and squeal. She was quick to fear but not to take offense; you could say that she had thin courage but thick skin.

Her cheerfulness, though out of place, was something of a saving grace in this abandoned city. But Wizard Boy was both too embarrassed and not honest enough with himself to admit it.

Just imagine what would have become of him if he'd been thrown into this situation all alone. It wasn't a pleasant thought.

"I can think of some other people who would be a lot more suited to this sort of place than we are."

Wizard Boy's offhanded grumble brought an expression of genuine weariness from Rhea Fighter. "Yeah, those rats and those bugs were so big... And then there were those slimes. Ugh, I don't like them."

There were many opponents in this world who couldn't be handled simply by swinging a sword around. The fact that some of those opponents were just sewer-dwellers was beyond pathetic...

"...All right, pipe down. I'm gonna give the signal."

"Yeah, I know." By the time she whispered this to him she had already slid her sword smoothly from its scabbard. "Any old time."

The two of them had reached the far end of the sewer, where the brackish water slipped out of sight. The sewers had been created by humans or dwarves or somebody else, but what lay ahead was different. The water flowed under the rocks, off to become the tributary of a great river somewhere. The boy studied the water, dark as ink—in fact, he practically glowered at it—and lifted his shining staff.

He waved the staff twice, then three times—big, sweeping motions as if it were a brush and the light were paint, and he was drawing in the air. After making this portentous movement a couple of times, stirring the empty air, he waited a moment, then repeated the process. An onlooker might not have known what he was communicating, but it would have been clear that he was communicating *something*.

One thing, however, would have puzzled any observer. Namely, who could there be to receive a signal from the far edge of a polluted stream in a dead city?

"........"

"........"

"…Nothing happened."

"No shit!" Wizard Boy groaned, wishing he could run away from this moment. He couldn't, however, so he didn't. Instead, he bit his lip and repeated the movements with his staff a fourth time, and then a fifth, desperately sending the signal.

There was no response—not that he even really knew what he was hoping for.

"…Um. I don't guess maybe you've got the order wrong or something?"

"No way," Wizard Boy snapped. "Even if I did, they'd still notice it."

"Yeah, but…" Rhea Fighter started to say something, then stopped, offering only a "Pfah" and a click of the tongue. She could complain all she wanted, but even the lackadaisical rhea understood that if nothing happened, then you had to do something about it yourself. But she didn't feel like there was the slightest thing she *could* do about it.

Every last stupid little thing here is all Ol' Teach's fault! Looking to vent some of her anger, she gave something by her foot a good, hard kick. She didn't even know how it had managed to ride the stream all the way down here: It was an old, rusty metal helmet. Released from otherwise being destined to sit there until it turned to dust, the helmet smacked off some nearby rubble with a great *clang*. It rolled into the water (*ploosh*), leaving behind it only the echo of the impact.

"Oops… Ha-ha…"

"Listen, you…" Wizard Boy eyeballed the girl, who flinched a little, perhaps expecting a storm of rage. But before he could say anything, everything else was drowned out by a heavy, wet *shlop*.

The two of them froze, and then, as if on cue, they looked in the same direction.

It was a hand.

It stuck up out of the stream, sending ripples across the dark water, grabbing firmly onto the shore. Next (*shoop*), up came a heavy body. The thick, sticky water went flying almost like mud.

There was a cheap-looking metal helmet. Grimy leather armor. You could almost mistake it for Living Armor or an undead monster. But it was an adventurer, and he worked his way onto dry ground.

"It's just as our information indicated. At least it appears to have been correct." The man didn't even glance at the boy and girl, but shook himself like a wet dog coming in from the rain. Then he turned his back to them and stuck his hand back under the water, his arm tensing with exertion.

What he pulled up was a muscular body covered in armor—a hulking man with a greatsword across his back.

"Wouldn't have occurred to me to think they didn't trust us. That info came from the quest giver, didn't it?"

"Even if the quest giver is telling the truth, there's always a possibility that unexpected circumstances could have caused the path to collapse."

"There *was* a possibility, but it didn't happen, did it? So, no problem."

"Indeed," the first man said, his metal helmet nodding up and down. "No problem."

"It's nothing *but* problems…!" This came from the third and final form to emerge from the water. This person jumped out of the river as smartly as a salmon, even the ripples he made looking neat and attractive. He was a handsome man who had somehow managed to sling a spear across his back, and the moment he was on land, he held up his sopping hair. "It's great that you have rings that let us breathe underwater and all, but I never want to wade through a river of sewage again!"

"Did the rings not do their job?"

"Not the point."

"I see." The man in the middle helmet, Goblin Slayer, nodded, sounding somehow slightly disappointed. "We will have to find ourselves another way home, then."

"Not the point, either. I'm not just sayin' this for my own amusement— Ahh, forget it. Oh…"

"Hey there. Sorry about all the noise." While Spearman tried to sort out his hair, Heavy Warrior managed to spare a glance at the boy and girl as he checked his equipment. The two kids, watching in some amazement, found themselves pinned to the spot by his look. Then again, you wouldn't have to have been a born coward to feel the same, seeing this group emerge from the water.

It only lasted a second, though. Heavy Warrior came over to them like a lumbering bear, then squatted down so he could look them in the eyes. "So, we've linked up, just like we planned. And you guys got your stuff done safely? Nice work." His voice was rough, but his tone was kindly. He patted them each on the shoulder with his powerful hand. It was almost painful, but also exhilarating.

"Well, y'know." Wizard Boy sniffed as if quite pleased with himself, and even Rhea Fighter puffed out her generous chest proudly. These rookie adventurers had earned praise from a Silver. It didn't happen often. Which meant...

"Maybe this adventure was just a little bit over our heads?"

The rhea girl's whisper cut to the heart of the matter, but the boy greeted it with a snort. He couldn't admit that he had been thinking the same thing—it would simply be too embarrassing.

§

Another city destroyed.

It was not, of course, at the hands of goblins. Any adventurer who said it was would be a laughingstock. Only the thoughtless or the ignorant believed goblins were as threatening as all that.

Anyway, you didn't need goblins to destroy a city. There was an endless array of monsters in the Four-Cornered World who could do that. A dragon attack would do the trick, or a rampaging giant, or a dark elf's plotting, or a demon's domination, or, at specific times and in certain cases, all of these things at once.

Such occurrences were common enough in the never-ending battle between Order and Chaos. But there wasn't a god, ruler, or adventurer who wouldn't try to do something about it. Adventurers, for example, would find out exactly what monster had destroyed the city, and then go try to pay it back in kind.

So, we find ourselves with not one, not two, but three such devil-may-care adventurers.

And what were these three doughty daredevils? MHF, MHF, MHF: Male Human Fighters all. The kind of party that would make an onlooker grin, or put their hand to their forehead, or look up at the ceiling—but here they were to try themselves against this ghost town.

They had been told that another party had gone ahead to do some investigating. As such, they ought to link up with that party and see what they had found out. Via a familiar, they agreed to set a meeting place, but where should it be? For that matter, how were they supposed to get in? This was different from doing reconnaissance, or even from going in to topple the leader of the place.

In theory, they could simply kill the guards and everyone else they encountered; then they would certainly not be "spotted" in a practical sense. More realistically, though, they would need to conserve their resources as they infiltrated the area.

Heavy Warrior had accepted the quest, and Spearman had agreed to go with him with hardly a second thought; Goblin Slayer had required some dragging, but came along. Three heads together were said to be as good as having the God of Knowledge by your side, but the conclusion they came to was...

"So, we will traverse the sewers to gain access, yes?"

"Seems like it's got the best chance of success. Just have to be careful our gear doesn't get washed away."

"You've gotta be kidding me..."

...like so.

They dove into a river, walking along the bottom, until they were finally able to pull themselves up onto dry ground again. It was the sort of thing adventurers with countless quests under their belts were perfectly used to; and they immediately set about checking over their equipment. They would hate to fumble things at some critical moment because their gear was fouled up with gunky water.

One could do nothing to influence the gods of Fate and Chance, but that was no reason not to be prepared.

"You really had breathing rings..."

"I got my first from someone I knew long ago. It was a gift."

Quite some time past, there had been on the western frontier a wizard very knowledgeable about magic and the Gate spell and so on.

When Goblin Slayer mentioned it, Spearman realized that he, too, vaguely remembered such a person. From his first year or so, perhaps, back when he was a newly minted adventurer...

"Huh, izzat right," he said.

"I haven't had many chances to use it in this way."

Spearman decided not to think about what *other* ways there might be to use a breathing ring. He was sure he didn't want to know. Instead, he started wiping off his armor and getting his hair in order.

"So, what's the situation?" Heavy Warrior asked, trying to move things along.

"We did our best to get a read on it," the red-haired wizard boy said. He still had the lankiness of youth, and he possessed a certain fiery forcefulness, but that was all. As he unrolled his map, Heavy Warrior observed how well the boy communicated the information they needed.

Wonder if he studied a bit under a certain scout, Spearman thought with a smirk.

To learn. To grow. To take your first step away from being a complete novice. It could hurt to realize how inexperienced you were, but it could be invigorating, too. He'd gone through that phase, as he well remembered, and this headstrong young man touched his heart for that reason. But it rubbed him the wrong way how the boy gestured *Sit down* to the rhea girl with a wave of his hand, without even looking at her.

Got a ways to go still. Spearman smiled to himself, and tossed his waterskin, wrapped in oil paper, to her without a word.

"Oh, um..." She blinked her big eyes and ducked her head as if embarrassed. "Thanks."

"Don't mention it. Just remember to breathe—if you can give a good swing of that sword when you need to, that'll see you through." He gave her an affable wave and went back to checking his stuff. He quietly kept her in his peripheral vision, though.

After a moment's hesitation, and with a touch of embarrassment, she took a couple audible gulps from the canteen. He wasn't very good with rhea ages, but he figured she was still a kid. Give her a little time to grow up, though, and she might turn out to be quite a woman.

Can't be draggin' your feet, boy, he thought. He saw the way Wizard Boy's eyes went from Heavy Warrior to the girl and then to him, and he grinned. Wizard Boy promptly dropped his gaze and tried to focus on his explanation—just went to show that the guy had a lot left to learn.

"Okay, executive summary time," Spearman said.

"Don't make me do all the work. Pay a little attention sometimes…," Heavy Warrior replied, annoyed, but Spearman brushed him off with a quick apology and, with his spear in his hands, inserted himself into the conversation. Neither of them *actually* thought the other wasn't listening. Of course not. Spearman just wanted to make sure he was clear on the details.

"It seems there are hostages." Goblin Slayer's explanation was concise and to the point, if never anything else. His gloved fingers flexed, working over the papyrus map. Some of the cartography left something to be desired, but for a Porcelain or Obsidian, it was pretty good work.

"Two locations appear to be confirmed," Goblin Slayer continued. "We cannot leave them here. We cannot allow them to have hostages."

"Occult ritual, it sounds like," Heavy Warrior added, and Wizard Boy put in, "They're gonna sacrifice them," his expression grim.

"Huh." Spearman didn't sound unduly concerned. *Yeah,* he seemed to say, *that's pretty much what you'd expect from the forces of Chaos.* "Hey, we let them get away with this and the world is done for, right?"

"Maybe." Heavy Warrior shrugged. Goblin Slayer's metal helmet nodded. "At the very least, this town was destroyed."

"Meaning failure's not an option on this adventure. Tough spot."

Captives, sacrifices, hostages—the point was, there were two places with people who had been captured. Spearman tapped a point on the map with the butt of his spear, asking if this was where they currently were, and Goblin Slayer nodded. Well, then.

"How about we just follow the road? Start with what's closest?" offered Spearman.

"No dice. We can't bust into the leader's place hauling all the captives with us." Heavy Warrior, for the time being the party's de facto leader, stroked his chin thoughtfully. "This isn't some anecdote about slaying a dragon, either. I want to hear our scout's opinion about where they're likely to be hidden."

"Hmm," Goblin Slayer grunted. "There are several possibilities… However, we won't know until we check."

"Start with the closest spot, then. Stay flexible after that…"

"Play it by ear, huh?" Spearman said, shrugging. "In other words, just what we always do."

"Hey, that's how adventuring goes." Heavy Warrior clapped his huge hand down on Spearman's shoulder, ignoring the other man's aggrieved "Hey, that hurts."

The young boy and girl could only watch in amazement as the adventurers fell into formation as if they were completely used to it. The two of them looked at each other, and then Wizard Boy gave voice to the question in both their minds.

"…You guys decided awful fast… To rescue the hostages, I mean."

"Thought we were gonna just leave 'em here?" Spearman grinned.

Wizard Boy shook his head quickly. "No, no, I don't mean—"

Well, it was understandable. Helping hostages or would-be sacrifices was a good deal of trouble.

"I don't understand the point of not helping them," Goblin Slayer said quietly, to which Heavy Warrior made a sound of wholehearted agreement. Spearman nodded, too. "We're adventurers 'cause we want to be," he said. "We ain't just mercenaries."

If it was *just* a job, it was just about efficiency; if all they wanted was enough food to keep them alive until they died, then they each could have just stayed home. They could have been farmers, or slaves, or prostitutes—all regular folks who lived out their days without incident.

But they were looking for something else—that was what had led them all to become adventurers. Of course they wanted to avoid danger if they could. They weren't eager to die. And yet…

"When all you think about is efficiency or profit or advantage or whatever, when that's the only thing in your head—you're done for, kiddo," Heavy Warrior explained, in a tone that suggested that (as party leader) he was talking in some measure to himself as well. "You start to look at everyone—your comrades, your friends, your enemies and allies and everyone—in terms of nothing but how strong they are."

It was unlikely that the young man and woman quite understood what he was saying. But they grasped, certainly, that it was something important.

Hmm. Rhea Fighter tilted her head slightly with a sound like she was puzzling over something difficult. "...In that case, they wouldn't really be your friends or comrades anymore, would they?"

"And that's why it'll get you killed." Heavy Warrior smiled like a shark. "You'll be all by yourself."

That's why such people were called munchkins—in a word, idiots. Yes, there were those who mistakenly believed a real pro knew that the most efficient thing to do was simply to kill all the hostages. But any such person would undoubtedly invite destruction upon themselves before long. It would be impossibly selfish to think you could heedlessly abandon others and not expect to be abandoned yourself.

"You want to focus only on what's most advantageous or not, if that's all you're interested in, join the army. Don't come adventuring," Heavy Warrior said.

"Look, there are those who can go it alone, sure, but we're not talking about the exceptions, here," Spearman added, picking up on Heavy Warrior's theme and adding a little twist of his own. Almost to himself, he continued, "You fight in the coolest possible way, you die, and they make a song out of you. That's what I became an adventurer for, anyway."

That was reason enough to help any hostages. This was the truth for them. For these adventurers.

Goblin Slayer didn't say anything. He simply grunted, and then let out a "True enough." Perhaps the only person who could have guessed at his expression hidden under that helmet was the girl from the farm.

"Listen up," Spearman said in an achingly light tone, pounding the grimy leather armor with his fist. "You oughtta be thankful to me and that elf girl of yours, eh? For teachin' you what a real adventure is."

"...I see."

"Damn right you do. Am I wrong?"

"No," Goblin Slayer replied, shaking his head almost with resignation. "You are absolutely right."

"All right, enough with the sermons," Heavy Warrior cut in, trying to cover for himself. And that was where the conversation ended. The adventurers resumed wiping down their sodden equipment, unwrapping waterproofed bundles of gear, putting everything on, and getting into formation. They lit the lanterns hanging at their hips, and their soft glow began to suffuse the gloom of the abandoned sewers.

Now they would proceed, they would kill, and they would get the loot. Hack and slash was the beauty of adventuring.

"You kids okay getting home?" Heavy Warrior asked, easily lifting his broadsword as the younger adventurers prepared to head off into the dark.

Maybe we should go with them. Maybe I want to go with them. Wizard Boy fretted about it for a moment. The very fact that he was fretting was a fretful thing to him. Not long before, he would have nodded without a second thought. Back when he had just become an adventurer. But what about now? *No, I can't.*

There was the issue of how many spells he had left. How tired the girl beside him was. Enemy strength. Enemy skill. He'd just been told not to look at things purely in terms of power, or points, or advantage and disadvantage. But from that perspective...well, if they went along, at least they might make helpful meat shields.

That wasn't what he wanted. Even less did he want his partner, the girl, to die that way. In any event, he should focus on getting home, not on putting up a show of strength.

And so, the boy answered, "We're fine," in a very sharp voice. "That old fart gave me some magical paints. We just need to draw a tunnel or something and we'll be out of here."

"You suck at it, though, so we might not have a real tunnel for a while yet!" Rhea Fighter laughed out loud, earning herself a "Shut up!" and a jab in the side from Wizard Boy. Even this only made the mage more annoyed, though, because he hurt his elbow bumping it against something far more muscular than he had expected.

"But you guys better listen up!" he shouted at the others as they turned to leave. He seemed to be letting out everything he had held in. "We'll be taking on the next one, so leave some for us!"

There was no answer. Spearman just grinned and started walking; Heavy Warrior raised a hand without even looking back. Only Goblin Slayer stopped and spoke. "Do you think you can do it—slay a dragon?" The question was so quiet.

The boy shook his head reluctantly. "...Probably not yet."

"I see." Goblin Slayer nodded, too. Then he thought for a moment, as if he felt he should say something. "Me, neither."

"...Heh."

"Do what you can."

"...Sure."

The three adventurers vanished into the sewers. The last thing Wizard Boy and Rhea Fighter saw of them was the light from their lanterns, and even that was swallowed up by the darkness before long. Left by themselves, the boy and girl were silent for a moment, straining their eyes against the blackness, unable to see anything.

After a moment, the rhea girl whispered something. With her water-skin still in her hand she said, "...Y'know, they really are cool."

"...Yeah."

He hated it—it nearly killed him—but he had to admit it was true.

§

"And they say nobody knows where the servant went."

"Huh." Heavy Warrior's response to Spearman didn't sound terribly interested. "I was sure it was going to turn out that he'd become a monster and was eating people, and you were there to kill him."

"That's because you're a muscle-brain who thinks with his broadsword. C'mon, Goblin Slayer, your turn next."

Even though the party was trekking through the sewers of a town that had been destroyed by monsters, they didn't feel unduly nervous. They didn't know what they were really dealing with, or where the enemy might be located, or how many of them there were, or whether there were traps, or even, really, what their opponents were after.

But that was all in a day's work.

©Noboru Kannatuki

An adventurer knew how to remain vigilant without becoming twitchy about every little thing. That was Spearman's personal philosophy anyway, and it seemed Heavy Warrior and even Goblin Slayer shared it.

"Very well." There was a grunt from beneath the metal helmet. "In that case, eight ways to kill goblins without making a sound..."

At that moment, however, Goblin Slayer broke off. The grimy sewer pathway had stopped, intersecting a rapidly flowing waterway that was like a huge river. Ordinarily, a scout like him wouldn't have stopped walking or talking if that was all he was faced with. The issue was the small but prominent boat floating there.

It didn't look unusual at first glance. It would allow them to ride the river and continue their journey. The map Wizard Boy had produced didn't extend beyond this channel. Based on the size of the blank space, though, it was clear that the current led to a room with one of the living sacrifices. It was a highly convenient coincidence. And that led to only one conclusion.

"Suspicious," Goblin Slayer intoned.

"Got that right."

"Mm."

Goblin Slayer nodded solemnly and then approached the vessel, checking it over quickly. There were no holes, and no stoppers. It didn't appear to be booby-trapped—just a normal boat.

"I cannot speak to possible magical traps, however."

"This is why I keep tellin' you to get better equipment." Spearman smirked, then had them wait a moment and began rifling through his items. He was able to reach remarkably far into his bag for its small size. It was clearly magical in some way, as was the small wand he pulled out of it. "A Silver oughtta at least have something like this along. Watch and learn."

"I'll try," Goblin Slayer said from inside his helmet. "I haven't given much thought to using enchanted items against goblins."

"Listen, we ain't talkin' about goblins, all right?"

"Besides, items like that always have a limited number of charges. Can't expect it to be powerful *and* last forever," Heavy Warrior teased. Spearman only gave a little cluck and waved the wand gently.

"Lumen." To their surprise, the wand began emitting a faint glow. Spearman drew something in the air with the tip of the wand. It appeared to be the outline of a butterfly or some such; the particles of light scattered, drifting onto the boat.

"Nothin'..."

"In other words, it's enchantment-free."

The boat continued to rock in the water in front of them, looking exactly the same as it had before. A wand of Detect Magic wasn't infallible, as Spearman well knew. He tossed the item back in his bag, then with one easy motion, jumped onto the boat. That it didn't even wobble under his weight was a testament to his nimbleness.

"Guess that's really all that's left, huh?" Heavy Warrior was the next to board, and this time the boat listed noticeably. Between the broadsword on his back, the armor all over him, and his own not insubstantial physique, it was inevitable. That Heavy Warrior himself didn't so much as sway, let alone lose his footing, was likewise thanks to his well-trained muscles. Most physical obstacles could be dealt with through sheer brute strength.

"Hmm." Goblin Slayer was the last to step onto the gunwale. The boat pitched under his weight, but not much. Easy to control. He picked up the oar that lay at his feet, and then tilted his helmet. "Who will row?"

"Not sure we need to. We're going with the current—when we undo the rope, it'll just carry us along, right?"

"Besides, having someone row would mean one less hand if we need help. Somebody was nice enough to leave this boat here for us, we might as well use it." Heavy Warrior shrugged as he worked to undo the diligently secured rope. "If we wind up in a trap, we'll just bust our way out. More fun that way."

"I see," Goblin Slayer said, and then nodded. "Yes. You're right."

§

And indeed, it was a trap.

"Dammit!"

"Ha-ha-ha-ha-ha-haaaa!"

Spearman cursed, Heavy Warrior chortled, and Goblin Slayer was silent as they all leaped from the boat.

The moment they had arrived at the terminus of the rapids and the room of the living sacrifice, a net had come plummeting down over their heads.

No, something like *a net,* Spearman thought, reevaluating the situation as he hit the ground and saw the white, sticky thing flying through the air. Whatever it was that caught the oar (flung by Goblin Slayer as he rolled away), it wasn't a normal net. It was *webbing.*

The space, which appeared to have once been a cistern designed to prevent rainwater from overflowing, was no longer serving its original purpose. At the center stood a cross of crucifixion, with an array of blasphemous words and symbols carved into it. And then there was the gooey white stuff everywhere in the room.

"If nothing else, it doesn't appear to be goblins," Goblin Slayer said, rising unsteadily to one knee.

"Yeah, no shit," Spearman growled.

"When you're right, you're right. This looks like a spider's nest." Heavy Warrior kicked at the sticky stuff with his boots, his face contorting into an animal-like snarl. He didn't have to look back to know that the little boat they'd arrived in was completely covered in the stuff. It had fallen on them from above—or been fired. They would have to work their way through the goop in order to get out of here, but the enemy wasn't going to give them the time.

Yes—the enemy.

They saw a pudgy man bound upon the cross: a sacrifice to be. He lacked even the strength to whimper—but there was something else there, too. Something in the subterranean gloom, in the corners of the ceiling, along the edges of the room, hiding with bated breath. Spearman didn't know whether there was really anything as ambiguous as an "aura" that one could detect. But his intuition as a warrior who had faced death and lived to tell the tale, time after time—in other words, his experience points—said...

It's there.

No question, no doubt: It was there. And the other adventurers knew it as well as he did.

"My teacher... My master, told me a story of encountering spiders in the dark, but it was in the way of a boast," Goblin Slayer said softly, as he sank into a deep, cautious squat. "What do you think?"

Spearman gave a snorting laugh, thrusting his famous spear out in front of him. "If I kill him in one hit, he's a shrimp. If not, he's tough stuff."

"Easier to fight than to plan," Heavy Warrior agreed, hefting his broadsword. "Let's give it a shot and see what happens."

Even as he spoke, he slashed through some of the webbing, cutting it down with an audible *shoop*. It couldn't precisely be said to sound like a sword racing through the air; it was too heavy a sound for that. But the gummy response from the blade was abundant proof that the webbing was stuck on it.

"Well, this sucks...!" Heavy Warrior spat, but he wasn't actually that upset about it. Why? Because he had a different role to play.

"........!"

The man in grimy armor ran through the dim chamber, flinging a knife that he held in his hand. The silver streak would have pierced the throat of any goblin it was aimed at, but instead it bounced off the stone floor with a dull clatter. Just before this moment, though, Goblin Slayer, looking around quickly, had called out: "It's going to jump!"

"Yeah, I hear ya!"

The dark shape sprang upward—and Spearman took aim at the air, where there was no escape.

A spider—knew it. A terrible, eerie spider like something that had been torn from a nightmare, then twisted and pulled into some bizarre shape. "Spider" was the closest word they had for it, but if *this* thing was a spider, then all the other spiders of the world would cower before it.

Spearman let these thoughts run through his mind as he took one step, then two, then three, getting just the right distance to throw his spear, and then—

"Bah!"

—clucking angrily as his vision filled with gooey webbing, just as he was about to launch the weapon. He placed one hand near the butt of the spear and gave it one good spin like a giant windmill. By the time the web went flying off into a corner of the room, the spider had hidden itself once more in the dark.

"It seems," Goblin Slayer said sharply, "that this one is tough stuff."

"Dammit," Spearman growled, looking in the direction where the spider had disappeared. He might have been cursing the gods, or the enemy, or himself. Presumably not his companions.

He stared as hard as he could into the corner of the chamber, but saw nothing in the darkness, and heard no sound. But the aura, or the miasma, or the feeling of the uncanny—if such things existed, Spearman was overwhelmed by them right now.

Even if he hadn't been, it would have been too much to think that the monster would conveniently run away. Goblin Slayer, his sword out and his round shield up in front of him, seemed to feel exactly the same way.

The three warriors spoke quickly, never ceasing to watch for the slightest hint of their enemy.

"What should we do?" he asked, his voice sharp and brief. "Shall we use fire?"

"Not out of the question, I guess..." Heavy Warrior was picking the last strands of webbing off his sword, groaning to himself. He stole the occasional glance at the man on the cross. "But we might torch our hostage, too, and nobody wants that."

"Think it's a good moment for a little magic?" Spearman suggested, but Heavy Warrior promptly replied, "No." None of them were eager to resort to magic too quickly in this den of a servant of Chaos.

"I need a little time," Heavy Warrior said. "Can you make some for me?"

"You're the leader," Goblin Slayer replied with a nod. "We'll try it."

"Yeah, follow the you-know-what," Spearman said, but despite his tone, he didn't object—and that meant all that was left was action.

A human warrior can't be expected to see into dark corners or discover hidden enemies. He can only go forward, attack, keep the enemy's hands full, and kill; these are a warrior's bread and butter.

Spearman and Goblin Slayer, without so much as a word to each other, jumped into action at exactly the same moment. They flew like arrows from a bow—well, such a description might have made High Elf Archer laugh, but they were fast and true.

"…!"

Once again it was Goblin Slayer who took the initiative. He reached into his item bag, pulling out an object and throwing it wildly. In the gloom in one corner of the chamber, the massive spider-like creature once again burst into a leap, launching upward with its eight knees and eight legs. "——?!?!?!?!"

A wordless screech came from its mouth. This was immediately after Goblin Slayer's projectile burst with a dry sound, scattering some kind of reddish-black powder everywhere. It was a bug repellent made of pepper and mint, not that the spider had any way of knowing that.

But that was hardly enough to subdue this creature of Chaos; the spider flew into the air—

"Take—this!!"

—where Spearman let his spear do the talking. It pierced clean through the webbing the spider spat out in self-defense, and then clean through the spider as well. It was Spear Fighting 101: Let centrifugal force and gravity do the work.

This simple physical blow was enough to slam the spider's soft body into the stone floor. Though of course, even this didn't deal a critical amount of damage. The creature bounced along like a ball, curling up as it came to rest on the ground. It bit through its own webbing with its poisonous fangs and hissed at them. None of them knew if monsters communicated anything with their cries, but if so, the meaning was clear enough: *I'll kill you* or *You're never leaving here alive*, something of that nature.

"Hey, that's our line."

Kerack. With a sound like a huge tree breaking in half, Heavy Warrior rose, his own fangs bared in a wild grin. The gloves on his hands glowed with magical power—and in his hands was the boat, freed from the webbing.

"Try this on for size…!!"

The spider could spit webbing; it could try to jump; but there was no longer any way to protect itself from this simple act of violence.

A second later, the monster disappeared under the boat like a bug crushed with a rock. There was a sickening squishing sound, and green goo splattered everywhere. Eight twitching legs were the only evidence that this monster, the giant spider, had ever existed.

"Order up!" Heavy Warrior cried triumphantly, removing the ogre gloves that had bestowed his monstrous strength. For a Silver-ranked adventurer, to have a magic item like this was just par for the course.

Spearman, though, scowled in Heavy Warrior's direction, his annoyance evident on his face. "That was reckless. What would we have done if you'd put a hole in our boat—how would we have gotten back?"

"Bail and row, buddy," Heavy Warrior said evenly. "Or we could have just done the underwater thing again."

"Spare me..." Spearman groaned; Goblin Slayer, meanwhile, was approaching the cross at a bold stride. The man bound to it was slumped listlessly; his entire body appeared swollen. He was breathing in shallow gasps, though, so he wasn't dead. That meant they could free him and find out what was going on.

Goblin Slayer crouched behind the cross, using a small item of his own devising to try and pick the lock on the cuff restraining the man. Heavy Warrior watched from over his shoulder. "How's it look—think you can open it?" He wasn't asking so much as confirming.

"No problem."

"Everyone in this room's been to a lot of trouble. Better see if we can get the story." Spearman jogged up to the cross so that he was in front of the man. He peered into the captive's face, observing his cloudy eyes and half-open mouth. He was alive. But that was only to say he wasn't dead. Would he be able to talk to them?

"Think this guy might need some healing before he's gonna be in any shape for an interview. Maybe that stamina potion I bought from the receptionist—"

—*would be a good idea*, he was about to say, but he was interrupted by the man, who spontaneously inflated like a balloon.

"Huh?"

Then he exploded.

Bits of the captive went every which way, while dark fluids spattered all around. Blood, brains, chunks of internal organs—well, if only spattering was the only thing they had done. The hunks of meat that had gone flying now began to twitch and quiver. They squirmed, crawled forward, writhed with an unmistakable will of their own—and began to slither toward the adventurers.

"Shit—slimes?!" Spearman, who had taken the full brunt of the explosion, tore a monster off his face and slammed it to the ground, then stepped on it as hard as he could. If that thing had made it down his throat, it would've suffocated him, an awful way to go.

The man they had found was either only what was left of a living sacrifice; or else a sick trap. Or perhaps both.

"They got us good. Ugh, the guy who thought this stuff up is either a genius or a complete moron."

Heavy Warrior, watching Spearman try to keep both the slimes and his frustration at bay, cackled aloud. One silver lining: Virtually no slimes had ended up behind the cross. Spearman was the only one who had suffered any of the impact, and he was the only one now surrounded by slimes. "Well, hang in there. I've gotta get this boat back on the water before the slimes melt a hole in it."

"And you think that's funny?!"

"Hrm…"

Spearman continued to wield his weapon even as he argued with Heavy Warrior; he was perfectly used to fending off slimes. Goblin Slayer had one eye on the fight, but tilted his head in curiosity. "Why didn't you use that wand when you approached the cross?"

"I told you, the thing ain't all-powerful! For example, it can't help a guy if he forgets to use it…"

"Dumbass!"

§

The boat was safely back on the water, having avoided any holes being either punched or melted in it, and now it was skimming along nicely. The spray in their faces as they zipped along felt pleasant, defying the fetid air of the devastated town. Heavy Warrior himself was leaning easily on the gunwale; he kicked his legs out and let his body relax.

How he kept his broadsword always in his hand, though, so that he could use it at a moment's notice, was suitably impressive—or perhaps we should say only natural.

Yes, it was the natural thing for a seasoned adventurer to do, and as such, Goblin Slayer was no different. He sat down and let the current carry the boat. With his helmet on, though, it was impossible to discern the look on his face.

Only one person looked really annoyed—it was Spearman, of course, drying his hair with a cloth. "Geez, that really sucked...," he grumbled.

"Hmm," Goblin Slayer replied seriously. "It didn't seem like that much of a problem to me."

"We have different standards, you and I."

"I see."

Goblin Slayer might have felt he was being quite serious, but to Spearman his answers always sounded diffident, and he clucked his tongue.

"I see." "Is that so?" "Yes." "Yes?"

No wonder he drives that elf girl insane, he thought. He felt like his own vocabulary was shrinking the more time he spent in Goblin Slayer's company.

"Not that I really care, but somebody needs to make sure the boat keeps going the right direction." Spearman gave a defeated sigh and sat down on the floor of the boat, clutching his spear. Truly was it said that a boat left only a thin plank between a man and a watery grave, but at least they would probably have a few minutes before they drowned. Six seconds was enough to get in a move in combat. Even in two seconds, there were things you could do.

"I don't want to turn into one of those cautionary tales about a boat capsizing while the captain and the crew are all mesmerized by candlelight or something."

"I have a bad feeling about this."

"Don't say that." Spearman scowled at Heavy Warrior's idea of banter, then gazed ahead at the waterway, which seemed to go on forever. "Okay, so where's the next sacrifice chamber supposed to be?"

"It shouldn't take long," Goblin Slayer said succinctly. Not just anyone can be a good mapper. Some adventurers are suited to it and others aren't. Goblin Slayer seemed to have a compass in his head; even Spearman had to grudgingly admit it. "If there are no problems," Goblin Slayer added.

"Hey, solving problems is our business," Spearman said, sounding a bit crabby. *I don't like all this extra trouble, though,* he thought. He noticed how the words emerged as white mist from his mouth, and added, "I thought it was getting cold—guess it'll be winter soon. Feels awful early."

"Some wine, some firewood, a nice dinner. I'd love to be celebrating a nice, normal Yule," Heavy Warrior said.

"But we're crawling around in the sewers," Goblin Slayer observed. Maybe it was time to get back at him a little.

"You need to think of a gift, man," Spearman said with a nasty little grin at Goblin Slayer (whose expression he couldn't see). "I heard, you know. You really give her a bag full of money that one time?"

"No," Goblin Slayer said, the helmet moving slowly back and forth. "Not long ago, I gave her a dragon scale."

So it had come to dragons. Spearman snickered in spite of himself. This guy had goblins on the brain, and what did he claim to run into?

"It was fake, right? I mean, how much did you pay?"

"I found it," he replied. "And it was real." His declaration had a frustrating directness.

Strange things happen, I guess. There were many mysteries in the world—and as such, Spearman decided to cut Goblin Slayer some slack and change targets. "What about you?"

"What, you mean am I gonna get something for the kids?" Heavy Warrior shrugged in annoyance, but the gesture was itself annoying to Spearman.

"Not the kids. The woman."

"A drink'll be plenty."

This was getting ridiculous. Heavy Warrior's impassive face made it impossible to tell when he was being serious. Spearman shook his head dramatically—or perhaps theatrically. "Ugh, now here's a man with no pride. Is this another one of those 'After I'm finally king' things?"

"Surely I need to at least be a knight before I could hope to have a princess by my side…"

"Think she counts as a princess?"

"As far as I'm concerned." Heavy Warrior let out a breath, then eyed Spearman. "If you're so smart, what about you?"

"I'd give something to that receptionist, no question," Spearman said, his best adventurer's smile on his face. But then it changed to something tinged with longing. "But I'd hate for anyone to think I was trying to bribe somebody."

A daughter of the nobility and an adventurer would be one thing; but this was a Guild employee and an adventurer. Too much treasure, too many nice meals, and suddenly you might find you were inadvertently causing trouble for the object of your affection. It wasn't necessarily a bad thing to give a gift to show one's appreciation, of course; that was no bribe. But Spearman always struggled to navigate the subtleties of bureaucracy, noble society, and nobles who were also bureaucrats.

"Not what I meant," Heavy Warrior said with a frown. "I was talking about your party member. You owe her a lot, right?"

"Er, yeah. Good point…" Spearman scratched his head. Of course, it wasn't that he hadn't given it any thought, but he'd had other things to worry about.

"Better give her gold or silver or jewels—you know, something awesome. Something befitting 'The Frontier's Strongest.'"

"Shaddup." Spearman laughed. "I'm happy to spend the big bucks on her, but price isn't the only factor, you know." When you found something you thought would make a good gift for someone, money was one way to get it. But you needed more than good intentions, and sometimes it wasn't enough to give a woman an expensive accessory. "Besides, we get more jewels than we know what to do with from treasure chests. You really think she needs another one?"

"Fair enough…"

It was bad enough as a novice—but when you reached the upper ranks of adventurer-dom, the worries only got worse. After all, experienced adventurers were so used to seeing gold and silver and jewels that they were practically inured to them. Take care of a couple of monster hunts and you could come home with enough loot to fill a large chest.

Ordinary people might assume that meant you had "made it," but many adventurers didn't feel that way. You might find a flood of treasure, but you equally found that it flowed through your hands like water as you paid for gear for the next adventure; and anything you had left over just sat around. Because no one became an adventurer *merely* to make money and live a cushy life.

"Hmm…"

Spearman turned toward the soft grunt to find Goblin Slayer looking at him. "I wonder if I should get something for the others," he said from within his helmet.

"Yeah, just to show you appreciate them," Heavy Warrior said. Then, not a question, just confirmation: "You *do* appreciate them, right?"

"Yes." Goblin Slayer nodded immediately. Then he slowly got to his feet. "But first, we must make it through the next chamber."

With an enthusiastic shout, Heavy Warrior grabbed the oar—it was a ten-foot pole—and pulled the boat up against the passageway. It rocked with a dull *bump*, which Spearman took as his cue to hop out onto dry land. "So," he said, "what's next?"

§

"So it wasn't goblins."

A pack of ordinary monsters was practically beneath the notice of such richly experienced adventurers. They had approached the great white hulk thinking it might be a snowy mountain, but it had turned out to be a giant slime—a ridiculous story if there ever was one, but it was over almost quicker than it could be told. Of course, Spearman was still scowling throughout the entire thing.

"Eh, it'd be kinda dumb if goblins showed up in the middle of this evil plot or adventure or whatever this is," Heavy Warrior said, crushing the remains of some unidentifiable creature under his foot. If they'd had a proper wizard or cleric with them, they might have been able to find out what it was, but…

Hey, if we can kill it, doesn't really matter, Spearman thought. Though a sage might be scandalized to hear Spearman say it really didn't matter to him. Anyway, a dead monster was a good monster. No reason to think any more about it.

"We need to prioritize any survivors," Heavy Warrior said.

"Mm. I'll investigate," Goblin Slayer responded, approaching the cross at a bold stride. Spearman grabbed something out of his bag—a wand—and waved it quickly. *"Lumen."*

The command word activated the item, surrounding it in a gentle haze of light. Suddenly, the cross began to glow as if lit by innumerable candles, shining through the entire room.

"...Hell of a magical reaction, geez!"

"That's because they were doing a magical ritual. Of *course* the sacrifice would exude magical power."

"I see. So it's *not* all-powerful indeed."

"Well ex*cuse* me!" Spearman snapped at Goblin Slayer.

"Can it," Heavy Warrior said. In the end, there was no way to be sure if the cross was booby-trapped except to check it up close, so he set about undoing the binds. The would-be sacrifice was wounded, badly beaten, and absolutely out of strength—but alive.

As such, Goblin Slayer lost no time, checking her over with quick, firm probes of his fingers. Her skin was bluish and dark like a shadow. Her hair was like flowing silver. Her chest was ample. And her ears were long. Not every female dark elf was well-endowed, but many people had the impression that they were. It might just be a bit of mistaken lore left over from the ancient ballads; Goblin Slayer didn't know the truth of the matter.

But if nothing else, even he could tell that yes, she was a dark elf.

"Heyo, miss—still breathing, huh? If you can talk, that'd be great, but if not, that's okay, too—just glad you're still with us." Spearman, who had left guard duty to Heavy Warrior, was likewise not hesitant to approach the woman. He knelt and undid the last of her restraints, then hefted her up, the very picture of gallantry. "And if you could not explode on us, that would be even better."

"Explode...?" the woman said, her breath ragged. "I don't know what you mean."

"Hey, I hardly do, either. It's all good." Spearman gave the dark elf an overcoat. While he made her comfortable, Goblin Slayer surveyed the area. Heavy Warrior casually tossed over a stamina potion, which Spearman gently and graciously helped the woman to drink. Potions were an important resource, but the party didn't regard this as a waste. The woman took one mouthful of the stuff, then two, then coughed gently. Her eyes fluttered open a little wider. "A human warrior, a human warrior, and…another human warrior? What are you even doing here?"

"We're on an adventure," Goblin Slayer replied. Well, at least he kept to the point.

The dark elf woman blinked, surprised, but then her lips turned up in a sarcastic smile. "And now adventurers, huh? I just can't win…"

"Wondered if there was anything you'd like to talk to us about, young lady," Spearman prompted, which the woman seemed to find amusing. Maybe the stamina potion had given her a boost, or maybe she was just trying to put on a strong front. Whatever the case, she spoke with the air of someone reproving a naughty child. "I'm probably at least ten times older than you, punk—maybe a hundred times."

"And yet, all women are beautiful, and all 'young ladies' in my eyes," Spearman replied with a completely straight face. He could have been speaking to someone who had been hideously burned, and this young warrior would still have made the same pronouncement with the same conviction.

"Gods." The dark elf let out an expansive sigh, but a smile tugged at her cheeks. "It's really nothing to write home about. Surely you all have an inkling by now?"

"Sure—I figure someone wants to summon a demon or revive a Dark God or something," Heavy Warrior said with a nod.

"Yeah, an apocalyptic crisis, the end of the world. The usual." Spearman shrugged.

"I have at least confirmed that it's not goblins," Goblin Slayer remarked.

The dark elf let out a breath, not quite the sigh she'd sighed a moment before. She eyed the men suspiciously, then shook her head. "I think you've got the idea. They said they didn't want me to die in one fell swoop—they wanted me to suffer."

And suffer it appeared she had. They could see the wounds on her skin even in the gloom.

"I was supposed to be the offering. They said it would, you know, reach the gods, or summon the gods, or whatever."

"Hmm," Spearman mumbled, not sounding particularly concerned. Then he looked at the others: "You heard the lady. Dark summoning ritual. What do you think?"

Heavy Warrior waved his hand as if to say the backstory didn't really interest him. "We charge in there, we kill whatever needs killing, and we go home. Simple." The three of them at least seemed to agree on this.

"What's really of concern is the enemy strength," Goblin Slayer said from under his helmet. He turned to look at the woman. "Do you know anything about it? Any information you could offer would help."

"There's some alter-planar monster that runs the show around here. A demon or something, a nasty piece of work. He has some kind of special trick up his sleeve, too. But..." The dark elf woman fell silent for a moment, and when she went on, it was with a self-deprecating tone, almost apologetic. "Well, you can see it—he doesn't have a lot of other security. Even this room... Even me... I'm just a diversion."

The three adventurers exchanged glances.

"Oh! Is *that* all?"

This time the dark elf woman looked genuinely confused. But there was nothing surprising about any of this to the warriors. It was, in fact, the most predictable thing in the world.

"I guess he thought we were the main event," Heavy Warrior said, his face hard.

"Gee, I'm honored." Spearman shrugged, but he did seem pleased.

Goblin Slayer didn't say anything, presumably because he thought there was no need. It was the reaction of men who had long ago accepted the fact that they were no heroes, and weren't bothered by it in the slightest. Nothing said you had to be a hero. Nothing said life was pointless if you weren't.

In fact, some people went the opposite way and tried to claim that heroes themselves were meaningless. But it was those who stood at the very forefront of all the nameless warriors—which included these three— -who were the heroes. That was what made heroes so admirable. To act as a diversion for such a person—how could anyone be dissatisfied with that?

"...Chaos wants to slop everything over with one single color. Order paints with all the colors of the rainbow," the dark elf woman said melodically, looking up at the stars. The tune was elegant, but not in quite the same way as that of a high elf. It was a beautiful melody that seemed born of nature itself. "So perhaps we should switch their names around."

"That is mere wordplay," Goblin Slayer said, dismissing the woman's idea. "Changing their names wouldn't change what they are, nor what I..." He closed his mouth and swallowed the words he had been about to say. After a moment, he resumed slowly, "...What *we* have to do."

"There's lots of people who don't understand that... And I'm sick of going along with them," the dark elf woman murmured, then narrowed her eyes. "I'm going to live my own life, my own way," she said softly. Although she added, "That's if you're going to let me out of here alive, of course."

"Hey, we already gave you a stamina potion—why would we kill you?" Heavy Warrior said with a shrug.

"And someone so lovely, no less!" Spearman added. Goblin Slayer was silent.

That was enough for the dark elf. She didn't know if she ought to sympathize with having one's plans upended by adventurers who thoughtlessly charged straight in, or if she found it laughable. She got to her feet, stumbling slightly—and then cast the overcoat around her into the air.

"Best of luck, adventurers! Surely you'll accept such good wishes even from me?"

The voice was a whisper in Spearman's ear. Then, naked, the woman receded into the dark, until it seemed she had never been there. Once the coat had settled to the floor, there wasn't so much as a silhouette left in the subterranean darkness of the sewers.

"So it's a monster behind all this. One with something up his sleeve,"

Heavy Warrior said as he picked up the coat—he noticed there was no body heat in it—and tossed it to Spearman. "...Wonder how far we can trust her info."

"Everything a beautiful woman says is true," Spearman quipped, catching the coat, folding it neatly, and putting it back in that seemingly magical bag of his. It was stained with the dark elf's blood and traces of whatever had defiled her, but he paid it no mind. This coat had a purpose, a purpose it served when it was of help to a good woman.

"And even if it isn't true, we have no way of finding out," Goblin Slayer added.

Spearman heard what he thought was a quiet groan from the man. "What, you got a problem?"

"No." The metal helmet shook slowly back and forth. "My plans for how and where to evacuate the captives have come to naught."

At that, Spearman burst out laughing, clutching his belly mirthfully.

§

To every dungeon, and every adventure, there is an end. Whether that's the master mage who waits in the deepest depths of the fortress, or the great warrior who rules from the highest heights of the tower. There's always a climax.

""""""""We're impressed you made it this far, mortals.""""""""

In the case of this adventure, the climax was this creature—this thing. It was like something out of a nightmare, freakish enough to make one doubt one's own sanity.

It was, in a word, an eyeball. In fact, many eyeballs, countless eyes in a wild array, squirming and writhing over one another, all attached to one single lump of meat. But collectively they had a will of their own, reaching out pedipalps like optic nerves, the eyeball buried at their terminus rolling and leering. The single giant eye twitched constantly in every direction, a hideous grinning mouth open beneath it. Its voice seemed to echo itself; the sound had to be more than physical. The thing must have been insinuating its disgusting thoughts directly into their minds.

"What would you say on the threat scale—fourteen?"

"Maybe if you were right in its damn house. Around here, thirteen."

"I have killed one before, but it was not easy."

"Hey, it ain't a goblin, right?"

"Maybe."

Somehow, faced with this creature whose name one would tremble even to speak, the three adventurers were unfazed. The thing presided over the chamber with its high ceiling, floating above a magic circle inscribed in dark blood…

…but a monster was a monster.

If it had a body—a body that could bleed—then it could die. There was nothing that couldn't be killed. This was a truth Heavy Warrior wholeheartedly embraced, and it had never failed him before. He grabbed his broadsword with both hands, planted his feet solidly on the stone floor, and let the strength flow into his muscles.

Beside him, Spearman gave a spin of his beloved spear, then thrust the pointed end directly at the monster. Goblin Slayer drew his sword with its strange length, raised his small, round shield, and settled into a deep fighting stance. It was just what he had done since the first time he had battled goblins on his very first adventure.

""""""""Ignorant fools. Do you not even have words?""""""""

"Might've used more of 'em if I ever planned on begging for my life." Heavy Warrior grinned like a shark, and the battle began.

The trio rushed forward, fanning out to attack the enemy from three different directions. This was just the right thing to do when your enemy could use magic. A frontal assault might be thinkable if you had a big, solid shield, but the last thing you wanted was for the entire party to be wiped out by a well-placed fireball.

This, though, was certainly not an enemy who was going to be undone by such basic tactics.

""""""BEEEEHHHOOOOOOOOOOOLLLLLL!!!""""""

The eyeballs that squirmed on the ends of the pedipalps blinked one after another, unleashing blinding rays of light. They lanced through the room like streaks of white paint flung from a brush. The stone floor exploded where they struck, or else began to melt and bubble.

Disintegrate, Death Ray, and then Disintegrate again. The

©Noboru Kannatuki

adventurers didn't so much as cry out as they faced down the deadly beams. One of them let his armor do the talking; another trusted to his physical agility; and a third rolled along the ground. No sooner had their weapons come to bear than they scattered again.

"Is this thing trying to kill us?!"

"I think it *is* trying to kill us…"

"I agree. Not that I care."

Spearman began the banter, Heavy Warrior continued it, and Goblin Slayer brought an end to the conversation. Whose weapon struck the blow doesn't really matter here. The important part is that several of the bug-eyed monster's pedipalps went flying, severed from the writhing mass, and landed on the ground.

Needless to say, the actual damage was minimal. This monster had nearly as many pedipalps and eyeballs as an ordinary person had hairs on their head—an almost limitless number. But *almost* limitless isn't the same thing as limitless.

"Thing's gotta die eventually," Heavy Warrior said, and it was true—but it was true of the adventurers as well. All those beams of light—get caught by one of those, and that would be the end of you. No one could survive that.

For this otherworldly servant of Chaos, though, they were only a patience-trying distraction, a waste of time. Imagine if you're trying to get down to work, but you notice your desk is dirty, and then when you go to wipe it off, you find it doesn't clean up as easily as you expected. You don't want to put off work in order to clean it, but leaving it dirty nags at you, too.

""""Let's give you a little playmate, then.""""

Thus, the servant of Chaos didn't hesitate to sacrifice one of its pieces to gain the advantage.

Shhmm. From deep in the darkness came an earth-shaking rumble— no, it was the sound of hoofbeats. Two, three, four. They sounded at regular intervals, and then their source was revealed.

"A dullahan?"

"No, not quite, I don't think…"

Admittedly, it looked like a dullahan at first glance. For one thing, it didn't have any head. It was wearing armor. And it carried a sword—much like a knight. But it was substantially larger than even Heavy Warrior; the equipment it wore was of a size no human could have supported. All of it, though, was covered in dark reddish splotches that might have been rust or might have been blood—the equipment was in such disrepair, it was hard to be sure.

Only the dark bluish color visible at the seams of the armor bespoke the owner's former glory. The tattered cloth, bearing the symbol *omega*, that passed for a flag likewise gave no hint as to the knight's former identity.

And yet—look at him. He was nothing like a run-of-the-mill dulla-han. He was what remained of a once-proud warrior, one who had fought for his glory in the ancient days of the Age of the Gods. How many dozens, how many hundreds of the forces of Chaos must he have buried with the blade in his hand? How brightly must he have made his name to shine among the stars? Yet now, all that was only legend, myth—here blasphemed and defiled.

Now he was nothing more than a Chaos Marine.

"Is that the little trick the lady warned us about?" Heavy Warrior said, sounding downright pleased. This was getting interesting.

"The BEM is our real goal," Goblin Slayer replied. "Other than those beams, it should be manageable somehow."

"Man, pain in the neck..." Spearman growled, then he took off one of his gloves and slipped a ring on his finger. It glimmered like a shooting star. It chiefly granted him two things: immense agility, and incredible strength. Spearman didn't normally wear the ring because most of the time he used his other magic items. When he didn't need to make hair's-breadth escapes, they were often better.

"I agree completely," Goblin Slayer said with a nod, and pulled a potion bottle from his pack. It was a secret draught that would increase his agility. It was expensive as potions went, but he had never been a man to begrudge his consumables. He pulled the stopper, then tossed it through the slats of his visor, swallowing it down in a couple of quick gulps before tossing the bottle aside, breaking it. He'd heard the effect lasted only a minimal amount of time, and he had brought it along as an experiment. There was one thing about it he liked: that if goblins stole it, they could be relied on to immediately drink it, and with its brief period of effect, it wouldn't cause any serious problems for him.

"What are you going to do?" Goblin Slayer asked.

Heavy Warrior looked down almost disdainfully at his smoking armor and said, "Couple of hits won't kill me. So I'm just gonna bull through!"

He'd actually taken a direct hit from one of the beams earlier, but evidently he had shrugged it off. Some considered the human warrior to be the epitome of someone with no special talents, but that was just because they didn't know any better. Killing off a warrior who had trained and trained to toughen himself was no mean feat. Thus, this one who couldn't be beaten down and hardly knew the meaning of the word *fatigue*, went on the attack.

That in itself made him a major threat on the battlefield.

"""""Just because one is immortal is no reason to waste time. Now your lives will burn."""""

At his master's command, the Chaos Marine raised the uncanny blade in his hand. It seemed to be both a hatchet and a sword at once, and it rang out with an unearthly roar. The weapon spun. It moaned. It was none other than an enchanted blade, forged by one of the great smiths of antiquity. It hungered for the flesh of its enemies, a weapon to be feared.

Faced with this blade that had made its name in the Dungeon of the Dead, Spearman…laughed. "That's supposed to be my line, sucker."

He charged in again. The adventurers didn't need to say a single word between them to coordinate their actions. The Chaos Marine met them head-on, and the battlefield was filled with flashes of light. In the middle of it all, Spearman found time to touch his fingertips lightly to the stud in his ear. He was perfectly well aware, of course, that the eyeball monster's eye could suppress magic spells. Thus, this was the spell he used:

"*Arma…manga…offero.* Gift magic to weapons!"

He ran like lightning between the clouds of steam and smoke rising from the flagstones, his enchanted spear biting into armor. The amber-coated cutting tip glowed with a strange light; its sharpness increased. But even this weapon wasn't quite enough to overcome the Chaos Marine's armor class.

"Damn, that's hard stuff!"

"Don't worry about it, just beat the hell out of him!"

Heavy Warrior, for his part, must have attracted the monster's gaze (or was that multiple gazes?) and taken the heat rays, for he emerged from a cloud of smoke, unscathed and closing the distance. His broadsword came down with all the force of a sledgehammer. But even that wasn't enough to shake the Chaos Marine, who stood as if made of steel. The floor was slightly scuffed where his feet had slid with the impact, but now he brought his sword howling upward.

"Well, now!" Heavy Warrior just managed to dodge the cleaving blow. Let it be said that he "just managed" precisely because he was Heavy Warrior. Any ordinary person would have been cut clean in half.

Spearman wove through the sparks from the strike, hopping backward to trade places with Heavy Warrior.

"Hold your position," Goblin Slayer said.

"You've gotta be nuts…!" Heavy Warrior cried, but he nonetheless threw himself into another exchange with the headless knight with all his strength. His sword met the spinning enchanted blade with an earsplitting screech, but it never wavered and certainly didn't threaten to break. "We're on…different…levels!"

"Indeed." Goblin Slayer was able to take all the time he needed to find his aim. He slipped through the chamber like a shadow, then he dropped his sword to the ground and flung something with his now free hand: a fearsome throwing knife, itself twisted into a terrible shape. He released it with an underhand fling and it went whining through the air, describing a great arc. An instant later, it had found a chink in the knight's armor, biting into his wrist.

This was on a different level from the sword Goblin Slayer normally used.

"_____!!!!"

Was that a scream? It was hard to tell. There was a sound like metal cutting metal, and the hand came flying off, sword and all.

"Now you're mine!!" Spearman said, not about to miss his opening.

He moved his grip on the shaft of his spear, shortening the length, then drove home a brutal blow from point-blank range. His target: the arm of the Chaos Marine, now exposed by the loss of its hand.

It felt like he was stabbing a pile of gravel, but the weapon tore through the wound—and Spearman wasn't finished.

"*Sagitta…quelta…raedius!* Strike home, arrow!!" The tip of the spear released Magic Missiles one after another, a deluge of blows from that most basic of offensive spells. These arrows ignored armor class and always hit home; now they ran roughshod inside the armor, battering the body of the servant of Chaos.

"_____?!?!"

Three times the Chaos Marine jerked like a broken puppet, and then he was still. When Spearman pulled his weapon back, it was followed by a mass of wirework and green stones with runes carved on them.

So this must be one of those, whaddayacallit, golems, Spearman thought. If nothing else, it couldn't hold a candle to the warrior of old who must have once worn this armor…

""""""Seems you can't rely on antiques."""""" Maybe it was just the humans' poverty of comprehension that made it seem there was a hint of annoyance in the supernatural voice. The death rays lashed out again, filling the air with their light, and Spearman avoided them by the skin of his teeth.

It was thanks to his ring. Otherwise, he would have been in a world of hurt. He clucked his tongue and dove for cover behind the closest available thing—the Chaos Marine's hulking corpse.

Goblin Slayer, the effect of his potion apparently having worn off, followed, and then Heavy Warrior slid in behind him. The metal of the armor, forged by the ancients, would resist both the deadly magical eye and the petrifying gaze.

For the first time since the battle had begun, the adventurers were able to take deep breaths.

"What do you think?" Goblin Slayer asked.

Heavy Warrior, whose body was covered in scorch marks, replied seriously, "I think it freaking hurts."

"I have painkillers if you want them."

"Nah, it'd blunt my strength. What I need is to keep kicking. Give me a stamina potion."

"Mm." Goblin Slayer produced a bottle from his pack; Heavy Warrior opened it and drank it down, then flung the empty vessel into the air. The instant it emerged from the safety of the armor, a bright beam of light vaporized it.

""""You may hide and you may plot, but you cannot run from my all-seeing eye!""""

"You heard the…thing. Guess we can't hide," Spearman said. He grimaced; the voice made his ears bleed. "And we can't take it out in one go."

Naturally, they knew they couldn't hide forever. If nothing else, the BEM would eventually move to flank them. And if they simply chased one another in circles around the armor, not only would it be ridiculous, it would become a matter of who got tired first.

Goblin Slayer grunted quietly. This didn't seem like such a difficult problem to him.

"So, we destroy it."

"Sounds good."

"Works for me."

With the strategy set, the adventurers leaped into action. Heavy Warrior had on his Ogre Gloves, while Goblin Slayer had wrapped cloth around his armor to prevent him from sliding. Spearman touched his jewelry again, speaking the words of the last spell it could muster.

"*Oleum…mare…facio!* Birth a sea of oil!"

The anomaly occurred above the stones. Did the BEM understand what it was? And even if it did, did it have time to understand why the adventurers had done it? So long as it was floating in the air, the Grease spell would be completely meaningless against it.

Meaningless—until a vast silhouette overwhelmed the supernatural sight an instant later.

"Hrrragghh…!!" Heavy Warrior bellowed, shoving the Chaos Marine's body at the monster at incredible speed.

Fools. The rift that passed for the BEM's mouth opened in a hideous smirk. It need simply dodge the oncoming object. The ceiling was too low to float over it, but there was plenty of room to the left and right. Get around behind them, and that lump of metal would be a ball and chain that would slow down the adventurers. *This* time the BEM would flood the humans with death rays.

The monster began to float, confident it had its enemy cornered.

"Bug-eyed *idiot.*"

Suddenly, the BEM discovered it was being driven toward the wall; its huge eye widened in surprise.

There was a dull impact. The creature never figured out that it was one of the adventurers striking a hammer blow.

"Get in close with the first move. Hand-to-hand, we've got the advantage," Spearman said as if it should have been obvious. Heavy Warrior laughed. Goblin Slayer was silent.

No better time to attack than when the enemy was about to stumble right into your range. And if it was obvious where he was going to go, then you didn't even have to work for it. It was as simple as that.

The BEM was stunned, but only for a second; it soon regained its bearings. The damage was minimal. But this was without question a critical moment in the fight.

"BEEHOOOOOLLLLLL?!?!?!"

An otherworldly cry escaped the creature's mouth. The hulking armor that had smashed into it had crushed half the BEM's eye, splattering a horrifying fluid everywhere.

The creature wouldn't die yet. It wasn't dead. But that was the best that could be said of it. No longer able to float, it settled to the ground, where it tried to crawl along—did it want to run? To fight back? Perhaps it didn't even know, twitching and thrashing, howling and screaming as loudly as its alter-planar voice was able.

"""""You damnable barbarians…!!!"""""

"You're not wrong, but you're not quite there, either." Heavy Warrior grabbed the ancient sword, the Cusinart, that lay at his feet. The weapon howled for joy to be hefted by a new master, quivering to complete its mission. "It's damnable *great* barbarians!"

And then the monster whose name one hesitated even to speak was reduced to a simple lump of meat.

Then it was over. The fell air—the miasma—whatever you wished to call it that had settled over the deserted city thinned and dissipated. The circle carved into the floor, which had glowed with magical power, faded; parts of it were gouged away now, and it no longer functioned.

That was the end of the adventure. Heavy Warrior cleaned off the blade and returned it to the former warrior of the gods. He wanted to see the Marine with his glory complete, be he alive or dead.

Maybe Spearman understood what Heavy Warrior was thinking, or maybe not—in any event, he snorted softly. "You like that nickname?"

"Yeah." Heavy Warrior stood with his chest out, unabashedly proud.

Spearman seemed less than impressed, but Goblin Slayer nodded and said, "I also like that legend."

§

"Huh! Gold coins, silver coins, more ancient currency than you can count... This thing was rolling in loot."

"Monsters like him like to hoard."

"Hrm."

After the battle came the looting.

It fell to Goblin Slayer to unlock the treasure chest, while Spearman set to examining their haul with glee.

Wouldn't it usually be the scout who gets excited about this sort of thing? Heavy Warrior thought, taking in the odd moment, but then he smiled and shook his head. The three of them were all warriors, so it shouldn't have surprised him, no matter who got excited about what.

"If that thing happened to be hoarding any books about how to pump up your muscles, I want 'em. Any luck?" Spearman asked.

"Here's a tome bound in human skin," said Heavy Warrior. "I'm not sure, but that seems like a bad sign. Still want it?"

"Nah, pass."

"I'm not interested," added Goblin Slayer.

"Cool, we'll hawk it when we get back."

The book was one of only a handful of such ancient texts in the world, but to the adventurers it was just another source of income. It was much the same with the enchanted swords they found: A rookie adventurer might have been thrilled, but for these old hands?

"I've already got a few at least as strong as that thing…"

Unless it possessed some extraordinary hidden power, to a Silver, such things were hardly worth keeping as spares.

"Can't be really sure until we get it all identified, but it looks that way. Damn, no spears…"

The most commonly enchanted weapon is a sword, though axes can be found sometimes, and occasionally a hammer. Those seeking spears or clubs are more likely to be disappointed than not. Sighing deeply, Spearman grabbed a random longsword and tossed it to Goblin Slayer. "How about you carry at least one enchanted sword with you? It's totally lame for a Silver not to have *any* magical weapons."

"I don't need it," Goblin Slayer said simply. "I would be in trouble if goblins stole it from me."

"Argh, you're hopeless…"

"How about you take that staff? Make a nice gift…"

"Nah," Spearman said, shaking his head in Heavy Warrior's direction. "She says she doesn't need a staff."

"Hmm…"

Well, that happened sometimes. Every adventurer had their own loadout. Everyone had things they wanted; that was why they went on adventures. If someone was interested in weighing the potential and merit of various weapons, then let them. As for everyone else, as long as they liked their gear, that was enough.

"You remember back when you started, and the smallest magical sword or spear was enough to send you over the moon?" Heavy Warrior asked.

Maybe it went to show how fortunate they were these days, or maybe they'd become inured. Heavy Warrior felt a twinge at the memory of his first one, when he'd stolen the weapon from a hobgoblin he was fighting. A goblin with an enchanted sword—he didn't know whether to find the incongruity draining, shocking, amusing, or delightful.

He'd put off that first broadsword for a while, relying on his trusty longsword instead. He wondered what had happened to the enchanted blade. He was pretty sure he'd tossed it in his chest at the inn…

"Geez, all this treasure, and nothing we really need."

Heavy Warrior wasn't always sure how to feel about the place at which they had arrived. They'd climbed a long way, that much was certain. But when he looked up, there seemed to be an endless way yet to go.

Sheesh. Knighthood, kingship—still a dream within a dream.

"...But does it really matter?" The remark caught him by surprise—it was Goblin Slayer, who delivered his comment in his usual nonchalant tone.

Did it really matter if they didn't bring home a bunch of treasure? It wasn't like they had cleared out every last chamber. And just because the ringleader was gone, it didn't mean the other monsters and traps would instantaneously disappear. And it wasn't just here underground—the undead walked the earth above as well. This former city was well on its way to becoming a dungeon.

And what was more...

"We were told to leave it."

Heavy Warrior exchanged a look with Spearman. Spearman grinned. Heavy Warrior knew he himself was grinning, too.

Shortly thereafter, the adventurers set out for the surface. It felt good, rowing the boat upstream against the current of the polluted water, knowing in their bones that they had been victorious. Then they had to go under the water again, following the underground stream until they got back to land, and yes, it was a pain in the neck. But Heavy Warrior took the time to organize his thoughts as they went. He knew the boy and the girl had to be camped out, waiting for them to show up again. So, when he saw them, he would put on his proudest, coolest face, and as nonchalantly as anything, he would say:

"You called it, kiddo!"

Just like the hero in the old story.

CHAPTER 6

LI'L HERO VS. THE UNDEAD KING

"Hiiiiyah!"

A girl came tearing through space with a shout much more cheerful than seemed warranted by the underground gloom. Her equipment shone, and in her hand was a sword that seemed to contain the light of the sun.

She was in a crypt deep underground, someplace that could have been anywhere in the Four-Cornered World. The swirling miasma, the fell mist, were as nothing compared to those on the surface, but the walls and floor here were covered in terrible, rotting flesh. The way the stuff throbbed, almost imperceptibly, suggested that this might indeed be the inside of some living creature.

Surely no one would guess that this was directly below the mountainous peaks known as Wyvern's Roost.

But the black-haired girl—the hero—glanced around and then declared, "Looks safe!"

"I don't care how safe it is, I don't think I approve of you charging right in," complained a female fighter who followed her, though she sounded gallant doing it.

Finally, there came a youthful woman holding a staff—a sage, walking none too confidently. "We *did* use my crystal ball to check that it was safe…" In her hand she held a precious gem, which she now tossed into her bag like a toy she was tired of playing with.

"...Regardless, it was quite a stroke of luck that we obtained that Gate scroll."

"And that it happened to have these coordinates written on it!" Hero kicked at the flesh around her like a child kicking a snake they'd found in the grass. "Wonder who'd build a place like this."

"In an old song, it would be some ancient wizard or something, but there are a lot of people in this world who keep themselves and their abilities quiet." Sword Saint looked around, furrowing her eyebrows. It was a very unsettling place. She was used to dungeons by now, but that didn't mean she was comfortable in them.

"Whatever the case, it means there was in this world a wizard with a true gift of foresight," Sage noted.

"An even better wizard than a certain someone I know?" Hero said, nodding emphatically. She owned four or five Gate scrolls, but if you didn't know the coordinates, they weren't that much use. But if there was someone who had known from long before the danger that would befall this world...

"The Four-Cornered World's a big place, huh?"

"...I suppose, but what matters is where we are and what we're about to do," Sage replied, her expression never twitching at Hero's joke. Instead, she started pulling items from her bag, more items than it seemed should fit in a bag of that size. In fact, the bag itself had seemed to come out of thin air.

They weren't exactly items she had prepared specifically for this adventure—but *stuff* does accumulate when one travels. A wonderful thing it was, to have excellent items on hand.

"I'll start preparations," Sage said.

"Roger that!" Hero chirped.

There were potions, of course, along with every kind of secret brew for boosting stats. There was the potion of supernatural strength, which temporarily bestowed power nearly akin to that of the giants who had helmed the storms in the Age of the Gods. And a decoction of invulnerability that granted resistance to virtually every kind of spell, albeit only for a very brief time. There was a whirlwind potion that gave one the agility to dance through the sky like a colored wind; a draught of mind-reading, which granted the ability to perceive the thoughts of those around you. And then, the holy water from the Valkyrie, the goddess of battle, which could grant the blessings of the gods merely by drinking it down.

There was a magic scroll that would show the path to your destination from wherever you were, and another that let you know of any traps or dangers on the way. And there were baked goods—said to have once been the food of the gods—that only the royal family of the high elves was permitted to make. Plus, further provisions, granted after supplication to the gods, that bestowed the vitality of a hero.

Many other things there were, too, so many that we would run out of paper if we tried to list them all. Each one had a legend of its own, each something the average adventurer couldn't expect even to lay eyes on in their lifetime. To purchase any one of these items at market—if one ever appeared—would take enough money to buy a warship.

And these young women went through such items like water; made of them their daily bread.

"Awfully convenient," Sword Saint said, tossing aside an empty bottle. "Just stinks how short the effect is."

"We've got lots more. In fact, you start to get tired of this stuff, even if it is delicious," Hero said. Then she exclaimed, "Oh yeah!" and dug her favorite seasoning out of her bag. It was a powder, rather like salt, but the moment it tipped out of the little jar, it sparkled in the most beautiful way. This, believe it or not, was a magical spice, and it would provide the delicious flavor its owner craved. It wasn't much, just a little something, but—

"This really makes the difference!"

"Hey, mind if I have some?"

"........Me, too."

—it got rave reviews from the three women.

Sage got her food a little later than the others, delayed by all the many scrolls she had to read over. Despite her waifish appearance, Sage had a robust appetite, and Hero wondered if maybe that was why Sage was so much more *developed* than she was.

Or maybe she's using some sort of secret magic spell, Hero thought, licking the crumbs of the baked treat off her fingers as the others passed the seasoning around.

"You can use it for up to ten meals per day, so we can each have some to spice up our breakfast, lunch, and dinner!" Hero said.

"That's probably not quite enough uses for a rhea," Sage remarked.

"But you're not a rhea...are you?" Sword Saint said.

Sage responded only, "...Hee-hee-hee."

"She's a real mystery!" Hero said.

It was a pleasant little chat, but too brief to be anything more than that. They did a quick check of their equipment, and then Hero exclaimed, "All right!" and jumped to her feet. "Now all we have to do is go save the world!"

She sounded like someone headed off on their very first adventure.

§

"DAEEEEMOOOONNNN?!?!?!"

"Kreeeaaaahhhhhh!!!!"

Each time the colored wind blew through the room, the unearthly walls of the dungeon were painted with filthy demon blood. What was this that traveled so quickly, faster than sound? Was it the wind—a whirlwind—a scorching wind? Anyone who waited to find out would be cleaved clean in two.

No matter how far away, the wind could engage with a minor action, and in its next major action it would bash, bash, bash. An absolute weapon that cut through the layers of space. Any who survived its attack were sliced down by the katana that followed it.

They moved like a lightning storm through an abandoned field. These demon mobs couldn't slow them down for even a second. That didn't stop them from trying, of course. From every shadow they poured forth, from every angle they attacked, spilling out, fangs bared, seeking to steal the girls' lives.

But would the veteran Sword Saint let them? Ah, that was another story.

"The shadow at your feet!"

"...Mm."

Sage reflexively lashed out with her magical force-sword, striking a single decisive blow. The death rattle of the shadow demon that had sought to sneak among them and catch them unawares was already behind them as they pressed forward, forward, forward. The scroll they had opened showed them the way, and they knew where every trap was located. The blessing of the goddess couldn't reach the deep heart of this dark fortress, but these adventurers weren't so soft that that was enough to stymie them.

That was precisely why the goddess, ruler of justice, had chosen this hero to regain the crown. The chance to be her champion would have been an honor for any adventurer. The legend they carved would become as scripture to other adventurers, there was no question.

As they passed the umpteenth intersection, Hero saw an enemy detachment approaching from ahead. "Ooh, here comes a serious group!" she called.

On they came, creatures out of the pit as if from a nightmare.

"What's the plan?" Sword Saint asked, jogging up to Hero with her sword in her hand. "Hmm," Hero said softly. It wasn't that she was unsure. The monsters were scary, yes, but it didn't really bug her too much. She could just charge forward and carve open a path. She knew that was her role. But there were three of them fighting—and many more behind them. Three heads were better than one.

"...I wanted to conserve my resources," Sage said, holding up her staff. "But time is short."

"All right, take it!"

They didn't slacken their pace as Sage intoned two words, then three. "*Ventus...semel...concillio.* Winds, for this moment, converge!"

On the instant, the momentum of the oncoming army of demons subsided. The creatures in their tens and their hundreds—but not their thousands; there weren't as many as that—clawed at the air, arms and legs flailing as if they were drowning. It didn't matter whether they had wings. This was Float. It didn't function like ordinary flight.

Once the demons were caught up in the air, Sage ruthlessly pronounced her next word.

"*Restringuitur.* Extinguish."

Then the wind showed its fangs.

The demons, having been lifted to a high place, suddenly found themselves back in the grip of gravity and were smashed down against the ground. As the great sage who once brought an entire flight of dragons crashing out of the sky said, "Push a god from a high enough place, and if he can die, he'll die."

As for gods, so certainly for demons. "Those ancients sure knew what they were talking about!" Hero cackled. They ran down the path, strewn with bodies burst like ripe fruit, with nothing to stop them.

"I kinda expected more of them, though," Hero said as they rushed from chamber to chamber, from one fight to the next. She'd been imagining the evil cultists' secret hideout would be packed to the brim with monsters. She was practically relieved that this wasn't the case.

"Our opponents must split their fighting strength as well," Sword Saint said, running beside her. Despite having just fought a series of battles, she hadn't so much as broken a sweat. Hero was nearly envious of this, her awesome friend—she nearly felt like she could have fallen in love with her herself.

"The human-wave strategy only works if you can bring the requisite forces to bear at the time and place where they're needed," Sword Saint continued.

"Uh… Meaning what?"

"Meaning if you can do it, it's not just thanks to your soldiers, but also to everyone who makes the weapons and provisions, and everyone who transports them, and everyone who plans the operation."

"The king did his part. And the adventurers, too. And lots of others," Sage added. She would add anything at all, if it put Hero's mind at ease.

"…Wow, guess we can't lose!" Hero chirped, and then she forced herself to smile. Sword Saint and Sage nodded. The two of them knew. They knew this little girl was speaking as much to herself as to them. It was time for the hero to do her part.

Her part: two simple words, but such a great burden. Even though the chattering masses might never think of it.

To save the world wasn't a duty anyone should have to shoulder alone.

"Yes—everyone is out there doing their damnedest for us," Sword Saint said.

"…And so we shall do ours," Sage agreed.

They would do everything they could. With her friends' words to hearten her, Hero promptly said, "We sure will!" and grinned.

§

When they kicked down the door (*bang!*) and entered the great room, it seemed to be packed full of all the darkness in the entire world. Things that had once been people were scattered about, slowly being absorbed by the pulsating walls of flesh. The walls rose and fell slightly with each throb, and Sage finally found the conclusion inescapable: "…This entire dungeon must be some sort of new body."

"And so it is," came a chilling voice that echoed off into the darkness.

That thing's not of this world, Hero thought. It was obvious from the air that filled the room. It was altogether too cold here for any human to survive.

"I'm impressed you made it so far, heroes."

At the far end of the room was an altar—or perhaps a throne, or perhaps some sort of gallows; it was hard to tell. Darkness wriggled there in the shape of human beings. And there was a wizard, his upraised staff sparkling like a jewel, his clothes as dark as if he wore the night itself.

His face, though, was inhuman. He looked more like a dull white skull. A lich or a wight, perhaps; someone who through the practice of magic continued to cling to this world even after death.

"Your arrival I anticipated, but you're here early. Yes, twenty times sooner than I expected." His voice sounded like dry wind, blowing through the branches of a dead tree. No living thing could make such a sound.

Even confronted with this terrible voice, Hero only snorted and grinned. Twenty years, twenty months, twenty weeks, twenty days, twenty hours, twenty seconds? *Doesn't matter—who cares about his dumb prediction?*

The undead king turned his pallid eyes, like blue-white flames, on the sword of legend, which shone with a soft glow like the first breaking of dawn, and waved his hand. "To be clear, I have no special interest in destroying the world or any such thing."

"You say, as you attempt to flip over the board," Sage replied. Her voice was always even, nearly nonchalant, so much so that even her friend Hero wasn't always sure what she was feeling. But the cold edge in her voice, Hero recognized.

That means she's totally pissed, she thought.

"Yes, for when I do, this land will itself become one corner." The undead king made himself comfortable in his throne, seemingly unaware of Sage's mood. From a corner of the Four-Cornered World, one would be able to see three sides—beyond the board. One would be able to planeswalk, in other words.

The undead king spoke of the very heights of magical achievement, but Sage's tone was unchanged. "You'll kill countless people doing this. Many have already died. People we can never get back."

"All things that live will die," the undead king said as if he understood everything in the world. As if to say that, having understood these things, they were disposable.

"I'm afraid we can't have that," Sage replied flatly. "The world is too vast for you to claim that you know all those who live and all those who die."

The world you claim to have no need of is so pitifully small.

The two, who must have been among the foremost spell users in the entire Four-Cornered World, locked eyes. A battle between mages is conducted with words, meaning this was in its own way already an exchange of spells.

The wizards of old might have spread cards covered in fearsome spells before them, but neither Sage nor this necromancer had yet reached such attainments. One said such attainments were not necessary—while the other said it was the world that was not necessary, if its sacrifice could propel them to those heights.

Even without any further words, the course of this battle was clear as a burning flame.

"This is dumb…," said Hero, who had been listening quietly, but now, finally able to bear it no more, spoke up in support of Sage. "I knew we shouldn't have bothered listening to you. We should've just chopped you up."

"Hey, it's only polite to listen to a person's last words," said Sword

Saint, as though chiding the young woman. (Well, not really *as though.* She was.) "Not much more he can hope for, considering we've come to kill him."

"This is the part where the villain's supposed to say *I'll at least spare your life* or *I'll give you half the world,* or something, right? Except...I guess that would be our line now." Hero guffawed, and Sword Saint could only shrug agreement. It was true: They were the ones who had assaulted the place, and their enemy who stood to die.

They had come to kill him. No more and no less than that. It was clear who held the upper hand here.

The necromancer's fingers creaked faintly as he grasped his staff. He had cleared the wyvern out of this nest; he had prepared the ritual; he had created the undead army; he had conceived and implemented the entire plot. To have the ritual into which he had poured all his pride dismissed as "dumb"—well, naturally he was angry.

For all these reasons, Sage felt compelled to say: "You seek to overturn the board and aim for the Beyond with a lump of dead flesh. And why? Because you couldn't get there with your own power. *That's* what's dumb."

That was why one who had already flown beyond the board had seen through it all. A gift from that mage, combined with the swirling destinies of many and various people, had led to this moment.

All was a chain of cause and effect.

"I'm sure you think you're very clever, but I believe I know what that evil and cursed god would say." A slight smile played over Sage's lips. *"Your plans are neither perfect nor decisive."*

These words appeared to strike the critical blow.

"I thought perhaps I would make you immortal, so that I could spend eternity humiliating you to pass the endless time..." *Thrum.* A shadow rose before them. The shadow of death. The terrible Dungeon Master who assaulted the Four-Cornered World. "But I see it would be better to hang your severed heads from a post!"

"Just try it!" Hero yelled. "I'm ready for you!"

The battle began.

§

Spells flew, light flashed, life and death intertwined. To say it was a battle that beggared the imagination—well, that would be the easy way out, but I crave your indulgence as I make an attempt to describe it.

It was a battle that beggared the imagination.

It was Sage who made the first move: "*Caelum…carbunculus…concillio!* Stones of fire, come down from the heavens!" A meteor shower appeared near the ceiling of the great room, raining down. As one comet after another crashed into the ground, spewing flame, Sword Saint and Hero charged straight forward. Sword Saint's sword couldn't quite reach. But did she care? Hero's blade, the shining sword of the sun raised high above her head, was what really mattered here.

"_____?!"

Yet her movement was ever so slightly slower than it should have been. It was only a matter of a second. The most minor of Hold spells.

"Blood to sand, flesh to stone, soul to dust."

Hero felt the terrible realization all through her body. It was a petrification curse. She gritted her teeth and tried to save herself against the piercing cold in her back. Sword Saint lunged forward to protect Hero should the moment come when she was no longer able to move…

"Aren't you just a pain in the neck!" she cried, and from the ground emerged a mountain of swords, a forest of blades. It was a sword wall. Anything that crashed against it would be torn to shreds.

I'll do everything I can…to push through! That indeed was the pride of a human warrior. Without a moment's hesitation, Sword Saint dove into the fray, drawing her sword, letting her own blood fly like a banner to which the others could rally.

"Most impressive…!" The display earned Sword Saint the praise of the undead king, although he seemed to mean *impressive for a wild barbarian.*

Sword Saint clucked her tongue, not caring that it wasn't very ladylike. She wasn't happy that her opponent still had the wherewithal to sneer. He was supposed to be screaming in terror, gripped by the fear of knowing his head was about to be lopped off—anything less was failure.

"I'm good to go now!" Hero called, regaining her balance. "Take a step back for me, will you?!"

"I'm not done with you yet…!" Sword Saint howled, but Hero glanced at her and nodded, then stepped decisively forward. There was no distance to close. A single step was enough. But as she took that single step, a withering spell assailed her.

"*Shrivel where you stand. Wasting in the wilderness, thirsting after rain, scorched by the sun.*"

"*Mors…adversus…anima!* Death, be reversed to life!" The king's attack was rebuffed by another spell from behind her; she had nothing to fear.

"Meddling little…!" The undead king gesticulated broadly with his left hand, the one not holding his staff, then pointed at the oncoming girl. "*A sword the trump card, and a dark staff; when eight splits in two, the one left is the Grim Reaper's hand!*"

It was an incantation of instant death; an awful hand reached out to squeeze Hero's heart—but Sword Saint, shining, smashed it away.

This still, though, provided just the opening the undead king had been looking for. Hear his words of true power!

"*Magna…manus…facio!* Form, magical hand!"

"Hrrnnghh?!" An invisible force field formed a rampaging fist, smashing into Hero, and the young girl couldn't hold back a scream.

She struggled. She kicked with her one free leg, gritting her teeth, trying to resist with all her might. Her bones creaked. Her joints cried out. It was hard to breathe, and she felt something bitter work its way up into her mouth. "Argh… Agghh…!!"

It hurt. So had being struck by lightning, and burned by flame, and the petrification of just moments ago—but now she was scared.

But…scary and painful…that's all this is. She kicked at the air, forced the strength into her arms, and with a mighty effort she held on to her sacred blade, she kept fighting. That was why she was still there, why Sage's spell arrived in the nick of time, just as it felt Hero's internal organs might be crushed.

"*Arma…fugio…amittimus!* Weapons, flee and be lost!"

If a hand can hold, a hand can slip, so Fumble was always going to have an effect. Hero tumbled through space like a broken doll, but she just managed to get her feet under her and land standing up. She forced strength into her quaking legs, rising and trying to regain

©Noboru Kannatuki

composure on her snot-streaked face. "I thought I was gonna die…!" she said.

"Well, you haven't yet," Sage replied, wiping away the blood that dribbled from her mouth, a consequence of the Overcasting. "I was just in time."

Hero somehow managed a smile. She knew she should have been the one to take on the army of foes earlier. Heh! "I wouldn't have minded if you'd been just a little quicker…!"

She wiped away the tears in her eyes (a biological response), then got a better grip on her enchanted sword before launching herself once more at the shadow.

All the while, Sword Saint held the front line alone. With the strength of a Storm Giant, she was powerful enough to take on any wizard, no matter how fearsome. She was bleeding all over, a pitiful sight, but so what—blood was just a sign you were still alive. She'd lost a bit of her long hair, her pride and joy, but she was safe.

The elves say that to steal even a single strand of a maiden's hair, or to make a single scratch on her unblemished skin, is to pay with your life, she reflected internally.

"I see. I thought you were doing surprisingly well—you've been granted tremendous strength." The undead king chuckled to himself. He turned his staff toward the oncoming Sword Saint—no. Hero was on her feet, too, and charging forward, and Sage had gotten her breathing under control and had raised her own staff. The necromancer was confronting all three of them.

"*Magna…remora…restringuitur!* An end to magic!"

A freezing wave attacked the young women. It was almost possible to *see* it reaching into their bodies, eliminating the various powers they had been granted. The giant's strength, all the various magical resistances, the wind-like speed, the sharpness of the swords—everything.

Counterspell: a spell that canceled all other magic, a decisive play in a battle between wizards.

"Your work was feeble, O sage," the necromancer said. But Sage said nothing; she didn't rise to the bait. Or perhaps she was unable to say anything. Perhaps it was all she could do to cling to her staff now…

Sword Saint answered instead. "So? What about it?"

"Hrk?!"

Her blade tore into the necromancer's chest as if to say this was all dumb. The undead king immediately produced a force-blade from his wand, slashing at Sword Saint again and again. He was no master swordsman, but he let his physical strength as a high-level undead substitute for skill.

Sword Saint was covered in wounds; she should already have been in danger of her life—but she shuffled her feet, weaving between her opponent's blows, sliding past one and then another by a hair's breadth. That was all she did, and yet it was critical.

She changed her angle to get a better target. Shuffled her feet. Changed her angle. Shuffled her feet. They were only the slightest of movements, but they were enough to forestall the necromancer's attacks.

"Heh-heh!" Sword Saint chuckled, and she moved like flowing water, first right, then left, slicing, stabbing. The undead king widened his eyes in astonishment at this display of the *danse macabre*.

The woman clutched a katana in her hand. A perfectly ordinary thing, at least as far as swords from the east went. That was its only distinguishing feature. The slightest of cracks and chips were visible in the metal of the blade, but otherwise, it was completely unremarkable; just...

"A steel sword...?!"

"I don't much care which weapons are supposed to be better than which others," Sword Saint said with a smile—she almost sounded like she might stick out her tongue like a kid. If the one who had once used just such a blade in the Dungeon of the Dead could have heard her, he would have laughed.

She didn't know whether it was some famous, legendary blade, and she didn't care. Her belief—her faith—could be summed up in just a few words: "A sword that won't break, that won't bend, is a good sword. And it's why I'm going to win!"

"Curse you...!!" Yet even as the undead king spat the words, the light of the sun began to peek into the darkness of this deep chamber.

It was Hero: Her shimmering armor was fouled with filth, her steps were unsteady, yet still she raised high her sword. Sword Saint's blow had been powerful enough to destroy the ghost that moved the corpse.

The rotting undead that was left was never going to be able to escape. Instead, it glared hatefully at the blade of sunlight. "Damnéd pawns of the gods…!"

"Are you trying to say you lost because there wasn't anyone in control of you? You think you would have won if there was?"

The necromancer might wish it were so, but he was just being a sore loser. And that made him look pathetic. Hero gripped her sword with both hands. She couldn't seem to summon the strength. She gritted her teeth and tried again.

That was when the voice of the goddess of battle rang out. The spell on which Sage had been focusing all this time, silently weaving with utmost concentration, was finally complete.

"*Ennoia… Iao… Aurora.* Wisdom… Fire… Dawn!"

Strength returned to Hero's ravaged body. She could fight again. She could lift her sword again. The pain and the fear still remained, but this was enough to go on.

"Even you will meet destruction one day! Let them revere you, let them worship you—in the end, you will return to dust!"

"I guess." Hero had the strength to laugh now. Why not? They all said the same thing, more or less. Like they had all agreed on it ahead of time. "But not now!"

If she was defeated now, the world would fall into darkness. How could she ever face those who had helped her? There were the soldiers and the other adventurers, their families, and many people who had nothing at all to do with any of this—not to mention her friends, and her. That was why the undead king and his ilk all said the same things—because they didn't know any of those people. That was why they could so calmly talk of destroying the world, of killing people—even think it was the right thing to do.

They believe no one would come save the world if that person weren't being controlled by the gods? If the necromancer really felt that way, then there was nothing she could say to convince him otherwise. *And in that case, there's just one thing for me to say—one thing for me to do—on behalf of everyone.*

Just before she unleashed a blow to summon the dawn, she exclaimed: "Take this, you fiend!"

It was as if the sun had exploded.

Of Starting a Goblin-Hunting Scenario

His eyes fluttered open to the chirping of the canary. His body seemed immensely heavy, the ceiling above impossibly far away.

"Hrm…" He grunted softly and sat up. The bed creaked beneath him.

There was a chill in his room that suggested it wasn't yet too late in the day. He might have overslept, but only by a little. That he had overslept at all, though, was a problem.

His old friend was watching him with a smile from the window. "G'morning! You really conked out, huh?"

"Hrm," he grunted again, nodding, and then he stood and quickly pulled on some clothes.

I must have been very tired.

He realized that his friends—it took him a second to think of them that way—had invited him to do something he wasn't used to. And going on an adventure that was certainly no goblin hunt really took it out of him.

An adventure…

He felt his lips arch ever so slightly at the word.

"Ooh, you look happy about something."

"Do I?"

"I certainly think so."

"I see."

She also appeared to be happy, for she was smiling. He studied his old friend for a moment, searching the empty air for the words, then finally he said: "Aren't you cold?"

"Hah, I'm plenty warm, thanks!" Then she spread her arms proudly.

Ah. I see.

"New woolen clothes?"

"Yep. I knitted them myself."

She loosened her work belt and slid aside the top of her suspenders to show off her shirt. The wool was white and new.

He thought for a moment, went searching for the words once again, and finally offered the only ones he could come up with: "It looks good on you—at least, I think."

"Hee-hee-hee…!"

Apparently, that wasn't the wrong thing to say. The girl he had known for so long blushed happily and smiled again. "I knitted one for you, too—try it on later, okay?"

"All right. I will." He nodded, then looked across the room at the black shirt folded and placed on top of his chest. He had somehow been reluctant to touch it—and it seemed that had not been the wrong thing, either.

"Can it wait until after my quest?" he asked. And then, perhaps thinking that wasn't enough words, he added, "I don't want to get it dirty."

"Sure, that's fine. But you'll try it when you get home, won't you?"

"Yes."

He nodded, and the girl said, "I'll be waiting for you!"

He observed that this, too, sounded happy.

§

Grimy leather armor, a cheap-looking metal helmet, a sword of a strange length, and a small, round shield.

He passed through the door of the Adventurers Guild dressed just as he always was, to find the same people there he always did. There were Rookie—no, not anymore—Warrior and Cleric, conferring with Harefolk Hunter.

"We need to get some experience with flying enemies!" The former rookie was saying. "I want to at least be able to take down a wyvern!"

"Yeah, but this Roc or whatever is impossible. We'll get ourselves killed. Let's find something else!"

"Hey, I been thinkin', do adventurers really have to just hunt monsters all the time?"

When had it been that they had come to him asking about the proper way to use a club? It was an incidental memory for Goblin Slayer, but if it had been of some help to them, then good.

That reminds me, I used quite a few potions on that last expedition.

He had better make sure he was stocked up.

Adventurers Goblin Slayer knew called out to him as he went past on his way to the workshop. Among the established members of the Guild, he was well known as "the weirdo who's all *goblins-goblins-goblins.*" He wasn't quite sure how to take that. But there was no need to deny it, and it did not seem bad to him, so he let it be.

"Hoh, look who's back." The boss of the workshop, a man short and stout enough to be mistaken for a dwarf, eyeballed the metal helmet with his typical suspicion. "I haven't finished putting that armor you gave me back together. What, did you run into a goblin who can use Disintegrate?"

"No."

"Thought not. Never been a goblin like that, never will be." The man laughed, a sound like rocks crashing together. It occurred to Goblin Slayer that he had now known this man for a fairly long time.

The boss started taking his order—first potions, then everything else he had used up, quite familiar with the process. He took down the items in a notebook, informed Goblin Slayer of the price of each, and then glowered at him from his one good eye. "You, boy... You could stand to buy a decent sword every once in a while. Something with a little history."

"I have found your southern-style throwing knife highly useful."

"That right?" He *hmph*ed, then said more quietly, "Guess it doesn't matter. It was a nameless blade that carved its way through the Dungeon of the Dead."

"Is that so?"

"Mm."

It wasn't of much interest to Goblin Slayer. He liked the old hero stories, but they had nothing to do with him. He was just taking some gold and silver coins from his purse when there was a commotion from the workshop. He moved his eyes slightly behind his helmet and discovered the apprentice boy and the padfoot waitress jabbering about something.

"Uh, isn't this a little big?"

"You think? I made it to my size."

"Well, you're— I mean, I appreciate it and all…"

"And that drink the other day was good, right?"

It seemed the waitress was in the process of making the apprentice boy try on the clothes she'd knitted. The knitting was a bit loose in places, and the size wasn't quite right, but he didn't seem displeased by them. Only now was Goblin Slayer realizing how close the two of them seemed.

He thought about it: He had come to know a wide variety of people, and yet there were still many things he didn't know about them. And that was only natural. To know everything about even a single person was no mean feat.

"Dumb kid, slacking off…" The boss rested his elbows on the countertop, watching the two youngsters as if he were at a play. After a moment he said, "How about you? Maybe you should try looking decent every once in a damned while."

"Is that so?"

"There was this elf girl buying a rapier here not long ago. A novice, seemed like a good kid. Even if her makeup did stink a little."

"Hmm," Goblin Slayer responded.

This wasn't quite the season for rookies, but new adventurers could show up any time of year. Goblin Slayer didn't give it much thought as he paid his money and went back into the Guild proper.

There were indeed many adventurers here. Maybe it was because winter would be coming in earnest soon: Everyone was here, and everyone seemed to be talking at once.

There were Scout Boy and Druid Girl watching Heavy Warrior and Female Knight with no small amount of exasperation:

"Ooh, is this...wine?! Hold on a second, just what do you take me for?!"

"You don't want it, that's okay with me."

"Hey, I didn't say I didn't want it. You gave it to me; it's mine now."

Beside them, Half-Elf Light Warrior gave Goblin Slayer a polite bow, which he acknowledged with a nod.

He had just gone by them when he felt someone clap him on the shoulder.

"Yeesh, his head's as thick as his armor. I *told* him to get her something a little more thoughtful."

"Yes, you did." Goblin Slayer nodded at the grinning Spearman.

"You, though, you better show that you can act like a real man. People pay a lot of attention to that when it comes to us guys, you know."

"Is that the case?"

"Damn well is."

If that was so, then had Spearman gotten anything for Witch? Goblin Slayer was just entertaining the question when she appeared, walking over to them in a way that emphasized her voluptuous body. Her cheeks were red as roses, such that even Goblin Slayer couldn't fail to notice it.

"Oh, my..." Witch blinked her long eyelashes. "Am I...interrupting...a nice chat?"

"Naw, just shooting the breeze," Spearman replied, moving away from Goblin Slayer with a motion like that of a carnivorous beast. "See ya, Goblin Slayer. We've got a date-venture!"

"I see." Goblin Slayer nodded slowly, then grunted, trying to decide what to say. He finally settled on "Be careful."

"Don't have to tell me twice!" Spearman grinned as if baring his fangs, then he gave a jaunty wave and set off happily.

Witch turned over her shoulder and said, "Fare...well," leaving only a slight smile behind her.

What *had* Spearman given her? It would have been barbaric to ask. Besides, even Goblin Slayer knew what it must have been.

§

"Orcbolg, you're *late!*" High Elf Archer called, looking up at him eagerly as Lizard Priest appeared to be giving her some kind of scolding.

They were along one edge of the ever-familiar waiting room. What had once been his spot had become *their* spot.

It wasn't that the five of them were joined at the hip. But it was always good to see the other four.

"Ah," Goblin Slayer said, approaching at his usual bold stride. "I didn't mean to be late. I'm sorry."

"Aw, don't give it a second thought, Beard Cutter. Long-Ears here just happened to get up a little early today."

"Complain, complain. We've all been so busy with our own things, I feel like it's been ages since we were together like this."

"Not sure an elf should use the word *ages* so lightly!"

The banter between Dwarf Shaman and High Elf Archer was likewise familiar—and it had been a while. Goblin Slayer listened to them with one ear as he looked at the others. Lizard Priest managed to appear relaxed even though he wasn't sitting on the bench. Priestess was sitting, her hands folded politely in her lap.

"Any trouble?" Goblin Slayer asked.

"Heavens, nothing of the sort. We were merely messengers, you see." Lizard Priest snaked his long neck from side to side, then made a strange palms-together gesture. "Although it seems our esteemed cleric and her companions have won much merit for themselves. I've heard the story."

"M-merit? I hardly think..." Priestess's voice had gone up an octave. "I hardly think it was that big a deal..."

Then again, she whispered just under her voice, *maybe it was.*

Goblin Slayer seemed to recall that High Elf Archer had dragged her off to some fortress or other. He noticed that her formerly pristine Sapphire status tag bore a few scratches and some stains—it was starting to look broken-in. He wasn't sure if Priestess realized it herself—but that was unmistakably experience accumulating.

"How were things for you, Goblin Slayer, sir?"

"It was not a goblin hunt." That much was certain. He quickly provided a summary of all the information he had grasped: "There was a strange monster there called…something or other. We've fought one before, and I have learned they're a lot of trouble."

"Uh…huh." Priestess looked at him blankly. That meant the monster could have been an ogre, or a demon, for example.

"Hmph!" High Elf Archer said, finally having had her fill of arguing with Dwarf Shaman. "Give us some *details*, Orcbolg! Begin at the beginning and don't stop until you end at the end!"

"I'm not a very good storyteller."

"And another thing. I'm not sure I like you suddenly deciding to go off on an adventure!"

"I don't believe it was sudden."

"Oh, it came right out of the blue. And let me guess—*today* it's back to 'Goblins, goblins,' am I right?"

"Indeed, you are."

"And there it is. *Sigh!*" She kicked her legs, a behavior most unbefitting a high elf, yet still just as elegant as you would expect from one. Her tone wasn't as sharp as her words, though, and her face was cheerful, as if to say, *That's life!*

"All right, hurry up and go get 'em," she said. "You know where to find us."

"Mm." Goblin Slayer nodded his metal helmet, then looked toward the reception desk. The rush for the morning quests was over and most of them had been taken; that would make things easier. He walked over, as ever, with no hesitation in his step.

On the other side of the counter, Guild Girl was rushing from one thing to another like an overexcited puppy. Suddenly, she noticed him standing there, and spun toward him, setting her braid wagging like a tail. "Oh, Goblin Slayer!" she said. She grabbed a sheaf of papers—it looked like she had specifically set them aside—and settled into her seat. Goblin Slayer looked at the papers to discover that, yes, they were the goblin quests.

"You look rather busy. No problems?"

"Busy is as busy does, and we're *always* busy." Guild Girl smiled, maybe a bit more wryly than she'd meant to. People tended to pay attention to the most visible things. "The world's in danger, there are goblins around, and the water town is in an uproar."

"I see."

"It's terrible, I tell you." She let out a small sigh, though her smile never slipped.

Goblin quests, well, those would always be with them. People sometimes said jokingly that every time a new party of adventurers formed, a goblin nest was born—and sometimes it felt like it was true. Most such quests were easily taken care of. A few weren't. And there was a mountain of other adventures.

"And we were thinking of doing something a little different for the winter solstice this year…"

"Is that so?"

"Yes, and, ahem…," Guild Girl trailed off, then played with her braid for a moment before she said, "…I might, perhaps, ask for your help…"

"I wouldn't mind," Goblin Slayer replied nonchalantly. He didn't have to think about it. Spearman had talked about repaying someone who's done so much for you.

And it only makes sense, he thought. It might not involve goblins, but hunting goblins was only his job. It wasn't goblin hunts alone that made the world go around. That was simply common sense.

"I'll help you," he said, and then he added with hesitation—unusual for him—"if you can make do with me."

Guild Girl's face lit up, and a smile blossomed on her lips like a flower. But, faithful to her task, she gave a sweet little cough and said, "So, what brings you here today?" The deliberately formal tone of the question sounded a bit mischievous now.

Goblin Slayer replied simply, "Goblins."

AFTERWORD

Hullo, Kumo Kagyu here. Did you enjoy Volume 12 of *Goblin Slayer*? This story brings us *just up to the point* where goblins appear and Goblin Slayer has to slay them. I put my all into writing it, so I would be thrilled if you had fun.

Still, twelve volumes—wow! And to think, I expected to wake up and find it all over, with dawn peeking through the window, three volumes ago.

This time we have a short story collection, so you get a taste of all the different adventurers going on all their different adventures. As a practical issue, the part of the world we know is much smaller than the part we don't, and there are a lot more adventures out there than just goblin hunting. Saving the world from an evil wizard or running through the shadows of the city are just as adventurous.

…Which is just what I'm always talking about here, so I won't repeat myself.

Take an example: In addition to a manga version, a tabletop RPG, and a TV anime, *Goblin Slayer* is getting a theatrical film. Naturally, there are going to be a lot of people involved, way more than I'll ever know personally. I don't even know all the people who are part of the production of these books. Think of everyone involved in promotion, planning, creating brochures and marketing materials, and now everyone who runs all the theaters.

These days there are even people involved in this series overseas, and I'm sure some of them do jobs I can't even imagine.

Then, of course, there's everyone who's been so kindhearted as to pick up these books—this is thanks to you, too. There's everyone who's supported me since the web-novel days, all the aggregator-blog admins. All my friends.

Each part of this series exists thanks to a wide range of people—the movie version obviously, but even this single book. There's Kannatuki, everyone in the editorial department... Boy, I'll never have enough pages for the entire list.

This is why I can never claim to have done it all by myself. If anyone says, "Kumo Kagyu got all the way to a theatrical release all by himself," that person is wrong. I can't tell you how lucky I've been to meet all the people I have, and how grateful I am for all of them.

Thank you from the bottom of my heart.

So, that means Volume 13 is next. I assume it will be a story about goblins showing up, and Goblin Slayer having to slay them. I'll continue to put my all into writing it, and I hope you'll continue enjoying it.

See you next time.

GOBLIN SLAYER

He does not let | anyone roll the dice.

Watch it on FUNIMATION | NOW

FUNIMATION.COM/GOBLINSLAYER

©Kumo Kagyu·SB Creative Corp./Goblin Slayer Project.